HOW
DID
I NOT
SEE

KALLY HAYNES

HOW DID I NOT SEE

The Book Guild Ltd

First published in Great Britain in 2021 by
The Book Guild Ltd
9 Priory Business Park
Wistow Road, Kibworth
Leicestershire, LE8 0RX
Freephone: 0800 999 2982
www.bookguild.co.uk
Email: info@bookguild.co.uk
Twitter: @bookguild

Typeset in 12pt Adobe Jenson Pro

Printed on FSC accredited paper
Printed and bound in Great Britain by 4edge Limited

ISBN 978 1913551 629

British Library Cataloguing in Publication Data.
A catalogue record for this book is available from the British Library.

To my son Danny & Chloe

ONE

In the underground car park, I slip into the red Bentley and slam the heavy door. Nick insisted he came with me for safety. But with confidence, I didn't feel I lied. I insisted I'd be fine. If I'm honest, I have to talk to my husband on my own. I want answers. *I want to hear what he has to say.* Driving into the centre of Birmingham city feels strange; the roads, for once, are empty. I guess it's normal for the day after Boxing Day. Not that it matters much. Still, I can't help but notice a man asleep on a bench; one arm dangles and beer cans roll underneath him – the afters of last night, I guess. I continue to cruise past the BBC building on the right and ease the brakes to stop at the traffic lights. My hands grip the leather steering wheel. *How could my husband do this? What kind of person is he? How did I not see? How did I allow it to happen?* I bite my lip, almost wanting to draw blood as a punishment to myself. Hands are clenched into fists and I bang the steering wheel. A menacing taunt echoes loudly in my head: '*She was born stupid.*' Even in death, my dad was right.

1

Powering the three-litre engine forward each set of traffic lights turn amber. A set of nerves jangle in the pit of my tummy; they scream, 'Go home. Go back.' But I don't. I have to know the real truth. And why would Nick lie?

Five minutes later I slip into an empty parking space on the opposite side of the King Edward Wharf apartments. My heart steps up its beat as I stare across the road to the canal-side tower blocks. A sigh escapes me, and before I lose my nerve, I fling the door open. Depressing dark clouds gather and pigeons scatter as though disturbed by an invisible murky force. *It's a bad omen.* With leaden feet I crush abandoned leaves as a hostile wind whips up my hair, leaving me almost blind. I shiver and clear wisps of blonde from my vision with trembling fingers. Then, quite unexpectedly, I'm distracted when I side-step chewing gum glued onto the footpath, as the substance triggers an old memory.

A child squealed, 'I dare you!' I kneeled in warrior mode and shoved the sticky texture into my small mouth. A game I thankfully grew out of. But what happened to her, the brave one? I give a despondent shrug and edge closer to the apartments. Why did I believe him? Why didn't I question him more? Trust, that's what. *I trusted him.* Susie, my best friend, was bang on from the start, and I curse myself for not listening to her warning. The thought set off another alarm shortly before I met my future husband. Why didn't I take any notice?

Amber, the clairvoyant, had cradled my watch in her hands, her eyes firmly closed, deep in concentration. I shifted around on the hard oak chair for a comfortable position but without much luck. A bowl of half-eaten cat food was next to a dish of water on slate tiles. Beyond the patio doors in the terraced garden, I spotted carp fish swimming around under a net, most likely to keep the cat out. A dream catcher of Native

American feathers dangled on one wall. Nervously I ran my fingers over the cold polished wood table and settled my eyes into the flicker of tea lights. The scent of vanilla smoked the air while I waited in anticipation for Amber's words of wisdom – well, ones sent via her spirit guides.

What did my future hold? Was Mr Right just around the corner? I'd had my fill of being a singleton: the never-ending disappointing dates, the long lonely nights spent on my own. I wanted to feel loved, I wanted to feel passion, I wanted to feel the arms of a strong man, one who'd protect me and not betray me.

'What's happening in December?' Her small, intense eyes questioned me.

I repeated her sentence like a dummy, 'What's happening in December?' I thought she'd be telling me. That's why I was there.

'Well…' she continued, holding my watch as her eyes connected with mine. 'Your life is going to change.'

I edged forward. 'How do you mean?' *Can she see something?* 'Change how?' I asked with a thrill of tiny pleasure.

Then, surprisingly, she shoved my watch back in my direction, and my elation melted to nothing. I straightened up and grabbed the leather strap. Last time she held on to it for much longer. How could she be finished? She'd only just started.

She jerked up and scraped the chair legs backwards; her expression was blank. 'I'm sorry, I can't see any more.'

My tummy fluttered nervously. *How can she do that?* I stuttered, 'But—'

She'd cut in super-fast. 'There's no charge – as I explained earlier, I can only tell you what I see, and now there's nothing.'

I forced words out: 'You said change? I don't understand.' *She can't do this.*

But Amber pushed her chair under the table like I was dismissed. So, with no choice, I left in silence and fumed that I would never to use her service again.

I stumble on the uneven footpath and it jolts me back to the present. I steady myself and fix a stare up to the seventh-floor balcony of my husband's apartment. Is this what Amber meant? My life changed, that's for sure, but not in the way I ever imagined. No wonder Amber shut up shop and practically booted me out. She saw something alright; she just didn't want to be part of it. And if Nick is telling the truth, then I don't bloody well blame Amber. Perhaps I'd do the same. There's a chance Nick might have got it wrong. Plus he stated the police didn't arrest my husband?

When I catch raised voices from above, I tune in. My husband barks out a suspicious snarl, 'What do you mean, you're pregnant?'

I struggle for breath. *Amy is pregnant?* The words echo around my brain and my heart begins a slow bleed. It wilts and dies inside me. More of his harsh words are spat out. I don't understand them; they're not sinking in. They don't make sense. It's a lie; it has to be. But only when Amy screams back does a scarlet rage gather inside me, exploding in my veins.

TWO

Our wedding photograph, dated 24th May 2014, sits proudly on the kitchen windowsill. A few people had commented on my skin tone. They assumed it was tan to complement my white satin dress. I'd just smiled and sort of agreed. The day was perfect: the sun was bright in a clear blue sky, the church behind us as we posed for the photographs. It sends warm tingles up my back when I pick up the photo. It's a daily reminder of my *perfect* life. Well, it would be, if only my period would miraculously fail to mark its presence promptly every month. At thirty-one, I should be with a belly full of life. Not barren, like a discarded wasteland. I sigh and replace the frame, patting the corners of eyes with a clean tea towel. To serve as a distraction, I concentrate on the spicy tones of velvet wine; it seeps into my veins like the blood I'm losing. When something rubs against my jeans, the touch softens my heart. I discard my glass and I swoop down to ruffle Timmy's tan fur, grateful for the diversion. They say dogs can pick up on your mood; how you feel affects them too, so I read. But how would I explain to Timmy the never-ending disappointment, the longing to create a baby with the man I love? It's what a woman is made for – to feel whole, complete with what nature intended. What life is all about, basically?

Greg embraced my dream even before I told him. It was almost as if he knew already. He's paternal, broody; his hands urge to caress over my full tummy. He craves our child to boast of loving parents, the same as his were. There's no wish to linger on mine. Having lost both sets of our parents, that was also part of our connection. Greg is family-oriented, and that's all I ever wanted, what I had been denied as a child: a family infused with love and warmth.

Stroking Timmy, it reminds me just how thoughtful my husband is. For shortly after we had wed he'd burst into the kitchen. He cradled a Yorkshire terrier, one he'd already named as Timmy. He was a rescue from the dogs' home. At first, I'd held back, not quite believing. When it had sunk in, I'd whipped him from Greg's arms and nursed Timmy into my bosom – almost like I'd given birth for real, nuzzling his fur with happy tears. Greg had known how I'd longed for a dog, having been denied one as a child on the account of Dad's career in the army, being constantly on the move. In some ways, Greg reminds me of Dad. That's rather strange, really, as he wasn't exactly a father figure. Thoughts on him are best not to dwell on, and I drown them out with gulp of Yellow Tail red wine.

Greg somehow thinks that by homing Timmy it will spurn on a baby, like karma. What you give out you get back – that sort of thing. Surely, after five months, a tiny seed should have boomed by now? It could be me. My fault. I don't want to go there, so I force my mind back to Timmy and recall the day of his arrival. His tummy was so soft and warm, like a wool-covered hot water bottle. I murmured, 'We need to go and buy baby stuff.'

'Timmy is not a puppy, you know.' Greg laughed light-heartedly.

I swung Timmy in my arms and added, 'I know that, but he feels like one.'

'Babe, I wish I could go with you, but I have to get back to work.' He shrugged. 'Sorry.'

I lowered my head and hid my disappointment. 'Okay.' But it soon evaporated when I locked eyes with Timmy as I tickled his belly. I hardly felt Greg's peck on my cheek as he left.

I break away from the memory and notice my wine glass is almost empty. *Karma has not worked its magic*, I think, picking up the bottle. Timmy barks to run free in the garden and I flick on the outside lights. The air is cold and bitter. A full moon glows from a velvet sky; the contrast is eerie when an owl hoots. I shiver and ease the door to.

From the window, I watch Timmy dart down the long garden, weaving in and out of trees. He brings on a warm chuckle. No matter how hard he races after squirrels, it's a lost cause. I've tried to explain to him, but I'm not sure he understands. And that's another thing I've noticed. How often I rattle on to Timmy. I'm not overly worried because I googled it, and guess what? All animal lovers do it. Maybe I should have drawn a line on the dog buggy. Not one of my best ideas. I couldn't help it, though, when I took Timmy on our first-ever shopping spree. Nor could I resist decorating his bedroom in powder blue and stencilling on cartoon characters of puppies. The revamp of Timmy's room had felt good. It was a reminder of my working days. It had also brought on a flash of regret. To be honest, I'd have preferred not to have given up my job until I fell pregnant. But Greg was full of persuasion for me to finish; he was certain we'd conceive soon. But I haven't, have I? Anyway, how can I go back to work now? There's Timmy to look after. It would be so unfair to leave him all day *alone*. I sigh and think, *Perhaps next month I could be painting a pink room.* Another wine is poured and I reflect on the fact that Timmy's bedroom was a great idea at first. However, I couldn't bear to be apart from him so he ended up in our bed. I wasn't sure if that was normal, so I googled it. Evidently, it's a common occurrence for there being three in a bed for the furry kind.

The pushchair now gathers dust in the garage. It had felt far too uncomfortable with the odd stares from strangers as I wheeled it over Clent Hills of Stourbridge with Timmy inside. To be honest, I don't think he was too impressed either. But I thought after an hour's walk he'd be tired and welcome a rest. I know I was shattered when we arrived home.

Timmy nudges open the door and darts back inside to the warm kitchen. Cold radiates from his fur and he laps up water from his bowl. I settle on a high stool and rest my elbows on the island. My finger traces a line across the black granite to the last dregs of Yellow Tail. Timmy has been walked twice today; now he's in his basket next to the radiator licking his paws. Automatically my fingers tap to the clock's rhythm, the endless drone, the sound so pointless. I wonder if the spikes are taunting me with their slow motion, and stupidly I will them to fast-forward to bring Greg home. He's been working such long hours recently. With the last of the red finished, I pause, wondering whether to open another bottle. Yellow wins with a large measure, but the smooth velvet taunts my conscience with unease. I should cut down, I know, and I promise I will. It's hard, though, to let go of the comfort that settles in my tummy, filling it with warm tones. It makes it easy to turn to happy thoughts, and I cast my mind to the fateful night of when I met my husband. Who wouldn't want to delve back in time over and over to glory in wondrous memories?

I was bored of the same crowd in the local pubs; they made it virtually impossible to meet someone special. So, I turned my luck to online dating; apparently, according to the internet, it was the new trend. It was surprising just how many singletons were out there, all on the lookout for their perfect match, that particular person to cuddle up to or walk hand in hand on a sandy beach with under the stars. To begin with, it had looked very promising. There were a couple of months of:

hi.x

hows ur day

what u up 2

Then frustration had kicked in until a decent, normal message landed in my inbox. I was pleasantly surprised – Jason was *hot*! And it didn't take me long to scrawl through his pictures at speed with lust in mind. We engaged back and forth in communication for weeks without actually ever talking for real. Jason came across as a gentleman with old-fashioned manners, and I had to admit I was quite impressed. His messages were articulate and interesting. He certainly believed in romance. And I imagined, had he been in the war, he'd have sent long, loving letters back home to his wife. *Which, in my fantasy, was me.* He wrote that his nature had stemmed from being raised by loving parents on their farm. A countryman with a warm heart appealed. Oh yes, he ticked all the boxes and was very much a possible candidate of being the *one*. At first I guarded my story, but then gradually I opened up. I felt I could trust Jason. There was stuff I did hold back on, though. That needed to be spoken about in person, if ever at all. Maybe one day. *Maybe not.* That was best left out until another time.

Finally, we agreed to meet on a Wednesday evening in early April. A hint of winter was still in the air even though daffodils were visible along the grass verge of the footpath. Promptly at 7.30, I steered my VWGolf onto the pub car park. Butterflies fluttered in my tummy as I scanned around, biting my lip. I should have found out what car Jason drove, then at least I would have known if he had arrived? I hung on for a bit in the hope of spotting him. But after around five minutes of tapping the steering wheel, I gave up and assumed he must be already inside.

There were logs burning in the grate as I stepped inside. A handful of couples were dotted around with one man seated at the bar. From his back view, I was certain it was Jason in dark jeans and a navy blazer. In one of his pictures, I was sure he had something similar on. My mouth suddenly felt dry and my hands became clammy as I'd crossed the flagstone tiles, heading for the gap between him and the vacant barstool. But it was a stranger who glanced up in surprise, not Jason.

Immediately I blushed and stumbled over my words, offering an apology. 'I'm…sorry… I thought you were someone else.' My flush burned as I was drawn into his sapphire-blue eyes and his smile produced faint lines across his forehead when he said, 'That's okay, and I don't mind a pretty lady sitting next to me.'

My heart had beat with rapid movement. Never had I been called that before, and as I made to move, he sounded disappointed, glancing at his watch. 'I think I've may have been stood up, actually.'

I tried to stop my mouth from gaping. *Him?* Was the girl mad? Or blind, even?

Before I could stop myself, I blurted out, 'I'm on a date too.' What had I said that for? I hid from embarrassment as I fidgeted with my clutch bag, then I pushed back my jacket sleeve to check the time on my watch. Standing so close to the stranger, I felt quite jittery and unnerved. Maybe Jason was huddled in a corner and somehow I'd missed him. I scanned the pub again and then gave a silly schoolgirl shrug. 'It looks as if mine hasn't arrived either.' Secretly, for some silly reason, I was pleased; I know I shouldn't have been, but I was.

'What a coincidence,' he marvelled. 'Anyway, you're very welcome to join me while you wait.' He then hesitated like he was unsure. 'That's if you'd like to, I mean?'

I averted my eyes and wondered whether I should wait with this stranger? What would Jason think, especially on our first date?

He appeared to note my discomfort and offered, 'I completely understand your predicament – first date, only to be found chatting to someone else.' He nodded to affirm this. 'Not the best impression. So when he arrives or… she, I'll up and go, saving you from any form of embarrassment.'

I couldn't help but laugh at his suggestion. 'It's a male date.' Not that it was any of his business. I just wanted to clarify that, for some unknown reason.

He offered his hand. 'I'm Greg Anderson.'

I ran my palms down the sides of my charcoal jeans to ease my clammy hands. 'Kate Taylor.'

His hand was soft but the handshake firm like it was practised, and the unexpected touch had unleashed a set of tingles in my body. I hauled back my hand, flustered, and stated, 'Gosh, it's hot in here.' As a distraction I wriggled out of my leather jacket and draped it over the back of the barstool, willing myself to cool down. What was up with me? I hardly knew the man? Why had he caused this effect on me?

The barman approached Greg. He then turned and asked politely, 'May I at least buy you a drink while you wait?'

I checked the time on my watch again, which showed 7.50. Jason was already twenty minutes late – hardly a good first impression. But what if he'd had an emergency? I thought quickly and supposed one drink wouldn't hurt while I waited a little longer. What was the harm in that? Besides, I didn't fancy sitting on my own. It was okay for men to hang around the bar, but for a woman, it gave off the wrong impression, so I smiled and accepted. 'Red wine, please. Thank you.'

'Any particular brand?'

I shrugged. 'You choose.' I decided to have one and if Jason did fail to turn up I was going to leave. As Greg chatted to the barman, I fanned my face with the back of my hand and then checked the dating app on my phone. I was surprised to see that he hadn't sent a message. How strange? He hadn't come across as the kind of guy to mess around. He was probably late for a good reason. Why not message? And I couldn't call him because we never exchanged phone numbers. He hadn't offered and I'd never felt it necessary to ask, as he always responded to my messages promptly. I could have sent him a message, but I was not the one who was late. Was I?

Greg handed over my glass and said, 'Have you been somewhere hot? You've got a nice golden glow.'

I sipped from the glass as I felt my cheeks burn.

'Sorry, bad holiday experience, I didn't mean to pry.'

I gave a small shake of my head and offered my usual response: 'White mum.' I also added a little shrug and hoped that would be the end of that conversation. People's reactions were funny at times, like I was going to taint their life. Greg, though, hadn't appeared to mind.

I return from the memory when Timmy demands attention by jumping up my leg. I stroke his fur, idly wondering whatever happened to Jason. After that night, he deleted his account, puff – gone without any explanation. Maybe he spotted me through the window, chatting and laughing with Greg? Admittedly it must have looked bad. Greg could have been a friend, or even someone I went to school with. Maybe Jason was the jealous type and stomped off in a huff? Or perhaps he cottoned on to my mixed colour, knowing there was no mistake of it being a tan. I take a mouthful of wine and think that I had a lucky escape. There was something quite unnerving in how his profile suddenly disappeared the way it did. Although the heating is on full, I shiver unexpectedly with a sense of unease at the silly notion that I'm being watched. I edge closer to the window and squint through the darkness. Could it be Jason? I chide myself. Why would he? He certainly made his intentions very clear. Even Susie remarked it was strange not to talk for real. She suspected he was married. You hear such horrors stories about online dating. I was lucky, very lucky, and truthfully, I'm glad to be out of that game. I fudge a smile at just how lucky I am to have found my *perfect* man. In one way, online dating worked its magic in a way I never thought was possible. The thought, though, is ruined when the feeling of cramps curdle in my tummy.

When Timmy barks from the hall, I jump. It's a sign Greg is home. He's early for a change, which is nice. The good feeling is then smashed and I sigh, frustrated, having to burden him yet again with the depressing bad news. I batter down possible responsible thoughts as Greg glides over and brushes a kiss on my cheek.

His voice hints at concern. 'You okay, babe?'

I avert my gaze as my chin quivers.

He slips his arm around my shoulder, giving it a tight squeeze. 'Hey… come on, what's wrong?'

Tears well up and I cry, 'It's never going to happen. I'm such a disappointment, a failure.' *I'm to blame, I'm sure of it.*

He steps back and yanks a packet of Silk Cut cigarettes from his suit jacket pocket. 'Come on, stop, you know I don't like to see you upset, and what about me?' He lights up and inhales a prolonged drag before dispensing smoke upwards, adding miserably, 'I feel the same too, you know.'

I force a faint grin. 'I'm sorry.' Then a sudden thought pops up, and with a hopeful stare up at him, I blurt, 'What if we went for tests… what's the harm in that?'

'Come on.' He jokes with a brief push to my shoulder. 'You know I only like you messing with my bits, and we don't want some stranger poking into our affairs.' He turns to get the ashtray from a cupboard under the Belfast sink, stating, 'How would you feel if it was your fault?' He nods to affirm. 'What then, babe? Could you live with yourself with that hanging over us? Meddling, that's what I call it, and I've told you before, let nature take its course, and besides, it's fun trying.' He pauses for a second before adding in a more serious tone with a shrug, 'But if you want to go ahead and have tests, then we will.' He snubs out his cigarette in the astray. 'You might want that, babe, but I don't.'

My flash of guilt is instant, and I touch his arm. 'Hey, of course I don't.' Why the hell had I mentioned that? How would he act, knowing it is most likely to be my defect? And going for tests would prove it. I curse at my stupidity. What was I thinking? I'm the last person to want to be examined, for God's sake. I claw back my mistake and place a smile on my lips. 'Yes, you're right, let's keep on trying.' *Bloody hell, that was close.* I need to be more careful in the future. Did too much wine loosen my mouth? That's another reason I need to stop, or at least cut-down. But it's hard, and then after one it leads to another.

Greg displays even white teeth. 'I'm always right, babe, don't ever forget it. And I know what's best for both of us. Trust me, it will happen, I promise.'

'I know, darling,' I say with reassurance I don't feel.

THREE

Timmy's urgent scratching on the bedroom door jolts me awake. He must be desperate, because it's only just getting light. Carefully I peel off the duvet so as not to disturb Greg and quietly I mouth to Timmy, 'I'm coming.' Slipping on my dressing robe, we pad across the fawn carpet.

On my return, climbing the stairs with two mugs of coffee, I mentally hug myself. Greg isn't due to get up for a while, meaning we have a chance to kiss and cuddle and much more. They say a woman's body is most fertile fourteen days before her next period, which, by the calendar in the kitchen, is now, the 27th October. My passion sinks, though, seeing Greg already showered and dressed, folding his striped tie in the dressing room. That was super quick?

'How come you're up so early?' He never mentioned anything last night, but there's a chance he might have. Perhaps too much wine has fuddled the grey mash of my brain and turned it into a red blob of forgetfulness.

Greg slips on his jacket. 'I told you, remember? It's the big day of the new showroom.' The navy pinstripe jacket hugs his straight broad shoulders and I long to rip it off.

A white lie makes its way out. 'Oh, yes, I do.' Because I don't want to give the impression that I never listen properly. Inwardly I sigh. That new car showroom is to blame, with all the never-ending changes of dates and the never-ending problems which keep my husband out on far too many late nights, working. His partner Gerry is useless. It surprises me that Greg ever went into business with him in the first place. Having never met the man, I'm hardly going to understand, I suppose. Secretly, I'm certain Gerry wants to sabotage our marriage. According to Greg, he'd wanted him to hook up with his sister. Greg, however, fell in love with me. He confessed a week after we had met; he knew I was the *one*. Anyway, I sort of agree with Greg – it might be best if I stayed away from the business and Gerry. My husband is fearful we'll get into a confrontation, as Gerry is still smarting over nothing happening with his sister and Greg. I suppose there's no need to visit, anyway, and like Greg moaned, he hasn't got time to spit, let alone chat with me even if I did call in. Sometimes though I can't stop a fragment of annoyance from creeping in – what if I wanted to go for lunch? At the start of our courtship, there was no mention of the new business venture. Greg had plenty of free time, with lazy afternoon pub lunches and then coming back here. The more I think about it – Gerry is to blame, alright, keeping my husband working long hours, and now, of course, the new showroom, making it even worse than it is.

Greg checks his cropped hair in the en-suite mirror; it gleams from Brylcreem, the man's equivalent to hairspray. When I hand over his mug, his sigh sounds jaded. 'I must admit I'm beginning to feel tired with all the long hours.'

I mirror his sigh. 'I imagine you are.'

He slips on his shoes, his grin slightly brighter. 'Hopefully things will settle down in a couple of weeks and I can spend more time with you, babe.'

Yes, that would be great, but didn't he mention the other day he'd be busier than ever with the new showroom? Or had I misheard? Tersely, I add, 'Thank God for that.'

With Greg almost ready to leave, my disappointment sinks in and I wander over to the window to gaze out. A woman pushes a pram with her bulldog trailing behind, watching her fills me despair as I think of the long, lonely day ahead. With no baby in sight, I'm beginning to miss my days at work. The novelty of playing housewife isn't quite what I expected, especially with Greg working such long hours. And who knows when I'll fall pregnant? It could be months or years. I dismiss the notion that wine or something else might be the cause. And I have tried cutting down – I have.

Waving Greg off, I offer, 'Have a nice day.' He darts over the gravel drive to a silver BMW, his choice of motor for this week.

Yanking open the door, he calls out, 'It's the big day, babe, remember, so don't bother cooking. Gerry has ordered a buffet.'

I bite my lip and force a faint wave. Only when the car disappears down the road do I allow tears to fall. How long is Gerry going to keep this charade up for? Secretly, I'd liked to have popped in to say a quick hello just to break up the day. I did mention it, but Greg said its business and not pleasure, and none of the other wives were going. I bet if Gerry was married, his wife would have been allowed.

That's not really why I'm upset; it's another late night. Should I be *worried*? Above the rooftops across the road, dirty dark clouds gather. I jump when thunder rumbles in the distance. The hairs on the nape of my neck spring up and I scuttle in. I slam the door and lean on it. Harsh rain batters the solid wood; it matches my flow of tears. My *perfect* life seems to have dissolved. Firstly Greg's long hours and zero sex. *What next?* The light in hall darkens and the walls appear to shrink in. There's a sense of *wrongness*, like something is *off-kilter*.

With a deep breath, I attempt to shake off the feeling and head to the kitchen for a warm drink. I grip the handle of the kettle. *Greg loves me.* Stop *this worry. He married* me. He fell for me the same as I did for him. He said he felt he already knew me on that chance encounter. We both laughed at how much we had in common, like his love for mint ice cream, same as me.

I'm being oversensitive. The new showroom is open now and Greg has assured me the long hours will stop. I'm being negative, and negativity attracts its kind. I must stay on top. Also, I have to believe my period will magically fail to make its presence next month, and after that Greg will kiss my full tummy. All will be well and *perfect* back in its rightful place where it belongs, where it intends to stay.

With a mug of coffee, I settle on the sofa in the lounge. My eyes cast around; they seek out the framed selfie of that freakily warm April Sunday afternoon seven months ago.

Susie and I relaxed in my small terraced garden around a mosaic table. The sun highlighted her auburn hair, and red lipstick stained her cigarette.

She placed her gin and tonic down to deliberate her statement. 'You hardly know Greg – are you sure want to get married so soon?'

I humoured her and flicked blonde wisps behind my ear. 'The answer to your question is yes.' I laughed half-heartedly and added, 'I think I know him now.'

She slapped my arm playfully. 'You know exactly what I mean?'

The taste of velvet wine savoured in my mouth as I explained, 'We're in love, and you can't say I don't look happy.' I wanted to have babies and a happy marriage. *Unlike my parents,* but I left that bit out. Sometimes stuff was best left unsaid or, better still, forgotten. Dead and buried like them, the loveless couple but the only family I had. *Had they ever loved me? Had they ever wanted me? But I know the answer to that…*

She blew the smoke away from my direction. 'No, I can't dispute that.'

'So, what's wrong then?' Or had she thought I was not attractive enough or good enough for Greg, the handsome, successful businessman? Was she secretly jealous? I knew she was married to Martin. He was a nice enough chap; he just blended in too much. Dependable was the word I searched for and found, whereas Greg was exciting.

She snubbed out her cigarette butt in the ashtray, her tone disapproving. 'It's all very quick. What's the rush? Why not wait at least a year? Besides, your plan was to start your own business, then marry and after five years start a family.'

I shrugged. 'I don't want that now and neither does Greg. As he said, why wait? That's what couples do when they have fallen in love.' A smirk appeared and I wiped a spill of wine off my chin. Almost like the dribble off of Greg that I'd wiped from my mouth that morning.

'What about your interior design company? I mean, you've got the shop all organised.'

I butted in quickly. 'I haven't signed the lease yet. Besides, Greg said I don't have to work.'

Susie shot me a look.

'What now?'

'Why give it up? You can still have babies later as you planned.'

'Greg's old-fashioned, and the thought of being a stay-at-home wife has grown on me.' And so had he, I mused. I wanted to lie in his arms forever. I wanted his wet lips to transport my body. He made me feel sexy. He made me feel like a real woman. He stirred up stuff I never knew existed, and I loved it. And I loved him too.

'That's the first time I've heard you say that.'

'Well, that's love for you.'

Susie turned her head like she knew best. But I had not cared because I'd found the man of my dreams. My prince in shining armour, the one I wanted to gobble up and keep until death we do part.

I'd been locked in the past for so long my coffee is lukewarm. I thought I'd conceive soon, perhaps Susie was right about the business. How many months or years do I wait? What if I never get pregnant? What then? Would Greg leave me? Quickly I dismiss the thoughts that know the real reason I might be unable to conceive. I shove them away and convince myself I've spent far too much time chained up in worry and that's the issue. Work, that's what I need to do. And when the blue line appears on the pregnancy test, I'll give up for good.

FOUR

The sun is deceitful and gives the impression of a warm morning rather than a cold November. Opening the back door for Timmy, I shiver. In the utility, I flick on the iron and pull out the ironing board. Mostly it's all Greg's to sort out, and this morning I've planned to discuss my return to work. I know what he said last time I mentioned it, but I've come up with an idea to fix that tiny problem. Timmy no doubt won't be that pleased, I'm certain.

Greg casually calls out, 'I'm going to the gym later after work. You don't mind, do you, babe?'

My head snaps up in surprise and I almost burn his shirt. The idea of work evaporates. Did I hear right? Greg's physique is already toned. What does he need to go there for? Plus that means more time apart. I dart into the kitchen and ask brusquely, 'What gym?'

'I might try Hartwell's Hotel. Plus it's got a swimming pool too.' He beams pleasantly. 'I'll join us both up.' He then adds, flicking crumbs of toast on his suit trousers, 'And there's a beauty salon with great reviews.'

Panic rises and I shrill, 'I hate the water, you know that!' *How could he forget?*

His expression dips. 'Sorry, babe, I forgot. I thought we could spend time together, that's all, and I need to relax after all the long hours I've spent at work.'

Sudden guilt overrides my alarm and I touch his arm. 'Sorry I snapped.' But he knows I hate the gym too, having spent so much time doing army exercises with my dad. But not wanting to sound ungrateful, I venture, with a strained smile, 'The beauty treatments sound good.' Next I press on to my real concern. 'But you don't need to use the gym.'

Greg reaches for my shoulders and his eyes lock onto mine. 'Babe, I want to look my best for you, and to keep this tone it requires work, you know.' The softness of his finger outlines my mouth. 'I won't be too late, I promise.' His touch triggers a quiver. 'Cook something nice, a romantic meal, and I'll bring back the salon's brochures.'

I wave my husband off and wonder over his words. Did he mean I need to use the gym? I size up my reflection in the hall mirror and frown. *Does he think I'm fat? I bet it's all that Yellow Tail hugging my hips.* Lately, one glass leads to another; the spicy velvet is addictive – same as chocolate, I guess. Another thought strikes. *I hope I'm not turning into* Mother? Why would I? I've no reason to.

Slipping on a waterproof jacket, I zip it up and check Timmy's coat. The sky is grey and hints at rain for our walk. The sodden Clent Hills is not on the agenda today, much to Timmy's disappointment as we head left instead of right and cross the road to the cluster of shops around the corner. Still, it's a fair way, but I imagine Timmy prefers to run wild without the constraints of his lead. We trot on I and muse that this is a much better way to keep fit rather than the sweaty gym. The idea of Greg at the pool nags at me – perhaps he forgot my fear. After all, he's working so hard, and to stay as trim as him you have to work out, I guess. I stop and pick up Timmy's mess with a poo bag. The beauty treatments could be fun – maybe a massage, perhaps a facial – that way Greg and I can spend time together. *He really is thoughtful, and I must try harder to stamp out my negativity.*

There's a queue inside the butchers. So I scoop up Timmy to wait in line. I half-listen to the woman in front. She's rambling on about her son Jason home for the weekend. For some daft reason, I tune in and wonder if it's the Jason who stood me up? Not that it matters – I'm just curious, that's all. But the butcher addresses her by a different surname to that of Jason, so it's not him. I then shiver with a feeling of unease like I'm being watched. I spin around and spy outside; the footpath is empty – just a couple of cars parked up, nothing sinister out there. Across the road is a black and white painted pub. An elderly woman hobbles in with the assistance of, I assume, her husband. The scene is endearing, and silently I chide myself over my silly imagination. Just as I'm about to face the front, I'm convinced I spot a shadow duck down in one of the pub windows. I'm distracted back when an old man in the queue nudges my arm. 'You're next, dear.'

'Sorry,' I say and return my attention to the glass counter. For a second I've completely forgotten what I came in for. But then I remember the steaks for our romantic meal later.

Outside I place Timmy on the footpath and nervously glance up at the pub window; nothing seems out of place. Who was I expecting see? Jason? This is all that woman's fault rattling on about her son, it reminds me of the horror story I read in the newspaper earlier about a serial killer. It rings like Jason. I shudder as I go over the details of how last week a young man drove over a hundred miles with the intention to murder a woman who'd left a nasty comment on his online profile. They'd been messaging for week. They'd never even met and she wasn't the first either to feel force of his anger as more victims stepped forward. The ones that are still alive.

I brood all the way home, and march on quickly. At brief intervals, I glance behind and try to shake off the feeling of disquiet. My fingers tremble, turning the key in the front door with a race to uncork a bottle of Yellow Tail. I convince myself I'm being overzealous to the extreme. What would Jason want with me now? And why would he want to kill *me*?

Later in the evening, I've managed shake off my wild belief of earlier, with the help of more Yellow Tail, of course. I flick on bedside lamps and their soft glow warms the bedroom. Before I pull the cord down for the Roman blinds I take a peek up and down the road. A man walks past, his dog trailing at his side on old paws, but that's about it.

With a mouthful of velvet wine, I rummage in the wardrobe. There's a black dress of smooth texture and a light stretch which I select. It clings to my portly hips and I sigh. It does, however, not stop another comfort sip of wine, and I wince, holding my tummy in. I turn to the side and then back again, but it's too much effort and I breathe out. I'm being paranoid. Greg's not mentioned anything about my weight before and I use my thumb to wipe the lipstick from my glass before draining its contents. *My husband wasn't concerned previously. Why should he be now?* Only last week he surprised me with silk underwear; he never complained that night. He moaned alright – more like groaned – and I fudge a grin, brushing away my insecurities.

At the granite worktop, I stand with my trusted friend Yellow Tail. A chef can't simply cook without it; take the late Keith Floyd, for example. I chop red onions, sip wine, I chop garlic, sip wine, I slice mushrooms and sip wine – it's methodical, a ritual, just like he did. I've watched so many of his cooking programmes I almost feel I enrolled in lessons for real. The steaks are swiped from the American fridge and battered with a steel hammer. Suddenly I stop to take a mouthful of wine and then after I curve a wicked grin; this candlelit dinner could lead to next month being the one where I fall pregnant. *It's got to happen sometime.*

Timmy stretches in front of the marble fire surround in the lounge. *Bless him*, and I leave him to his cuteness. I'm on a mission to the dining room. In the door frame, I linger and inhale jasmine from candles that flicker, anticipating romance. Crystal flutes gleam on a white crisp linen cloth. It's all very formal, with plates neatly lined. I remember the fun I had with Greg when he'd first shown me just how he liked the table set. The concept, I found, was quite endearing, well mannered. I'd compared him to previous boyfriends, ones who scoffed fish with chips out of wrapped paper, but I must admit, though, back then I enjoyed it. That life is in the past now, gone forever. Anyway, Greg said he wanted dinner parties to impress his new clients. I memorised his words of endearment. 'I want to show you off, babe, my beautiful, clever wife.'

A couple of hours later I snuff out the candles and slam the dining-room door. *What's keeping Greg?* My feet stomp into the kitchen and I grab my phone off the granite bar, punching in his name yet again. It's still switched off, and I bang my mobile down, almost breaking it. With nothing better to do, I race to the lounge and glare out the window like the action is going to hurry him home. I sigh and hiccup. When headlights eventually bounce off the wallpaper I storm into the hall and yank the door open. *At last.*

Greg heaves his gym bag from the front boot of the new Audi R8 but instead of being pleased with his new toy he shuts it like it's a huge effort. His shoes crunch over the gravel drive, but there's no joy in his step. He's clearly upset when he drops his bag at my feet. I'm caught off-guard with his tight bear hug as he cries, 'Babe, it was horrible.'

I stiffen and fumble from his arms. 'What was? What's going on?'

He sniffs and wipes under one eye. 'There was an accident by the gym; a little girl was knocked over.' A small sob escapes. 'There was blood everywhere… she didn't make it, babe.'

I go cold and grab his arm. 'Greg, are you okay?' But I don't wait for an answer, dragging him inside.

Questions speed through my mind. *How old was the child? What was her name?* Unwanted images flash up of her blonde curls spattered with blood; her broken bones twisted at the roadside; her mother, screaming, with her dead child in her arms.

Was it a drunk driver?

A hit-and-run?

I feel breathless, escorting Greg into the kitchen. 'Do you want a strong cup of tea?' He isn't really a drinker. On this occasion, however, he might need one. Anxiously, I offer, 'Brandy?'

His sigh is heavy. 'No, I have to go to the police station to make a statement.'

I gulp wine and whisper, 'Oh, yes, of course.' That's got to be awful. God knows how he feels. I wouldn't like to guess.

His eyes lock with mine. 'I had to rush back and tell you because I knew you'd be worried.' He shrugs with a forlorn expression. 'I forgot to charge my phone.'

I ask uncertain, 'Do you want me to come with you?' I don't think a drunken bystander is a good idea, though. Now I'm racked with foolish guilt, having guzzled so much wine and cursed his lateness, when all this time he was witnessing such an appalling incident. I can't begin to imagine what awful thoughts are cluttering his mind, the terrible trauma of it all.

The shake of his head is slow. 'No, babe it's okay. I don't want to put you through that.'

My shame deepens and quickly I reach for a glass and top it up with water. Stuff to sober me up. I bite my lip and offer. 'I don't mind, honestly.' That's a lie; I don't want to be witness to a parent's grief. What if it was a drunk driver? What if they whiff booze oozing from my pores? I'd be made to feel like the killer. What if it had been our child?

I'm startled when his phone rings from his jacket pocket. My husband's sigh sounds deflated. 'I bet that's the police calling me now.'

Weakly, I offer, 'Probably best not to keep them waiting then.' *God, that poor mother.* The whole family will be in bits. Tears lurk at their loss. Life can be so cruel at times. That mother will never see her baby grow up. Never see her get married. I bite my lip. *I'll drop flowers at the scene tomorrow; it's the least I can do.*

Greg's shoulders slump and his voice quietens. 'I'm sorry, babe, to leave so suddenly.'

I touch his arm to reassure him. 'Hey, don't be sorry, it's not your fault.' He must be devastated, and I cannot for the life of me imagine how he feels to be witness to such a tragic incident.

I escort him out only because I don't want him to get in trouble and keep the police waiting. I'm unsure what else to do, how to help him. They'll need witness statement as soon as possible. Right now I'm too scared to ask Greg for the full, gritty details. He'll have to relive his account of the dreadful facts again later. The last thing my husband needs now is to be questioned by me. And anyway, I'm sure the accident will be splashed across the local newspapers tomorrow. I can read the gruesome details then. That's if I want to?

I bite my lip, watching my poor husband cross the drive. *Why is heading to the boot? What's he doing?* He needs to get a move on; I'm sure the police don't like to be kept waiting. As much as I don't want him to go, he must.

I gasp in surprise when he straightens up, clutching a bunch of roses and champagne.

I'd completely forgotten about our night of romance.

'Oh, thank you.'

He sighs. 'I was looking forward to a cosy night in too.'

I mirror his sigh and reply, 'I know, darling, so was I.'

'Anyway, I must go, babe.' He then hesitates. 'I could be hours, so I don't want you to wait up and get yourself all worried – go to bed, promise.'

'I promise.'

The Audi R8 roars off and the tyres spit out the gravel. Only when the red taillights disappear down the road do I go back inside. Something niggles at me, but because of tonight's shock, I can't quite catch what it is.

FIVE

My eyes flutter open to my husband's empty side of the bed. Tiny hammers bang inside my head. For a second, I close my eyes again and remember why I'm alone. My hand strokes the soft sheet on my husband's vacant space and I breathe in the faint tones of his aftershave off his pillow. I miss the cuddle of his warm body. As a diversion, I stare at dancing particles from the sun's rays. They float through the open Roman blinds which I forgot to close last night. Timmy is asleep at the end of the bed. His presence warms my heart. For fake comfort, I drag the duvet up to my chin. Since the accident a couple of days ago, Greg's been depressed. He's also taken to using the spare bedroom. His reason is he's not sleeping well, tossing and turning. He insisted miserably he'd keep us all awake. I begged him; I didn't care. He was adamant, though. 'I just need a couple of nights alone to sort my head out, babe.'

I'm worried about his constant flashbacks of the terrible ordeal he went through. Plus Gerry is not helping, still cocking up deals with Greg then having to work late to sort out *his* mess. I've had to bite my lip on that – really, I have. I've no desire to further upset my husband and add to his troubles, one day though I'll have it out with Gerry. I know I will because the other day, I was unable to control my anger, maybe it was the fact I'd downed a couple of glasses of wine. But I was concerned about the stress Greg was under. So I demanded to know why he put up with Gerry. He'd shrugged and I'd practically had to force it out of him. He confessed his mistake of going into business with Gerry. And tearfully admitted he was unable to buy him out. I'd nodded at the thought. It made sense. Gerry needed Greg, but my husband didn't need him. It made sense to me to and I insisted he use my money to buy him out. All that money was just wasted in the bank, anyway, and without Gerry's mishaps, my husband could spend more time with me. I'd marvelled at my *perfect* solution. If only he'd not witnessed that travesty, then all would be okay. Quickly I chide my selfishness, thinking of the poor girl's mother. Admittedly I still haven't had the courage to search the news to read about it.

I'm thrown from my thoughts when my husband appears. He places a mug of coffee on the side drawers. 'I rushed back last night but found you flat out in bed with an empty glass in your hand.'

Guilt claws at me and I shift up, averting my eyes when his body sags on the bed. I bite my lip and briefly stare at pinstripe suit, murmuring, 'Sorry.' *How could have I gotten so drunk?* But old habits are keen to stay and not stray. I've tried, I have. But with the worry over the business and the accident – well, I need the soothing comfort. Not a good excuse, I know.

He ruffles my hair. 'So much for romance, eh, babe.'

I rummage through parts of last night. I'm sure it was after 1am. And I venture uncertainly, 'But it was very late – well, past one.'

His eyes widen in surprise. 'Don't be silly, it was around 9.30.'

That can't be right, surely? And silently I try to work out the time again, but with much of the night a *black hole* it's impossible. 'Oh... maybe I woke up and then fell back to sleep,' I offer lamely.

'I guess you did, because I took the glass from your hand and turned the telly off.'

As I feel a hot flush rise I'm grateful for the distraction from Timmy when he wakes up and bounds over. I bury head in his and ruffle his fur. I really must cut down.

'I'm going for a shower.'

'Okay.' After a slug of coffee, I drag myself out of bed and open the window. The cold air whips around my face but does nothing for my headache.

From the dressing room, I gather up Greg's rumpled suit. *This is what he had on yesterday?* I stumble back as it falls from my hands. *Why is he wearing the same clothes? What's going on?*

Greg makes me jump when he strolls in with a white towel wrapped around his waist. He rubs his wet hair with another towel and states, 'I have a confession, babe.'

I freeze, uncertain, when he mocks. 'Don't look so surprised, I haven't murdered anyone. I fell asleep on the sofa after I came up to see you. I had a few lagers, then puffed out like a light. It must have been them because it's the first night I've had a good night's kip.'

I scoop up his suit again. 'Well, that's good news,' I add, breathing his aftershave of lavender and birch with a hint of lemon. I linger for a second, allowing the aroma to kill my suspicion.

Timmy is curled up on the bed and I join him with my coffee. Greg fastens the buttons on his striped navy shirt. 'I think the lads at work are worried about me.' He casts his eyes in my direction. 'I can't seem to get that image of the little girl out of my head.'

In an instant I'm up and touching his arm, offering sympathy. 'It must be hard – I can't imagine how you feel.'

He pulls on his jacket. 'The police have suggested I go for counselling.' He shrugs with a sigh. 'I don't know what to do, to be honest, for a man it's hard to open up.'

I'm at a loss, and I think hard. 'So what have the guys said?'

He slips on his shoes. 'Steve suggested going around to his if I felt like talking away from work.'

Inwardly I offer a thank-you note to the salesman. 'Well, why don't you? It might help?'

He hesitates. 'Maybe?'

I urge him. 'You should go.' It hurts to see him struggling.

'I don't know, babe. I heard him mention it to the others, then someone suggested a game of poker might help ease the stress.'

Inwardly I clap my hands together. 'That sounds like a great idea.' Anything that will help keep his mind occupied from that dreadful night sounds good to me.

SIX

With my heart pounding, I drag my feet upstairs. At the top, I take a mouthful of wine, but it doesn't help. I can't seem to settle for some reason. Perhaps it's that it's my first night out as a married woman, maybe that's why. Or could it be that I don't wish to leave my husband on his own. Although he seems a bit more settled, I still can't help but worry about him. It's only natural.

After my shower, I turn the water off. Stepping out, I almost break my neck on the wet floor. I moan silently why carpet was replaced by tiles. Surely safety should override hygiene any day. After drying off, I slip on a robe, then wipe the steam off the mirror and open the window before I start to apply make-up. Anxiously I rummage in the drawer, undecided on which colour of lipstick to choose from. One slips from my clammy hand and I bend down with a sigh to pick it up. There's the temptation to polish off the wine to settle my nerves. As I'm driving, it's not a good idea. I need a distraction to fixate on, so I cast my eyes over the arrangement of silk roses on the side of the sunken bathtub. It backfires, when a sudden thought escapes. *I never did take flowers to the roadside of the accident.* I stare at my guilty reflection and force on mascara. To be truthful, I was too afraid to go because bloodstains could still be visible. I lost my nerve. And what if I'd bumped into the any of the family? What if they'd asked who I was? I'd have to explain that my husband witnessed the accident. It could have moved on to awkward questions, ones I can't answer. What if they wanted to know where we lived to say to thank you to my husband for his help? I don't even know if the police have caught the killer. And I've no intention of asking Greg, in fear of upsetting him all over again. For all I know, it could have been a young woman with a baby in the back of the car. She might have had a small drink and panicked, knowing if she was found out, prison was for her. I gulp wine to drown out the thoughts.

No, I made the right decision. I'd die if the family ever came around to the house and upset Greg. I'm sorry for their loss – really, I am – but my husband comes first. I place the hairdryer down and I shake my blonde hair. Another week and my roots will need sorting. I put that thought aside and think of Greg. He's getting through it, and the good news is he's planning to get Gerry out. I take a mouthful of wine as a victory and salute the mirror. Yes, goodbye *Gerry*. I can't help, though, to drift back to that dreadful night. Perhaps it's probably for the best if I don't search the internet for details of it. There's no particular need to see her sweet face imprinted on my mind, plus I've no intention of going through the same experience as my husband – admittedly not quite the same, but just as bad in my books.

I select royal blue silk dress from the wardrobe; I've only worn it once. It's teamed with silver high heels and a fake wrap. The thought of traipsing out as a married woman makes me giggle nervously, but a sip of wine helps that. Timmy, on the other hand, is sporting a sour face. I suppose it's going to be strange for him too – the first night without me.

I've dragged a small overnight case downstairs and left it right by the door, that way I don't go without it. I did that once – left my make-up bag on the bed. I was frantic when I unpacked on a girls' holiday. While my friends headed for the bar, I had to zoom into the Spanish resort to hunt down an open chemist. It was a right nightmare. On my return, I was all made up and plastered in face-paint when I eventually made it back to the hotel. The girls were plastered too, but not with powder and lipstick. They were loud, rude and very drunk. After that, I cut back my intake, but sadly it crept back, like an old lost buddy clinging to a weak friend.

I check my watch. Greg should be back soon, and I head to the kitchen for a refill. Minutes later I hear him stumble, cursing in the hall. He hops in, rubbing his leg. Mock hurt is written across his face as he moans, 'Babe, what are you trying to do? Kill me? I almost broke my neck over that case.'

My glass is filed away into the dishwasher. 'Oops, sorry, I left it there so I wouldn't forget it.'

He continues to rub his leg, asking uncertainly, 'Anyway, what are you up to?' He stands up straight, locking his eyes onto mine. 'Are you leaving me, babe?'

'What do you mean, leaving?' *Why would I be doing that?*

He sounds out with his hands. 'The case in the hall, where are you going?'

My head jerks forward. 'I told you, I'm going to Joanne's fortieth birthday party with Susie.'

His eyebrows ping together. 'What, that's tonight?'

'Yes, I told you,' I repeat, slightly confused. 'It's marked on the calendar.' I point to the date.

'Oh yes, sorry, babe, I forgot.'

For once he's failed to remember something instead of me;

it's a refreshing thought for a change. But perhaps I shouldn't be so quick to judge – after all, the accident must sometimes run back and forth in his head, no matter how much he attempts to fade out the visions. Suddenly I feel tightness in my throat. Maybe I'm being selfish to leave him on his own; he might need me. So I offer, 'Hey, I don't have to go. If you want, I can cancel.'

'Don't be silly, babe, you go and enjoy yourself, and you deserve it.'

I hesitate. 'Only, if you're sure. I don't mind, really.'

He holds out his arms in mock protest. 'I'm a big man – I can look after myself.'

I go to plant a kiss on his cheek but instantly he steps back, flapping his hand with an excuse. 'I'm all smelly from work, I need a shower and I've been moving desks around all day.'

I feel a stab of hurt but quickly I stamp it out. I don't want to upset his equilibrium, which appears balanced for the moment.

'I'll see you tomorrow then.' I'm distracted when my phone bleeps on the island. It's Susie.

Are you on your way XX?

I text back. *5 mins xx*

SEVEN

A hiccup escapes and I concentrate on judging on the sharp curves of the country lanes to Susie's chocolate-box cottage set in the village of Belbroughton. *Perhaps I should have laid off the wine*, I think, edging into the narrow drive. I spot Susie hovering in the hallway. Martin, her dutiful husband, wheels out her small suitcase. I roll the window down and suggest, 'Hi, that can go in the boot if you like.'

'Okay.' He shoves the case in, asking, 'You alright?'

I nod. 'Yes, good thanks.'

Susie fans her perfectly made-up face with one hand. 'I've had such a rush getting ready; I'm all hot and bothered.'

'Well, you can chill out now.'

'Honest to God, some customers think I've got no home to go to,' she moans, sliding onto the cream leather seat, closing the door.

I wave to Martin and slip into first gear, saying, 'Busy day at the salon then?'

'Don't ask, and tell me why I wanted my own business again.' I feel her gaze as she comments, 'But you wanted that too, didn't you?'

I keep my vision firmly in front and focus on the road ahead. 'Maybe I did, but that seems like such a long time ago.' I bite my lip. I'm guessing she's not heard about the accident. Or chooses not to say, which is fine by me. Greg's name was bound to be splashed around the news. *Successful businessman, witness to horror accident.* The thought of returning to work has been put to one side. Besides, I need to discuss it with Greg first. He is, after all, my husband, the one I make joint decisions with. Back in the day, I'd have happily confided in her. But I'm married now; it's different. It's my husband and I working together as a team – a bit like her and Martin, I suppose.

She checks her face in the overhead mirror. 'That used to be your dream, Kate.'

'A baby is still my dream,' I coo. I'd almost forgotten about that too what with everything going on. Somehow I don't think the timing is quite right at the moment, which is just as well, I guess, with my poor husband in another bedroom. Still, I'm sure it won't stay like this forever.

'That was only when Greg came along; you didn't seem too bothered before,' Susie says, applying another coat of lipstick.

I add lamely, 'Well, that was before I fell in love.'

Heavy rain pelts the windscreen and I flick on the wipers as she moans, 'Damn, I'll get soaked now if I open the window to have a cigarette.'

I pat her knee. 'I'm sure you can wait a while.'

'Yes, you're right, and anyway, I'm trying to give up – it's bloody hard, you know.' I feel her studying me as she presses on, 'Maybe if Greg quit… then, you know… just saying, maybe.'

I nod with a sigh. 'A baby… I know.'

'Sorry, I didn't mean to upset you. But you know me and my big mouth.'

I reassure her, 'It's okay, and don't worry about it. I try not to.' What a lie that is, and I consider Greg's smoking as not being the problem. But that's my secret, the one I keep hidden. Everyone has something to keep private. I bet she has. I bet my husband has a few too. He once told me he idolised his mum, and when she was alive he was a real good boy. I think of his cute childish antics. He most probably charmed his way out of a kicked football ending up with a smashed window and blamed it on his mate, silly harmful boys' stuff. The warmth inside fades; his background was so different from mine.

'Kate, Kate.'

I'm pulled back into the present as if on autopilot. 'Yes, I can see the lights have changed to green.'

Susie gently touches my arm. 'Are you okay?'

I give her a brief glance, changing gear. 'Yes, fine.'

'You can still start up your interior design business, you know, it's not too late. And if you did become pregnant, you can still work.'

My hands tighten on the steering wheel. I don't care for being reminded of my barren belly. I'm saved when her mobile rings. She opens her evening bag. 'It's Donna from work; sorry, I have to take this.'

I'm relieved. 'That's okay.' And I flick on the fullbeam, then ease the window down, rain or no rain. I need a drop of cool air as we cruise along Drayton Road through the darkness of the countryside.

Ten minutes later, with the rain easing off, I turn the Mercedes into the car park of the grounds of Creswell Manor Hall, set in seventy acres of tranquil parkland. It dates back three hundred years and I search for free space. Suddenly I slam on the brakes and do a double-take, my heart beating wildly. 'Is that Nigel? What's he doing here?' *Oh my God, how can I face him?*

Susie jerks forward. 'Oh dear, Joanne didn't tell me she invited him. Then I guess there's no reason to, but I have wondered why he is always hanging around the salon lately. I bet she's secretly knocking him off – he is, after all, a bit of a married tart.'

I grow hot and don't appreciate her thoughts. *Surely she's not forgotten?* 'I'm sure it was him, disappearing into the entrance.' And I can hardly concentrate on reversing into a tight space.

Susie exits the car. 'It's him alright, because there's his Bentley.' She then says, 'Oh God, sorry, I forgot about that night you spent at his.'

We drag our cases from the boot onto the wet tarmac and I moan, 'What if he's with his wife?' I turn to her and playfully beg, 'Do we have to go in?' But how can I go home? What excuse would I give? And I can hardly leave Susie. I should be barred from drinking at night, that's what. I need some sort of alarm…a *warning*, a voice, a nudge, just anything to scream, water needed! *Now.*

Susie lights up a quick cigarette. She blows smoke out the corner of her mouth, exclaiming. 'He's hardly going to confess to her, is he?'

Bits are plucked out from the dark hole of that night. I'd only gone out for a quiet drink with Susie at the Talbot Arms. Nigel came in at last orders; he'd just dropped his wife off at the airport for a friend's hen a party in Marbella. Susie had refused drinks at his, but I didn't. I burn at the next fragment of me naked in the swimming pool, him grabbing me and shoving me into the shower room. That's the real reason I gave the local pubs a miss: I was too embarrassed about bumping into him again.

Susie snubs out the cigarette with a red stiletto. 'He probably doesn't even remember; he's well known for his piss-ups.'

'Oh, gee, thanks for that,' I declare, tugging my case behind me.

She hits my arm playfully. 'You know what I mean. Anyway, that was almost two years ago, and besides, you're a respectable married woman now.'

I laugh and hook my arm with hers. 'Now you make me sound old and past it.'

Entering reception, I admire the bifurcated staircase with the vaulted ceiling. We take our place behind a young couple; the mother holds her little girl's hand. She bends to whisper something in her ear. The child covers her mouth and giggles. The scene is endearing, but then my heart drops when I remember the accident. I'm about to turn and ask Susie about it; she must have heard. Her salon is rampant with local news. Before I have the chance we're called to the front desk to checkin. Susie declines the offer of assistance with our luggage, as the bellboy is busy with other guests. She wants her perfume from her case and is not keen to hang around to wait.

As we ascend the stairs there's a familiar feeling of uneasiness, as though I'm being watched. It could be Nigel this time, certainly not Jason. I want to turn around, but I could lose my balance, as one hand clings to the bannister and the other drags up my case. When we reach the first floor I deliberately pause and peer down with a clear view of the reception. There's a man checking in. I don't recognise him, though. His dark tone suggests he is foreign. His tuxedo is tailor-made. Susie's habit is commenting on hair; mine is material. Suddenly feeling alone, I turn to see Susie sailing down the hall to our room and I rush to catch up with her.

Heading to the party along the hallway, we encounter Tom, who's a customer of Susie's. With his distraction as they chat, descending the stairs, I cast my eyes down for Nigel. I've certainly no wish to bump into him. Or could it be Jason? But why? And to be quite frank, I've had enough of this unsettled feeling. He had his chance and blew it. Perhaps, though, it's me and my silly imagination, the tendency to over think when all the time there's nothing there – the boredom of the brain more like it.

We advance into a room of the party and Joanne greets her guests at the entrance. We air kiss. I wish her a happy birthday, handing her over a card and present as my eyes dart around faces in the crowd. Susie and she catch up on salon gossip. It reminds me that Joanne is a colour artist, which is how I met Susie; we clicked straight away when she'd cut my hair. Good job, really, as I hardly knew anyone when I first moved into the area three years ago. When Nigel's name pops up that's my excuse to scuttle off to the bar. I've no desire to listen to another affair he is conducting, whether it is Joanne or whoever else. For some daft reason I glance over my shoulder, ready to jump to my defence should anyone challenge me. I'm being silly, I know, and I grab a flute off a passing waiter. I gulp it down to settle my nerves. As the waiter edges forward I follow and pinch another one. That unsettled emotion returns. I sense someone staring at me. So I spin around, daring to catch the offender. But it's not Jason or Nigel I catch across the other side of the room; it's the guy from reception. Stupidly I blush and focus on the swirls of gold blended in the royal blue carpet. *Don't be daft, Kate, he's probably searching for woman behind you. Why would he be interested in me?* As I mingle my way to the bar, I'm sure he's making his way over. Just in case he is, I attempt to concentrate on getting served quickly. Drumming my nails on the smooth surface, I try to attract the busy barman.

The stranger manages to slip beside me and politely asks, 'Hello, Kate, how are you enjoying the party?'

My tummy quivers and I dart a glance at the exit door. 'How do you know my name?'

'I overheard Joanne thanking you for her birthday present,' he says reassuringly, 'I'm a regular at the salon.'

I soften and relax. 'Oh, okay.' Then silently I quiz, *I don't recall Jo mentioning my name?*

'May I buy you a drink?'

Is he trying to pick me up? I flash a busy, tight smile, fiddling with my wedding ring. 'No, thank you, I'm fine.'

'Nice diamonds, have you been married to Greg long?'

My hands turn clammy. 'Greg?' I repeat like a dummy. 'Do you know my husband?'

His brown eyes cloud over as if deliberating on his answer. 'You could say that.'

The hairs on the nape of my neck spike. Before I can question him, I flinch when something wet and cold splashes against my back. I spin around just as a man staggers off. He is clearly oblivious about spilling his pint over me. I glare after him. *Drunken fool.* My dress is wet and already stinks of beer. Never mind him, though this stranger has unsettled me. The dress can wait a minute. It would be nice to get to know one of Greg's friends. Somehow he hasn't kept in touch with any of them. I turn around but find he's vanished. *That's odd. Why shoot off so suddenly?* I scan the room for him, but with so many party-goers it's quite impossible. After minutes of being jostled, waiting for him to return, I edge away from the bar area. I sigh, giving up, and head out to sort out my dress.

With my back to the hand dryer, I wonder over what the guy said. What did he mean? Or is it me with too much fizz making something out of nothing? I manage to blitz a spray of perfume down the back of my dress; it's still slightly damp but smells better than it did.

I grab a flute from the waiter and hunt down Susie. She must know that guy too. My friend is outside with a crowd of smokers huddled around a patio heater. A man standing next to her whispers in her ear. Her head falls back with laughter. For some reason, I feel a flash of irritation while I wait. But I've no desire to venture out into the cold. Instead, I hover around the patio doors and idly scan the room again for Mr Stranger. At last, Susie appears with a blast of cold air. The smell of smoke clings to her red dress. In a rush, I blurt out the details with his description: tall, foreign, wearing a tailored tux.

Grudgingly, I add, 'Handsome.' That should remind her, if nothing else, given the salon's rampant women's gossip.

She takes a long mouthful of gin like she's deliberating her male clients. Her head moves side to side, slowly. 'No. Can't say I remember anyone by that description. And I'd definitely remember a tall, foreign, good-looking male.' She chuckles when she adds, 'And the girls would have commented too.'

Yes, I agree with that, imagining her staff's playful banter. I sigh, dissatisfied, then suggest, 'Joanne must know him, surely? I mean, he spoke about her as if he knew her.'

Susie argues, 'Then so would I.'

I say, more to myself, 'Well, I find it odd.'

She offers a solution. 'Maybe he came to the salon once and he's a friend of someone, that's why he's here – that's all I can think off.'

Before I can speak we are interrupted by a ginger-haired male sporting a potbelly. He exclaims, 'Susie, how the devil are you? I haven't seen you in years since school.'

The night spills out with dancing and one drink glides down after another. All my thoughts about the odd conversation with the stranger become lost in the blur of champagne. Somehow, much later, we make it upstairs to our suite.

*

Greg runs from our house with the stranger screaming after him, 'I'm going to kill you…'

My eyes snap open and my heart thuds. There's a taste of panic, lying in the four-poster bed. *What's going on?* And for a second my thumping head won't function probably. *Where am I?* it screams. Then, gradually, the events of last night flood back. Susie, I note, is flaked out on the sofa under a loosely draped blanket, still wearing her stilettos.

EIGHT

Much of the drive home is a blur and Susie sleeps through most of it. I berate myself for drinking far too much and have to pull over to retch into the bushes. Eventually, her cottage looms ahead and I drop her off. Somehow I manage to get home in one piece.

The phase never to drink again races through my mind as I pull my case from the boot and drag it clumsily over the gravel drive. With unsteady fingers I struggle to insert the front door key; eventually I manage it, and Timmy bounds up to my tracksuit like I've been gone for years. When I bend down to ruffle him, the hall spins and I steady myself with the help of the wall. After being bestowed with wet kisses, I flick off the hall lamp as Timmy darts towards the kitchen to be let out.

As I run the cold water tap for the kettle I drift back to the strange conversation from last night. With a coffee in hand, I wander into the lounge and shrug; maybe the guy was a school buddy of Greg's? Why book in to stay overnight at a party only then to spend ten minutes at it? Perhaps he was called away on an emergency? Maybe I'm over thinking it all? The coffee does nothing for my raging headache and I think it might be a good idea to take a small nap. Hopefully I'll be in some sort of recovery for when my husband arrives home. No way do I wish for him to see me in this state.

*

When I wake, I realise I'm still in my tracksuit under the duvet, and I stretch out my legs. The hangover is lighter and more settled, thankfully. The central heating radiates a gentle hum and the street lights switch on, sending a warm glow into the bedroom. The pale cream tones from the walls blend with the bedcovers. Actually, when I think about this house, it reminds me of a rental home. So unlike my old terrace with splashes of bold colours; maybe I can use my creative outlet as I did on Timmy's room. Bring some life into the five-bed Tudor house.

The tranquillity is shattered by the ring of my mobile. It's under the duvet somewhere and I scramble to search for it. Greg's name flashes up. 'Alright, babe, did you have a good night then?'

His voice sends a warm tingle and I puff up the pillows to lean back for a comfortable position. 'Yes, it was nice, thanks.' I wonder whether to mention that guy. Would it be wise? He might get the impression I was chatting up a stranger. I don't want that – no way. *And I wasn't.*

There's a sound of him inhaling on a cigarette before he states, concerned, 'Babe, you sound knackered, and I bet you're hung over too.'

A sudden feeling of guilt pops up at his referral to my drinking and I attempt to shake the idea off. I've no reason to feel like that. It does, however, sound to my husband like I'm always drunk, and I do take umbrage when he jokingly mentions it. Admittedly it might be true *sometimes*. My offer is slightly strained, 'A little, I guess.' As a distraction to hide my shame, I ruffle Timmy's soft belly. He laps it up and stretches out his paws.

'Was it a late one then?'

Inwardly I wince, recalling a blurred vision of 4am on a clock somewhere. 'Not too late.' I don't want to give the impression I can't be trusted out on my first night.

Greg sounds amused. 'I thought you'd be dancing until dawn and need an early night tonight.'

That's exactly my intention, and I deliberate, 'So, what time will you be home then?' An image of my sexy husband naked in hot bubbles in the jacuzzi pops up, and I curl a seductive grin. Then, when I switch on bedside lamp, it reminds me of earlier when I arrived home. The light was still on and the lounge curtains closed. So I mention it before he has time to answer, 'I bet you must be tired too, getting up so early to leave for work?'

His sigh comes across as hollow, admitting, 'I couldn't sleep, and when I did, nightmares of the little girl's body splattered in blood were all I could see. In the end, I got up for work and left really early.'

For a second I seal my eyes shut and fight down the bile rising in an attempt to banish the image of his words. What can I offer? What can I say to make him feel better? How do I comfort him?

'You okay, babe, you still there?'

I'm so totally useless, and I mummer, 'Yes, I'm still here.' His devastation is beyond words. My poor *husband* is a broken man. And I try to rack my brain for words of comfort. Anything to help to banish his demons.

'And if I haven't got enough on my plate, I feel worse than ever regarding Steve,' he adds flatly.

My hand grips the phone and I cry, 'Why? What's happened now?'

'Well, he's only gone and gambled the money he saved up for his daughter's birthday.' He pauses before adding his confession: 'It was me who he lost to. But I swear, babe, I didn't know that at the time.'

I wince, exclaiming, 'Oh no. How much did he lose?' My eyes close momentarily, waiting for the dreadful sum.

I sense the shake of his head when he replies, 'Babe, you don't want to know.'

Suddenly I possess a suspicious thought and pose a question: 'Did Gerry play too?' I don't trust him one bit, as it seems whenever he's involved in anything it goes wrong somehow.

Greg echoes the name like he's not heard it before. 'Gerry?'

I feign surprise. 'Yes, Gerry, your business partner.'

'Sorry, I've got a lot on my mind. No, he didn't play. But now you mention him, I forgot to tell you, babe, he's not happy that I suggested buying him out with your money.'

'Hey… it's our money,' I remind him softly. And Gerry probably knows he can't cope without my *husband*.

'Hang on, Steve wants me.' Greg covers the mouthpiece and I catch mumbled tones but can't quite make out the words. 'Sorry about that.'

'What did Steve want?' I ask urgently. He must be in bits about losing his money, but before I have a chance to ask again how much, Greg's quick reply follows.

'He wants the chance to win his money back tonight. But I've already told him I'm staying in with you, babe.' He sounds remorseful, adding, 'I'm sorry, but his daughter will have to do without. I know that might seem harsh, but you're what matters most.'

I bite down on my bottom lip, knowing exactly what it's like not to have a birthday, let alone a present. So I ask with deliberation, 'When's her birthday?' Then, as an afterthought, I question, 'What about her mother? Surely she has money.'

'Sammy's birthday is in two days.' He then presses on angrily: 'His ex-wife is nothing but a vicious, nasty drunk, a royal right bitch.'

A sharp, bitter memory explodes in my head of mother's bloodshot eyes wild with furious rage. The walls close in and my temperature blooms. I unzip my hoodie and struggle over to the window to open it. The cold air sends a shiver down my back and I inhale a deep breath, stamping out painful childhood memories. I don't wish that life on anyone, so on this occasion, I can intervene and help a child to have a birthday. I beg, 'Greg, you must help Steve's daughter.'

'How?' he asks uncertainly.

My heart pounds as I propose my solution. 'You have play poker with him tonight, let him win his money back – it's the only way.'

There's silence like he's digesting the idea. 'I suppose I could try…but it might take a while, and will you be okay with that?'

I think of the little girl killed and the hope of happiness I can offer for this other child, Sammy. 'Just try not to be too late home.' It's the least I can do.

NINE

Timmy stays on the bed when I get up and tug the cords of the Roman blinds. The morning light filters in and I peer outside. Greg's car is not on the drive. He obliviously slept over at Steve's again last night, and I let out a heavy sigh of disappointment. His words from a couple of days ago echo in my mind. Now Steve's won all his money back and more, the excitement has spurned him on to enter a poker competition. His latest dream is to win a wad of cash to fly his daughter to America's Disneyland for Christmas. Timmy is nudged gently off the bed so I can straighten the duvet. I totally agree with Greg; the poker lark has gone to Steve's head. He can't be trusted and needs to be shadowed by my husband, who's fraught with worry. He blames himself; he feels responsible. Steve could lose everything, including his house. I pad downstairs with Timmy and let him out into the back garden. I've already googled gambling addictions and begged Greg to get help his salesman. I've read such disheartening stories of families who have lost everything to gambling. Some kids have even ended up in care.

In the garage, I uncover the black sack; the contents rattle with empty wine bottles. Out in the back garden, I carefully lower it into the wheelie bin, as you never know who might hear. Even though the neighbours' gardens each side are far apart, you can never tell. Dragging the bin to the front, I think how I've noticed Greta from next door regularly filling the council's recycling box for glass bottles. Each week without fail hers is neatly packed with one empty German wine bottle and three large Coke bottles. I'm sure she evens cleans them beforehand too. I've hidden our box in the garage and stuffed it with old newspapers, not that Greg's noticed.

As Greta's rabble of kids storm out and race over to the Porsche Macan, I scuttle inside. However, I allow the door to open just a fraction so I can spy. Her three kids are neatly turned out in royal blue uniforms – private school, obviously. I rub my barren belly with solid frustration and resentment. When I first moved in I'd waved hello and we exchanged banter a few times. Well, that's not quite true – she rattled on as I listened. Eventually, my warm smile dropped to a fake, tight one. I was fed up of her ramification regarding her blonde brood of accomplishments. Teddy, she confirmed, was going to be the next best footballer. Her middle daughter Delia with her fabulous voice was going to be in a girl band and, of course, tiny Pixie was going to be the next Kate Moss. And if that wasn't bad enough, now there's the new mum on the block. Who wheels her pram like a proud peacock past my house daily, it as if she's taunting me.

I run the cold tap for the kettle with visions of drowning her and next door's family. Then there's Steve's selfish wife, without a care for *her* daughter. The kettle lid is snapped. Some women just don't deserve to have kids. Who'd look after his child if his addiction took hold of him? We've plenty of room here, but that's not an option. Rigorously I clean the granite worktop. Next, I scrub the high-gloss cream units for non-existent stains. Feeling my phone vibrate in my robe pocket, I fold the cloth and dry my hands on a towel before I whip it out. It's Susie, and I mouth a silent thank you.

'Sorry I haven't been in touch. The salon has been so hectic, and after the long, hard, constant days all I've done is crash into the bath with a very large G&T.'

I turn down my mouth, remembering my working days, busy chatting to clients. Those wonderful, endless hours I spent gliding my fingertips over fabric books in search of just the right one.

She continues brightly. 'Are you still okay for lunch tomorrow? Believe you me, I can't wait for a day off and a lie-in. Anyway, enough about me, how are you? And how's married life treating you?'

I shrug. 'It is fine. I'm okay.'

Her voice hints at concern when she states, 'You don't sound it?'

By now I should have mentioned to Greg about my thoughts of regarding my return to work and telling her that I have. But with everything that's gone on, I haven't wanted to unsettle him. It also might remind him of our empty cradle, and after the little girl's death, I don't think the timing is appropriate. Plus he has the worry of Steve's habit. I do, however, confide about his poker habit as she takes a drag on her cigarette.

'What?'

'I know, Greg feels terrible and so do I.'

Susie snorts. 'Steve, gambling?'

She sounds as if I'm making it up and I glare at the phone. I then add, with a hint of sharpness, 'Yes, I just told you.'

Her tone sounds baffled. 'Kate, are you sure you heard right?'

A burst of irritation arrives, coupled with a headache, probably stemming from the after-effects of last night's wine binge. Now I wish I'd said nothing. 'Yes, of course I did.' *Why would Greg make it up? And what's her problem?*

'I'm surprised. Although Martin doesn't know Steve very well, he does know his brother, Andy, very well, and I'm sure we'd have heard something. You do know that Andy is very much into gambling, don't you?'

I rub my temples. I'm not happy with this line of conversation. 'Maybe I misheard.' Maybe I misheard a lot of things lately. Then, stupidly, I blurt out that I blame Steve for me hardly ever seeing Greg.

Her tone changes. 'Oh, I see.'

Instantly a siren goes off, implicating a tingle of unease. 'What do you mean by that?' Quickly I regret sounding so harsh and apologise. 'Sorry, I didn't mean to snap.' I suppose I'm taking my frustration out on her. But I miss my *husband*. And nothing has gone to plan like getting pregnant…and I'm lonely…

'No, it's okay… I'd be the same if Martin kept disappearing off twenty-four seven, and I'm surprised he's allowed the time off work.'

I remark, perplexed, 'He's not disappearing – I know where.' What did she have to say it like that for? And he can take off as much time as he wants. It's his business, but I don't bother to mention that.

In her silence I sense a funny suspicion, knowing exactly what she's going to say next. I hope I'm wrong, though. Really, I do.

'You don't think he's having an affair and using poker as an excuse?'

I want to pretend she never said that. I bite my lip and stare out the window. Angry rain belts against it and tears start to loiter behind my eyes. *What gives her the right to say that?* She's always hated Greg, though.

'Are you still there, Kate?'

There's a long, hard sigh before I choose my answer. 'You've never liked him from the start.'

She mirrors my sigh. 'It's not that I don't like him.'

'What is it then?' I say, more harshly than intended. *She's plain jealous, simple as.* Like Greg spat when I told him of her concern when I first mentioned his marriage proposal. She had made her mind up even before she ever met him, and the thought makes me snap: 'How would you like it if I suggested Martin was out having a fling?'

She responds back like I'm a child. 'But he's not the one out all the time, is he?'

I slam my hand down on the island bar. 'He's out helping Steve. The same as I'd help you if you needed it.'

Her voice softens. 'Okay…don't get upset. You're my best friend. I'm only saying it because of how it looks from my side, and you know I speak my mind.'

I sigh, slumping on a barstool. 'Why would you even think he'd do that? I mean, we're trying for a baby. And why do you think the worst when he's only out acting as a Good Samaritan?' I guess now isn't the time to mention the spare room arrangements either. Plus has she even read about that little girl and what my husband was put through? She was bound to have seen it plastered over the news. She could blame that on my husband too. She doesn't know him like I do. *Besides, I trust my husband.* How can she possibly make that statement, and on what grounds? He *loves* me. He's not going to *wreck* our marriage. Morning or not, I pour out a large measure of Yellow Tail and take a long gulp.

'Are you sure there's nothing else to tell me?'

I blurt out, indignant, 'No…Why would there be?' I drown more of the liquid in the glass as if to hide in it.

'Hey, I'm just looking out for you. That's what friends

are for. Damn, the house phone is ringing; it might be work. Sorry, I have to get it. See you tomorrow.'

I'm relieved when the conversation ends. Topping up Yellow, I want to call her back and cancel our Saturday arrangement. *How dare she say Greg is off having an affair?* What gives her the right to say that? She's plain *jealous*, jealous because she can't have kids. But somewhere in my wine-fuddled brain, I scream. *Maybe you can't either?*

TEN

Greg laughs, holding the hand of a tall, leggy, fair-haired woman. I cry out when they run into the sea and disappear.

I wake in a panic, heart thudding in my chest. My husband's side of the bed is empty. I reach out and battle with Susie's words. How do I know for sure where he is? Is there a possibility she's right? A horrifying river of thoughts cascade through me and I fudge through scattered memories. No, he's out with Steve playing poker, not running away with a blonde. He could make it home. Why keep staying overnight at Steve's again? Admittedly, he said it was closer for him to go to work. I wriggle up and wipe my watery eyes. The dream had felt so real, almost like watching a film. Sunlight flickers through the half-closed blinds. Timmy lounges on his back, his paws aimed up, snoring. Although I love my baby to bits, I can't dismiss the disappointment of waking up without my husband. I miss hugging him, feeling his warm skin next to mine. Thank God the stupid poker competition finishes soon. I tilt my head back and close my eyes for a second. A wave of nauseous washes over me; it's not morning sickness, that's for sure. Greg has assured me that the games are coming to an end. He didn't give a reason and I didn't ask. I'm just glad they are. I wish Steve had never mentioned it in the first place. And to think I was happy with it in the beginning. That was before I knew the damage it could cause.

Not to mention that I hardly ever saw my husband. I wobble to the bathroom and splash cold water on my face. Bloodshot eyes appear back. I'll just have to hope paracetamol will thin the wine from my veins. Maybe a hot bath will soak out the damage to my head too.

After slipping empty bottles of Yellow Tail into a black bin liner in the garage, I fill the kettle. Grabbing a mug from the cupboard, I recall Susie's wild statement. I fold my arms and lean against the Belfast sink. *What a nerve.* Fancy saying that? Abruptly I turn cold; in my drunken mode of yesterday, I'd fired off nasty texts to her. I bolt upstairs and grab my phone off the bedroom carpet. I'm almost too scared to check her reply. I gasp reading the words in capitals. *Shit.* Then, on closer inspection, I blow out a long, relieved sigh. *Thank God.* They were never sent. With fingers that shake, I quickly I delete the messages. I curse; never ever send texts when pissed. *I burn with shame.* Susie's my best friend – actually, my only one. I'd never have survived without her help when my parents died. I'm sure she didn't mean what she said. She has, after all, an overactive mind, and a mouth that speaks out before thinking. The one I'd admired when we first met. You always knew where you stood with her. I suppose if I'm honest, I'd like to be more like her: outspoken and fearless of hurting other people's feelings. However, on this occasion, I do wish she'd kept her wild thoughts to herself.

As I pour hot water into a mug, I rigorously stir in coffee granules. God, I dread to think of her reaction if I'd had sent the texts. Thankfully I didn't, but now I'm worried about lunch later. Do I want to listen to her banging on about my husband again? *Should I cancel?* But with an endless stretch of another boring afternoon, I dismiss the thought. Something about the poker game bugs me, and I try to catch it. I jump when Timmy barks. Silly me – I've only forgotten his breakfast. That happens sometimes when my mind drifts off.

After I sort out his food, I carry my coffee down the hall into the orangery with Timmy trotting at my side. It's a peaceful room with views of the fields beyond. I ease into the leather sofa and almost burn my mouth from the hot drink. A magazine on the low table catches my attention. I put the mug down. The front-page headlines screams 'Traded-in wife is the last to know.' Snatching it up, I scan the relevant pages. The tell-tale signs are clearly visible. Timmy curls up on my lap and idly I stroke his fur, reading. I feel for Claire, the woman in the article; she clearly loved her husband, who unfortunately buggered off with her best friend. There's a picture of her wedding day with her so-called buddy, the culprit, the maid of honour. The magazine falls from my hands. *Susie* and *Greg* – no way, now I am being *silly*. However, this article has set off doubts that were never there before. Her statement has unnerved me, and it triggers memories from my childhood. As fast as they come, I dismiss them. Greg's not like that. He's different. He's trustworthy. *He'd never hurt me.*

*

Later that afternoon I apply lipstick then press my lips together on a tissue. I stand back and check out my white shirt, jeans and wool blazer. With one last brush of my hair, I'm ready.

With my head bent dodging rain, I quickly ease into the Mercedes; I shiver, starting up the engine, and wait for a burst of warmth. The county lanes are sodden with deep puddles and bad potholes; I'm really not sure why we pay car tax. The council never seems to fix anything; I'm sure those gaps were there a month ago.

I pull onto Susie's drive. She's sheltering in the doorway of her thatched cottage. Dutifully, I aim the car as near to her as possible and stretch over to fling open the door for her.

She races over, moaning, 'Why rain now? It's been dry all bloody morning.'

I agree with a tiny laugh. 'Yes, how unthoughtful.'

Her mobile rings. 'Sorry, it might be work.'

Immediately I'm glad, and say, 'Go ahead.' Hopefully with the distraction she'll forget her assumption about my husband. Her call sounds like a delivery to her salon has gone wrong. I switch off to her agitated voice to concentrate on missing more gapping potholes in the road. We're headed towards the A458. Even though the rain eases off, I slow down. Some of the country roads are quite narrow with sharp bends. We're on our way to the Stable Bar in Bridgnorth for lunch. The previous time I came here was with my husband. The thought warms me. We'd strolled hand in hand down the cobbled side streets. We'd paused to read the menus before our choice of restaurant was made. *Of course he's not having an affair.*

I focus back on the road that leads to Severn Valley, split into High Town and Low Town. It's named on account of their elevations relative to the River Severn. We're dining in High Town if I can bag a parking space. As I'm about to turn right, I realise that I completely forgot about the Saturday market. Instead, I take a left and grin at my luck when I spot a couple walking towards a red Mini parked just a couple of bays down. A set of keys dangle from his hand.

Susie finishes her call. 'I can't believe how long that took to sort out, sorry.'

'Well, when it's your own business you do what you have to.' Unexpectedly, I experience a brush of envy. *I'd love to be in her position*, I think, edging into the free space. But hadn't I agreed to give up work? Wasn't that on the account of my husband's promise of babyhood? And yes, there was a great chance of it then with plenty of sex. That seems to have dwindled, though, what with one thing and another.

Susie glances out the window and remarks, 'How lucky is that to find a space, considering how busy it is, and it's stopped raining.' She turns to face me. 'I didn't mean to upset you yesterday. But as I said, it doesn't seem right with Greg off out all the time.'

I sigh and pat the leg of her dark jeans. 'I was about to add before you rushed off – the poker game stops in a couple of weeks. Anyway, come on, I'm gasping for a drink.' *Hopefully, that's the end of that.* My husband has insisted it would be all over soon. *And perfect will be back where it belongs.* Or should I say, my husband?

'That's great news.' Flinging the door open, she adds, 'I can't remember the last time I took a Saturday off, I can tell you.'

I'd like to say the same; instead, I urge. 'Come on, before it starts to rain again.' Thankfully she has shut up shop about my *husband* and her wild idea. *As if he would?* Perhaps working too hard has curdled *her* brain. I'm still miffed, though, if I'm honest, but I say nothing.

The cobbled footpath leads up to a black and white grade-II listed building now serving as a bar and restaurant. Timber beams line the ceiling and I breathe in sweet incense burning off a real log fire. A handful of people are dotted along the bar and we're served pretty quickly. We grab our drinks and choose a table next to the brick fireplace. I flop down, glad to be out, and run my fingers over the red velvet armrest while I sip Gulara Shiraz. Its smoothness glides down my throat like a youthful stream with the right hint of warmth. I know I shouldn't have ordered a bottle, but I couldn't help it. It's almost like a celebration to be out with company for a change. I'll take half of it home with me. I'm sure a couple of glasses won't hurt; besides, there's not much chance of getting pregnant at the moment, as it takes two to tango, as they say. *So wine now and then won't hurt,* I convince myself.

Satisfied, I scan the menu, taking another gulp. 'So, what do you fancy then?'

Susie is lost in her double gin and tonic. 'God, I needed that.' She studies the menu with an intent scowl. 'I'm not sure yet…oh yes, here it is, the slow roast shoulder of Bridgnorth lamb, mashed potato, cassoulet of roasted vegetables, butter beans, red wine, rosemary and mint.'

I order the same, as I'm afraid of making a bad choice. It's my Achilles' heel, and numerous times I've stared at my companion's dish with envy; so by having the same, there's no mistake. Susie waves to a young man heading in our direction. This doesn't surprise me at all. She's one of those people that can't go anywhere without knowing someone. She could travel to the moon and she'd know somebody. I sort of knowledge him, slipping off my jacket. I wonder whether we are too close to the fire.

'Kate, this is Ben. He used to work for me.'

His feminine hand darts out for mine. 'Hi!' But his attention is on Susie, who begins to deliver the latest gossip from her salon.

I lean back and cross my leg, listening as Ben flaps on. 'No really…oh, tell me more.'

I think Susie has now realised her mistake of engaging him. She's doing her best to be tactful, offering to call him later. He's obviously unaware, but perhaps the distraction is a blessing, as she might just revert back to my husband. I turn my attention to the yellow flames dancing in the grate. The rhythm is nostalgic and presents a warm image. On my last birthday, Greg booked a hotel room. The four-poster bed was lavish. Champagne was chilled in an ice bucket next to a vase of red roses.

I'm thrown from my reverie when the waiter arrives with our order. I'm surprised to see Ben still standing there.

His stance is wistful when he says, 'That looks nice.'

Susie asks, 'Are you not eating?'

'No, I only popped in for a quick drink and someone to talk to,' he adds with a lost expression.

'Oh,' says Susie, shooting me a sorry expression.

Guilt washes over me, and I offer, 'Why not join us?' Because lately I've known the presence of loneliness.

His bum is shot on the chair and his pint of lager shoved on the table. 'You don't mind then?'

I half-joke, asking, 'Would you like to taste my lamb?' What did I say that for? Guilty because I have food and he has none?

I'm relieved, though, when he shakes his head. 'No thanks, I know the chef, and he'll be able to rustle something up quickly.'

When he shoots off, Susie whispers, 'I'm sorry, I tried my best to drop hints.'

'I don't mind.' And really, I don't; the situation is perfect, as I top up my wine. It's obvious now that Susie will focus on him rather than my non-existent problem, should she have dared to have gone back to it.

'Anyway, I detect the real reason why Ben rushed over is because he wants his old job back, and of course, bumping into me is his perfect opportunity.'

A thought stands out that I wonder about. So I ask curiously, 'Did your staff know you were coming here for lunch?'

She frowns. 'What do you mean?' Her nod is then slow, confirming my suspicion. 'Yes, actually they did. And I can see where you're coming from. Of course, it was all planned in advance.'

I mock, 'You can't knock him for trying.'

Before Susie can respond, Ben arrives back with a dish piled high with a prawn salad.

'Wow, that was quick,' Susie says, bemused.

He produces a cute grin. 'Yeah, well, me and the chef, Chez, used to be lovers.'

Jesus, I almost choke on my mint lamb. Did I really want to know that?

'Well,' Susie comments, 'judging by the number of prawns he piled on your plate, my guess is that he's trying to get you back.'

His blue eyes widen in delighted surprise. 'Really, do you think so?'

Now we are subject to his drawn-out elaborate rendition of how he and Chez broke up. It's a sad story, and my heart drops thinking of my husband. Earlier this morning I'd tried his mobile a couple of times; each call went straight to voicemail, though. I'd bitten my lip and wondered whether to try the showroom, but I didn't want them to think I had no idea where my husband was. My guess is that he's still with Steve out playing some drawn-out game. I can't say I'm happy about the situation. But I trust my husband's words that it will be over soon. Still, I can't help feel a sinking sensation in the pit of my belly as I sip my wine. I sense something is not right. Not wanting to draw attention to myself I fake a smile at Susie and Ben, pretending to listen. *Is there a chance Susie is right?* As I slowly chew the lamb I have an urge to speak to my husband. I'm desperate to hear the sound of his voice. *I want reassurance.* I bend down and rummage through my soft tote leather bag for my phone. There are *no missed calls* and I sigh. As a distraction, I try to hone into Ben's flamboyant love story, but the snippets of his compared to mine adds to my disappointment. The once-delicious lamb dinner now tastes like dust, and I discard my knife and fork. The conversation then turns to Ben asking for his old job back. Probably as a clincher, he offers drinks.

'I'm okay,' I say.

Susie gets up. 'Go on then, Ben, but...I'm not saying that's a yes. I'm going out for a smoke and a think.'

He practically dances his way over to the bar like he's got his old job back already. Left on my own, I tap the side of the armchair and sigh. Susie's statement screams in my head. I cross my leg and bounce it up and down. I guzzle wine. I check my phone again. *Nothing.* Then a memory grabs my attention; it arrives like the grim reaper. On our honeymoon, we'd made friends with a couple who stayed at the same hotel in Spain. They'd invited us to the casino. Greg lied and explained that we'd made other arrangements. He'd told me later he didn't care for gambling, thought it was a mug's game. The memory flashes over and over. My hand shakes as I empty the bottle. I can't drink it fast enough. Through a haze of numbness, I hear my name called; the tone sounds urgent.

Susie is clearly distressed, rushing over. 'Kate, I have to get back to the salon.'

I shoot up from my chair, thinking it's to do with Greg. 'Why, what's happened?'

She races to the door; her words linger behind her. 'Someone tried to rob the till – we need to leave now.'

Driving on the wet road, my heart hammers in my chest. Susie is rampant on her mobile, firing off questions to her staff. I, on the other hand, feel a cold band of ice around my heart. I bite down a sickening panic. *Susie could be right, after all.* I grip the steering wheel and fight back tears. My loving husband wouldn't do this to me; he just wouldn't. There has to be a reasonable explanation. *There must be.*

The salon in the village of Belbroughton is surrounded by police cars and a crowd of onlookers. I drop her off as close as I can. I'm aware I'm over the limit and hastily speed off, more to get to my destination, the showroom. I don't care what trouble I cause. I can't stand not knowing any longer. It seems ages until I reach the high street of Stourbridge and I curse the traffic. Eventually, with my heart still banging in my chest, I turn left onto the showroom car park. I park up outside the glass frontage. The place appears empty, which is to be expected for 5.15. My legs wobble as I cross the tarmac, sick with nerves. There's no sign of my husband's car, but then again, he swaps and changes all the time. I bite my lip and shove open the door. A salesman is engrossed in his computer as I approach. Dave, according to his name badge, shuts down his system. He must be the new salesman Greg told me about.

I know what I ranted in the car, but in the here and now I feel the urge to be careful. So I do my best to hide my anxiety. 'Hi… I'm looking for Greg… my husband?'

Dave looks up in surprise. 'Oh, you're back early.' He jokes, 'London too much for you? I must admit I used to live there years ago.'

I sense fear within me. *London?*

Dave is oblivious, shoving documents into his briefcase. 'Far too busy for my liking and the cost of living, phew…don't even go there.'

He snaps his case down. 'Anyway, that's me done for the night. The boss said we could close early.' He grins. 'But then, I guess you'd know that.'

My mouth is dry. What the hell is going on?

'Oh, I'm sorry, did the boss want you to fetch something? Only it's the wife's birthday and boy, will I get it in the neck if I'm late. I'm the one locking up, being as Steve is still on holiday. Not that I mind.'

Silently I scream, *Holiday?* I grip the nearest desk and for a second I think I'm going to explode in shock. Somehow I manage to croak, 'When is he back?' Surely he's got the wrong *person*.

'You know what, those two weeks have flown by. He's back tomorrow.' He nods to affirm this. 'Anyway, sorry, I need the little boys' room, be back in a tick.'

'You do mean Steve Green?'

He turns around, puzzled. 'Yes, of course it's him. We don't have another Steve – not to my knowledge, anyway.' He appears to want to add something else but changes his mind, strolling off.

Greg lied. How could he? Hot tears sting and a million questions spring up. *Where is he?* More to the point, who's he with? The dream of him and the leggy blonde flashes back. I stumble outside and slip into the Mercedes. *London?* The black hole I'm falling down deepens. *Steve's on holiday?* Not out playing poker. Was anything my husband said *true?*

I have to get a grip and leave; I can't stay here. I manage to drive the car into the next road and park outside a newsagent sandwiched between rows of terraced houses. A cold band of dread circles like a vulture. *Susie was right.* Did she know something I didn't?

The shrill sound of my mobile slices through my thoughts. *It's Greg, I know it.* Frantically I rummage in my handbag. His name flashes across the screen. My hand trembles when I silence the ringtone, staring at the phone. *What's he going to say?* Does he even know I called at his work? *I can't talk now;*

I just can't. It's as if my mind is on delay mode, ready to shut down.

A text appears.

> Please, babe, pick up, let me explain. It's not
> what you think xxx

I bite my lip and my vision blurs. *He lied.* How is he going to explain that? More texts arrive. I turn the phone off. I'm too numb, too broken to listen or say anything.

I'm startled at a gentle knock on the side window. A man is bent down; he sounds concerned, asking, 'Hi, Kate, are you okay?'

How does he know my name?

His eyes twinkle warmly. 'It's Nick.'

I frown. 'Who?' I manage to ask, rolling down the window. His appearance has jolted me back to life.

'Nick, from Joanne's birthday party.'

Street lamps shimmer on and I notice a small gap between his front teeth. I blink, remembering, and wipe under my eyes. *What's he doing here?*

He peers in closer. 'You okay? You seem upset. Is there anything I can do?'

The betrayal of my husband flashes up in my mind and I sniff then turn to search my bag for a tissue. I blow my nose. I can't handle a stranger's intervention right now. I'm unable to cope with anything at the moment.

He presses on. 'You shouldn't be here hanging around on your own. Look, there's a pub further up. Come on, I'll buy you a drink. You look like you could do with one.' He mocks, 'I'm not an axe murderer, and besides, you know me – we talked for a while at the party.'

I don't remember whether we talked for long.

But I guess that's in the black hole, along with all the other stuff I can't recall. The thought of red wine hits the spot, and for once going home has no appeal. But I hardly know this person. Does it matter, after what my so-called husband has done?

Nick straightens, shoving his hands in his jeans pocket. 'Everyone knows me at the Moon pub. I'm Nick the Greek; my restaurant is over there.' He points to the end of the road. 'Come on, it's my night off.'

ELEVEN

My eyes flutter open. I'm nude in bed next to a naked man. I panic. *What the fuck! What the hell happened?* My heart thuds in my chest. I can hardly breathe through my dry mouth and desperately I search for memories. Bits from the showroom spring up, then Greg lies. Next is Nick, he'd held open the pub door for me to enter first. I'd gulped wine. I'd cried. I'd order shots and knocked them back. I search for more. There's nothing. I go cold with shame, listening to light snores sounding from Nick. *But is it him?* How would I know, with his back turned away from me? I delve into the black hole for more memories. *Nothing.* I freeze when he stirs and rolls over. I hold my breath, begging that whoever it is won't wake up. I'm in no mood for polite conversation or anything else. It's Nick… and fear prickles at me, remembering kissing his soft lips. Oh my God. *What have I done?* I glance over to the window, the early darkness fading. How long have I been here? I can just make out the time on my watch: 6.45. I scan the bedroom for my handbag. It's discarded on the polished wood floor next to a pile of my clothes. I ease out of bed, dreading waking *him*. My head feels horrible and bile rises. The room spins as I stumble to peer outside. *Where the hell am I? Where's my car?* I sigh, relieved, spotting it parked between a line of cars on the terrace street below. I scan left to right, unable to recognise the street. *I could be anywhere for all I know.* What I do know now is I have to get out of here, and fast. Hastily I throw on my clothes, grab my handbag and creep out into the hall. Clutching the bannister, I edge downstairs and silently slip out.

An elderly man strolls past with a poodle, a knowing glint in his eye. I bend my head in shame. I must look a right mess heading for my car. In my bag, I frantically search for my keys. I panic. They're not there. *Shit.* What the hell do I do now? I feel the heat rise to my cheeks. Silently I curse for not checking for them before I left. I race back to the front door and shove it. It's locked, just as I thought it would be. Then it opens and Nick is in his boxer shorts, seemingly amused, dangling my car keys. It's my final disgrace, and I rip them from his fingers. I fumble with my fob to unlock my car. With his no shame attitude on the doorstep like a Greek god I can barely get the key in the ignition. But something is wrong. My feet won't touch the pedals. He must have driven and moved the seat. Flustered, I spend minutes adjusting it back to the correct position. I know I glow the colour of beetroot, knowing he's still watching as I zoom off.

TWELVE

I roll down both windows. The cold breeze is welcome as I drive at snail's pace, fearful of blue lights creeping up behind me as I must be still well over the limit to drive. Reaching the end of the road, I take a gamble and turn left. Finally I recognise the Harp pub and I grip the steering wheel. *What have I done? I slept with another man. If* only I'd not parked there last night. *If* only I'd have gone straight home instead. I pull onto the car park, shaking. I stop and bury my face into my hands, sobbing. *I've wrecked my marriage.* How could I have been so stupid? *What's… wrong with me?* Suddenly I sit up and wipe my tears. Greg lied. This mess is his *fault.* Where the hell has he been? And who with? *'Oh my God, Timmy.'* I was only going out for a couple of hours…

Did Greg call again? In my drunken state did I call him? The black hole is darker than ever as I try to fish for a memory. Do I even have my phone? I delve into my handbag, my nerves shot to a thousand pieces. It's still switched off. *Is that a good sign?* I'm afraid…

Come on… Kate, shove it on. *Do it.* Nothing could be worse than sleeping with a *stranger with soft lips.* STOP. Think

properly. Breathe… Relax… Keep your guilty secret. *Don't tell.*
No one will ever find out. You're never going to bump into
Nick again, ever. Last night was a mistake. *A one-off.* Probably
best to stop drinking. I sigh loud and deep, pressing the phone
on. Greg's last call was 4am.

> Where are you?
> Please call me, PLEASE

He knows nothing. *I can do this.* It's him in the wrong, not *me.*
I head home and turn into my road, birds twittering until a
heavy lorry thunders past, drowning out their song. I could
have sworn I closed the gate. Edging in the drive, I take a
sharp intake of air, squeezing the steering wheel. Greg's Audi
R8 is parked up. My heart speeds up and my legs turn to jelly,
slipping out the car. *Do I look guilty doing the walk of shame?* My
fingers shake inserting the key. Hang on, I shouldn't be the one
shamefaced sneaking in. As Timmy jumps up and down eager
to see me, I don't know what to think anymore as I swoop
down, to accept his licks of love before bundling him up in my
arms. My heart hammers in my chest and I stand still, waiting,
daring to breathe. The house is silent as I creep towards the
lounge door, half-expecting Greg to jump out, demanding
to know where I've been. He's asleep on his armchair, mouth
gaping. I'm floored by fresh guilt and silent tears fall. Quickly
I wipe them away, remembering my secret pact to myself. It's
him who should be weeping, not *me. What's he done?* My head
pounds; I need sleep. I can't deal with anything right now.

I pull off jeans and unbutton my shirt before slipping
between the soft sheets, desperately wanting to forget last
night with Nick. Slowly then I drift off into a troubled sleep.

*

Nick is running after me calling, 'Kate…Kate…can you hear me…?'

I wake with a jolt, confused, expecting to see Nick. But it's Greg's face I see. I panic, thinking I've been rumbled about Nick. I turn my head, anticipating Nick naked beside me. I then breathe easy, recalling my journey home.

'Babe… are you okay?' Greg asks with concern, planting down a mug on the side drawers.

I nod, mumbling, 'Bad dream,' hoping he can't hear the banging in my chest.

He perches on the bed. 'Where have you been? I've been out of my mind with worry. And look, I can explain.'

The showroom memory floods back to me and I struggle to sit up. Grateful for the coffee, I take a sip and try my best to act normal.

'Those times I said I was playing with Steve, yes, I lied.' He pauses. 'Only because I wanted to surprise you.'

I screw my face up in disbelief. 'You wanted to surprise me by lying?' Who am I to talk, though, after what I did? Quickly I bury my head in my coffee, hiding heat rising to my face. Suddenly I freeze, smelling Nick's aftershave on my hand. *It's so different from Greg's.* Raising the mug to my lips, I pretend to take a sip. His fragrance is all over my hands. Silently I curse for not taking a shower. But all I'd wanted to do was climb into bed. How stupid of me for not having the thought to wash off Nick's scent.

When Greg touches my free arm, I jolt. *He'll smell it.* I know he will.

'Babe… come on, don't be like that. Let me at least explain.'

He mistakes my flinch, thinking it's him. I wish it was. *Act normal, Kate.* 'I, err…' *Think, Kate…* 'Surprise, you said? What surprise? I don't get it.'

'I'm in a poker tournament and the winning prize is a million pounds.' He stands up to pace the carpet. 'Sorry, I know I should have told you.' Then he stops and turns. 'But I'm almost there. That's why I've spent so much time away.' He sits back down to face me. 'I have more debt from Gerry.' He shrugs helplessly. 'I didn't know about them, and I didn't want to worry you. You do believe me, babe, don't you?'

I grip the mug with both hands. I want to disappear into my black hole. *Why did he lie?* If only he'd been honest. *Guilt* washes over me like an avalanche.

'Please say you forgive me, babe, I love you so much. I don't want to lose you.'

I gulp the coffee, wishing it was something stronger, and say, deflated, 'Why couldn't you have said? Why lie?' *Why?*

'I was scared, babe. I didn't want to let you down.' He checks the time on his watch. 'Damn, I have to go, I have a meeting, but I'll be back later.'

He reaches over to kiss my cheek. Instantly I turn my head and pray he won't pick up on Nick's aftershave, which I'm sure lingers in my hair too.

He draws back with a strange expression, staring down like he's scrutinising me.

I burn under his examination. He can sense my guilt. *He knows.* Can he hear the thunder of my heart? Know my fear?

'You seem different, babe. Did you spend the night with another man?' he questions lightly.

I freeze and force out a weak laugh. 'What do you mean?'

His eyes narrow. 'Where were you last night?'

'I…I…was out with Susie.' *I was.*

'Well, where did you go then?'

I shove the covers off the bed and urgently lie, 'I need the loo.' I do now with my bowels loosening. Hastily I offer to say,

'We went clubbing.' *Clubbing?* How childish does that sound, *dummy?* But it's the first thing I can think of.

'What club?'

I catch my burning reflection in the dressing-room mirror as I dive into the en-suite. 'I need to go – back in a tick.' I lean against the door and pray he won't follow to question more. I swallow hard. *He knows.* I have to confess. What if he wants a divorce? Tears roll down my cheeks and I wipe them away. He's going to hate *me*. I search the mirror for answers. *I've screwed up big time.* Now I know how my mother felt. *Just tell the truth, Kate. Get it over and done with.* On the toilet seat, I linger, stalling for time. After, I run the tap and watch water trickle down the plug like my *marriage*. Bracing myself, I open the door, but for a minute I'm confused seeing Greg naked in bed. *I don't understand.*

He pats the bed, smiling. 'I know you'd never look at another man – I was only joking – but the thought, babe, has turned me on.'

My insides churn, and if I didn't know any different, I'd swear that he really knows. I beg to take a shower, but Greg won't hear of it, dragging me into bed. I close my eyes, thinking. *This is not happening.*

*

As Greg gets ready to leave, this time I take a shower. Tears of guilt mingle with the jets of hot water. I scrub off my shame and curse at my mistake. Why didn't Greg tell me about the game? *Why lie?* Or is it *me* that's the liar now?

I jump when Timmy barks, and more remorse is added to the massive pile. *He must think I'm a terrible mother for leaving him all night.* Quickly I dry off and pull on a bathrobe. I give Timmy my best sorry smile as we head downstairs. He darts outside in pursuit of a blackbird in the garden. You'd think by now he'd know his chase is pointless. I sigh and close the French door, locking out the cold. The sky is a depressing dark grey, a mirror of my mood. *Greg lied. I lied.* It's certainly isn't the basis of a good *marriage. Neither is fucking someone else.* I feel a cold, clammy dose of remorse, watching squirrels chase each other. I bet they never screw up.

Timmy is let back in, the cold clinging to his fur as he shakes it. I switch on the glass kettle. When it boils I watch the steam curl like a genie, the master of wishes. I wish for last night to disappear. I wish I'd come straight home. I wish I'd taken Greg's call. Seated at the bar, cupping my hands around a mug, I glare at discarded grains of sugar mingling with drops of coffee; it's a mess, like my life. *How could I?* When the phone rings, I snatch it from my robe pocket. I don't recognise the number.

'Kate, its Nick, are you okay?'

I go hot and then cold, wanting the floor to open up and swallow me whole. I curse. *I must have given him my number.* 'I can't talk.' Cutting the call, hastily I block his number. What if Greg had been standing next to me? *What then?* Relax, breathe. He can't call again. My secret is still safe. Greg still loves me; my marriage is okay. I touch my tummy and then suddenly question, *Did Nick use protection? What if I get pregnant? Will I confess to Greg? Will I tell Nick?* I've jeopardised my marriage – *me*, not Greg. I stare down into Timmy's innocent face as tears blur my vision. *If only I'd picked up Greg's call.* If only Susie's salon wasn't robbed. On and on, the thoughts whirl and nag at me.

Later I turn to my trusted friend Yellow in hope to block out my guilt. I stuff a whole chicken and shove it into the oven. Peeling potatoes, my mind wanders back to last night. I put the knife down and drain Yellow as another tidal wave of shame descends. Greg and I made love earlier. How could I have refused? It happened so fast. I was lost in his arms, the passion like nothing had happened. What else was I supposed to do? Then I shudder. What if I pass on a disease? The front door opens and then closes, and I freeze. Guilt is etched across my face. *Act normal, Kate. You can do it. Forget the stupid mistake. It won't happen again. Put it out of your head. You can do it.*

Greg waltzes in, handing over a bottle of Yellow Tail. 'Something smells nice.'

I can do this. And I force out, 'Thank you.' Nervously, I wonder whether to kiss his cheek. Instead, I add the wine to my collection while Greg ruffles Timmy's fur. The scene would be endearing if Timmy was not so rigid. Maybe he's picking up on my distress. Greg slips off his suit jacket and drapes it over the barstool.

'Do you know what I fancy? A lager.' He pulls one from the fridge and asks, 'How long is dinner going to be?'

I open the oven door, avoiding his gaze. 'Not long.' Is it me or is he acting strange? He hardly ever drinks, but I always keep cans in for visitors. I start to feel unsettled. Could he have spoken to Martin to check up about my story? *My pack of lies.* Then it hits me…the *robbery*. Susie wouldn't go out after that. My heart thuds, closing the oven door, and I turn around like a startled rabbit, fearing the worst.

He rests on the barstool, pulling back the loop on the can. 'I thought I'd move out in the next couple of weeks when the competition starts.'

Cold trickles down my spine. 'Move out?' I say, shocked. *He knows?* This is it. My perfect life, shattered. Over. Gone.

'Yes, I told you this morning, remember, we both agreed I needed to be near the game if I've got a chance of winning.'

I repeat like a dummy, 'The game?' *What game? What's he on about?* Then, bit by bit, his words earlier surface. I cover my tracks quickly with a silly nervous laugh. 'Yes, of course, sorry, I was mentally timing the potatoes.' He did mention it, but I was too eager to grab a shower and scrub off Nick's sex mingled with his. Just the thought makes me shudder.

Pouring lager into a tall glass, his tone is measured. 'Babe, you seem upset, are you okay?'

I state, far too quickly, 'I'm fine.' As a distraction, I stir the gravy on the hob. The liquid reminds me of Nick's dark skin. I jolt when Greg gets up. 'I'll pop and get my laptop to show you places I'm considering staying at.'

He returns in an instant and rests it on the granite surface. He pops the lid open and proceeds to type. 'There are a couple of apartments in Birmingham I like with a five-minute walk to the casino.' He adds, evenly, 'Some nice places, don't you think?'

I take a glance and agree. Right now, Greg's departure is a welcome relief. It will allow me time for my guilt to fade. Then all this madness can be behind us and we can move on. Even Greg sleeping in the spare room is a respite – what if I called out Nick's name?

'Babe, are you listening?'

I get plates from the cupboard. 'Sorry, I'm concentrating on dinner, what did you say?'

'I thought we might celebrate.'

I'm stunned. 'Celebrate what?'

He grins, then sips lager. Wiping his mouth, he smoothly states, 'The win of one million pounds, of course. What else?'

I say, evenly, 'Oh yes, a million pounds.' I'd be more enthusiastic if I didn't feel so full of guilty shame. There's something bugging me, but whatever it is, I can't catch it. I'm far too wrapped up in worry about what I did.

THIRTEEN

From Stourbridge high street I edge slowly into the narrow brick wall turning by the car park of the Asian restaurant. The glass door swings open and I'm greeted with a smile from a waiter. Seated, I can't help but drum my nails on the black tablecloth, waiting for Susie. A week ago I'd packed Greg's suitcase. He'd acted like an excited schoolboy going off on his first trip. For once I was relieved for him to have gone.

I've also made a secret promise to quit alcohol. I can't be trusted around it, not after that *fateful night*. My glare is distasteful at the glass of *water*. First night and already I'm agitated. Wanting a distraction, I turn my attention to the velvet effect wallpaper; the smoothness, for once, holds no comfort and I return my gaze back to the glass with a sigh. Perhaps giving up alcohol could have its benefits, I suppose.

My mind then drifts off. What are the chances of becoming pregnant after sleeping with two men? I go cold at the possible nightmare. Whose baby would it be? I visualise a court case arguing the baby's DNA. Is it the *Greek* or the *English* man? Hearing laughter, I snap my head up. This isn't funny; it's no joke. I spot the guilty couple, giggling, their hands linked across the table. Their bond of love alerts me to my shame and I shove the glass away, desperate for a real drink. I drum the table and sigh. The house is empty without Greg and more boring than ever. We had lunch midweek, but he then had to rush back to the game. He did say he was doing well and was hopeful about winning. My fingers stop as I mentally reread his loving texts. They also relight my guilt. Hopefully in time they will diminish to dust.

Susie rushes in, overall apologetic. 'Hey, I'm not late, am I?' She then notices my water. 'What on earth is that?'

I flinch. 'What?'

'That.' She points her manicured finger to the water.

I grunt, 'Oh, that.'

She slips in the seat opposite, alarm sounding in her voice. 'You're not ill, are you?' Next, her hand flies to her glossed lips and her eyes flutter, excited. 'Oh my God, you're pregnant.'

The loving couple glances our way as if to share their good fortune too. I offer them a tight, forced smile. Then I whisper to my friend, 'It's nothing like that.'

'Something tells me I'm going to need a large gin and tonic.' She smiles uncertainly.

What's the big issue of giving up booze, like I can't do it?

Susie orders from a passing waiter and then questions, 'Are you sure you don't want a real drink?'

I force out my lie. 'Positive.' And to prove my point, I clutch the glass but make no attempt to drink it.

She settles back, folding her arms. 'I'm all ears.'

'I think it's a good idea to give up, that's all.' I've no intention of relating the real truth to her. That's my secret. Wanting to change the subject, I enquire about the robbery. I half-listen as her gin and tonic arrives and I stare at it with envy. I'm then irritated when the couple on the next table start deliberating which red wine is best. *Just get on with it.* Wanting a diversion,

I glance over at the entrance as one of the waiters greets four men who enter. They're ushered over our way to a table. I'm sure I know one of them. I do. Instantly I panic and duck down, pretending to delve into my handbag. *What's he doing here?*

'Hello,' says Susie, sounding bemused.

I take in his shoes and close my eyes in despair. I've no choice but to face him. I can't stay practically hidden under the table forever.

Nick's voice drips with charm. 'I thought it was you, Kate.'

I hold my breath and pray, Please don't say anything.

'Then again, I guessed it was, as I parked next to your car.'

My heart sinks. Did he have to mention that?

He then addresses Susie, stating mildly, 'Her husband's a fool to have gone off.'

My eyes widen and my face burns, dreading what he's going to blurt out next.

'And as I said, Kate, please call me if you need to talk. Anyway, have a nice evening, ladies.'

Susie leans over the table, demanding in a hushed tone, 'Greg's gone off? What's he talking about? Why didn't you tell me? How come he knows? And who the hell is he anyway?'

Her glass is snapped up, with me draining the contents down in one. After, I mumble, 'I'll get you another.' She glares at me, waiting while I signal the waiter, silently cursing Nick. *How dare he drop me in it?* In my haste, I order an Australian bottle of wine and a large gin and tonic.

Between slugging, I gush out what was said at the showroom, how I ended up in Nick's bed, the reason why Greg has moved out now and not gone off, as she put it. There's something else bugging me, but I can't quite catch it and I press on. 'As I said, I should have taken my husband's call instead of racing to stupid conclusions.' I sigh regretfully.

'Yes, I know my husband lied. But that was to protect me.' I grip the stem of my glass. 'But it was me who slept with someone else.'

Susie is silent. It's unnerving. I guess it is to be expected, though. After all, she accused *Greg* of having an affair. I wallow in wine, grateful for the comfort. I promise I'll give up tomorrow; right now, my need is desperate.

Finally, she leans over, her tone dark. 'I can't get over the fact you slept with a total stranger who you met in the street.'

Indignant, I blurt out, 'He's not a stranger.'

'Really,' she says with a hint of sarcasm.

'He's the guy from Joanne's party, so I sort of know him,' I add lamely.

'What? You mean the strange man you were going on about.' Her eyes narrow. 'Are you sure you're telling me the whole truth?'

I roll my eyes. 'What...are you suggesting that I gave him my number on that night and I arranged to meet him?' Admittedly it might look like that. However, I still press on, adamant. 'I told you, I parked up and Nick just happened to be there.'

'It seems a bit of a coincidence, don't you think?'

'I suppose it was a bit odd.' I hadn't given it much thought at the time, as I was too upset.

She takes a mouthful of her gin. 'So how does he know Greg?'

I'm confused and repeat her question like a dummy. 'What do you mean, how does he know Greg?'

She shakes her head in disbelief. 'Come on, Kate, you said he asked about Greg at the party.'

A cold band grips around my heart. *How could I have forgotten?* Wine is guzzled, masking my discomfort. I toy with the stem of my glass, eyes downcast, and shrug. 'I can't recall what he said.' *More like too drunk to remember.* I'm not going to admit that. I sound bad enough as it is.

Susie sighs. 'For once I'm at a loss for words.'

She's not the only one.

Then, lowering her voice, she asks, 'Did you use *protection?*'

I recoil, holding my breath, considering the implications. I kind of shake my head then bury it in my empty glass. It was just after my period too.

Her sigh is loaded. 'Why didn't you tell me sooner?'

I shrug hopelessly with no answer. I wanted to forget it, not relive it.

'Oh, dear…I need a cigarette.'

I'm tempted to join her, pouring the remainder of the wine down my throat. I bite my lip, daring not to think the worst. I then have a funny sensation that Nick is staring at me. With a sly glance his way, I'm right – he is. I flush bright red, snatch up the menu and pretend to study it. I'm sure I hear his laughter. Is he mocking me? But it was him who took advantage of me. He plied me with booze. He must have then dragged me back to his. I bet he remembers it alright. I bet he's not the one with a gaping black hole full of lost memories. *Will he drop me in it and tell my husband?*

I can't sit here any longer – we have to go. I can't stand the embarrassment. I drum my nails on the table, debating whether to get up. I decide to wait for Susie. It will be less conspicuous hovering in the aisle, demanding to leave. Just then Susie strides over, bearing a grim expression. *What's happened now?*

Before taking her seat, she signals the waiter for another gin and tonic. I still moan anyway, 'I think it's best if we left.'

Her command is firm. 'No, you need to listen.'

A cold tingle slides down my spine as I edge closer. *Greg knows.* My marriage is over. I've been such a fool.

'I've made some calls about this so-called poker game, and guess what?'

'What?'

She almost appears smug. 'There's no million-pound game. Even Steve's brother knows nothing about one either.'

The walls close in. 'I don't understand.' *No poker game?* I stammer, hopefully, 'There has to be. You're wrong. Why would Greg lie?'

Susie is adamant. 'Well, he's lied before… and I'm telling you from a known source. *There* is *no* private game.'

I drain my glass and pour another. *If there's no game, then where is my husband?* Her statement sinks in. I'm too stunned to cry, though, as pain curdles my blood, like how deadly cancer might feel. *Is Susie right and he is really having an affair?* What else would he be doing?

Susie reaches for my hand to offer comfort. 'Sleeping with Nick was wrong, but you must find out what your husband is really up to. Sort out what happened with Nick at a later date.'

I can hardly breathe. *My husband lied again.* And here I sit, racked with remorse. Like everything is my fault. I've been so swarmed with self-reproach I've fundamentally miscalculated once again. I got drunk because of *his* lies. I fell into the arms of a *stranger* because of that. I was hurt by Greg's lies. I made a dreadful mistake, sleeping with someone else. Greg's lies must have been calculated, though, no mistake there. Fuelled with alcohol, my rage simmers. And only then do I remember Greg's hate of gambling, which adds fire to my rage.

'So what are you going to do?'

I pull my hand back. 'I'm going to get drunk. Then I'm going over to confront Greg.'

She exclaims, 'What, go over now?'

'No, I'm having a drink first to calm down. Then I'm going.

I've just about had enough of his lies, once and for all.' *This is defiant Dutch courage spinning out orders.*

'I couldn't agree with more. But you need to go home first and sober up.'

As Susie settles the bill, I guzzle as much as I can. I stand up unsteadily. I grab the bottle and hiccup. Staggering out, I bump into a waiter, which sends his tray of drinks flying. I then trip but manage to steady myself on someone's chair, unfortunately spilling wine down their back. I hiccup once more. 'Sorry.'

Susie is right behind me. 'I'm taking you home; you're not in a fit state to drive.'

I hiccup again. 'I'm fine.' And I've no intention of going *home*. Not after what she's just told me.

Outside in the badly lit car park, she tugs at my arm. 'No, you're not.'

I struggle desperately to get away; the bottle slips from my grip. It smashes onto the tarmac; glass scatters, with everywhere stained in blood red. I cry, angrily, 'Now look what you've done.'

'For God's sake, Kate, calm down, and maybe it's a good thing that you dropped it – you've had enough. Now come on, I'll drive you home.'

No, I need answers, fast, and not via phone either. Susie is momentarily distracted when a man with a takeaway asks if we need any help. Grateful for the diversion, I fumble in my jacket pocket for the key fob. Lucky for me I parked the car facing out, which I calculate is going to let me have a fast getaway. In my haste to zoom off, I almost knock the man over.

Two white lines stretch ahead on the Hagley Road into Manor Way. I squint, unsure which one to take notice of. I blink and grip the steering wheel, crawling forwards. The traffic lights ahead change colour. What's the combination? Is green to go? Or is it red? A horn blasts, making me jolt. It's green for go, and I accelerate. Suddenly I feel sick. The brakes are slammed on and the horn blares are mixed with screaming insults. I fling open the door and heave out blood-red vomit. It hurts my throat, and after wiping my mouth, I shut the door. My head hurts, and I lean back and close my eyes.

FOURTEEN

In the distance, I hear shouts and banging. I blink, confused. My tongue is glued to the roof of my mouth. *Where am I? What happened? Why is a man in high-vis jacket peering through the window?*

'Are you okay? You do know you are parked just after the lights and have been since I started work fifteen minutes ago.'

I panic, scanning the row of shops on the left-hand side of Hagley Road. *He's right.* I must have passed out. The street lights are still on, but the roads are deserted. The time flashes on the dashboard: 6am.

'You're lucky not to have been hit. Can you drive?'

I nod my head, realising the engine is still running.

He rubs his hands together, stomping his feet on the road. 'You need to move your car and go home before the police see you.' He shakes his head. 'You're a very lucky lady.'

I mumble a self-conscious thank you. Then check the lights for green, powering the car forward. My mind is dragged back to the events of last night. *What happened?* Fragments dispense and my heart sinks. How can Susie be so certain there's no game? In the harsh cold morning, sort of .

sober, I question her statement. She's always accusing Greg of something, and without proof. I wonder about her motives – really, I do. She even accused me of taking Nick's number to meet up with him.

I stop at another set of traffic lights. Wolverhampton Road is to the left, with Quinton on the right. I'm heading straight to the city centre past Edgbaston. Further up along the dual carriageway is a service station. I pull onto the tarmac drive for bottled water. There's a rush of cold air when I open the door, making me shiver. My head pounds on unsteady legs and I zip up my leather jacket – not that it makes any difference – heading for the shop. The water quenches my thirst but does absolutely nothing for my throbbing head. I sit in the car and watch the trickle of early commuters speed past. Do I want to confront my husband? Do I want to make a fool of myself? Susie's haunting words about him having an affair attack my insecurity and I fight with demons in my head. *Is he or isn't he?* Is the game real or not? I need to find out for sure and put a stop to Susie's constant needling at my husband. To kill time I drive further up to a cafe; food has no appeal, but a strong coffee does.

The sky begins to brighten as I approach Five Ways Island and I head straight over to Bath Row towards the Chinese quarter. So close to my destination, and Greg; my heart flutters nervously. What will he think of me turning up? But, more to the point, is Susie deliberately trying to break up my marriage? Had it not been for her, I'd be at home now. And who did she phone? I battle with her words. Plus she seemed *smug* – that much I remember. Well, whatever her plan is, it's going to stop once and for all *today*.

For some strange reason I'm unable to find the entrance of the apartment of the Arcadian centre where my husband is staying. I grow frustrated and circle the block again. I scan between shops and restaurants in the Chinese quarter, searching for the car park sign. Then, suddenly, I slam on the brakes so as not to hit the car in front. When the traffic lights turn green, I edge forward and spot the entrance.

In the winding thoroughfare, I follow the sign to the apartments and park up. With shaking fingers, I check my face in the overhead mirror. Last night's make-up is long gone and I wipe black smudges from under my eyes. I don't look my best, I admit. Now I wonder whether this is a good idea – what if husband senses my guilty secret? What if Nick has already called him and told him? *What then?* I tug a brush through my hair in a nervous panic. *Don't be silly – why would he?* For what reason? He could have done it last night if he wanted to. To put my mind at rest, I check my phone. There's nothing from my husband but plenty of missed calls from Susie. I'll return her call when the truth is sorted out. *What if she is right? What then? Come on, Kate...Greg would never cheat.* I sigh. I did, though.

Reluctantly sliding out from the warmth of the Mercedes, I shiver. From the third floor, dull grey clouds hover over the city below. Workers then quickly pop up umbrellas; some race forward, dodging the sudden heavy downpour. I sigh again and turn on unhurried legs. The Dutch courage of last night has deserted me. I curse *Susie*; this is all her doing. I battle with myself whether to have a quick look and then head home. The glass-fronted door is pushed open. With the heat on full, I unzip my jacket. Abstract prints line the walls and polish hangs heavy in the air, almost like the cleaner has just finished; apart from that the reception is empty. *What do I do now?* I don't even know Greg's room number. I bite my lip and gaze around again. There's a vending machine in the corner. The picture of frothy hot milky chocolate looks inviting. I fumble in my bag for change. The hiss of dark liquid squirts into a plastic cup and I carry it over to settle on one of the sofas. I blow into the cup until its cool enough to drink. The taste of hot chocolate is sweet and creamy; it warms my tummy, and I wipe the edges of my mouth.

*

I must have dropped off because now there are four people in suits at the manned reception. The overhead clock reads 9am. I sit up suddenly, feeling conspicuous in last night's jeans. I decide to leave. *This was a mistake.* I stand up far too quick and wobble slightly. The lift on the far side pings open. My blood drains when Greg steps out, engrossed in conversation with a young woman. My eyes follow her long, straight blonde hair down a dark coat. They head for the apartment's other exit to the front of the building. I'm glued to the polished floor, gaping, taking in the scene, not quite believing what I see. In the revolving doors they go, and then they are gone. My head screams, *Do something.* My heart suddenly thuds, sending in adrenaline. I dart towards the side glass doors. Outside I almost stumble down the stone steps below. A harsh wind smacks my face and I shove wild hair from my eyes. They stand on the wet pavement, waiting to cross the road. The traffic man sign flashes from amber to green.

By the time I catch up I'm out of breath, and I croak, 'Greg.'

He makes no move and I panic, thinking he's deliberately ignoring me. My shout is louder this time.

He turns instantly, clearly shocked. 'What are you doing here?'

His companion tugs his arm, demanding, 'What's going on?'

I sound wild and out of control, frothing at the mouth. 'I'm his wife.'

'What the hell happened to you?' He grabs my arm. 'Are you okay? You look awful.'

I struggle from his gasp, trying hard not to cry, and point. 'Who's she?' *It's her. The one he's having an affair with. Susie's right.*

Commuters openly stare, but I don't care. Greg is clearly embarrassed, though, and promptly instructs the girl to go to the cafe across the road, telling her he'll follow soon. She's probably unimpressed but stomps off anyway, saying, 'Try not to be too long, Greg.'

I mimic her words silently. *Try not to be too long. Really?* Jabbing my finger on his chest, I rant, 'You…you lied about the game.'

'What are you going on about? Hang on, have you been drinking?' He screws up his face. 'You have, Jesus, I can smell it.'

Suddenly I stop, aware of the crowd that has gathered, and my face burns with embarrassment.

Greg drags me into a side ally. 'What's got into you? The booze must have numbed your hearing.' He grabs both my arms. 'You never listen properly.'

His statement lands on a nerve; it triggers that nagging thought. It transports me back to the morning when I'd raced under the shower to scrub off Nick's DNA. So consumed with guilty shame, I'd barely listened to Greg. He was washing his hands in the sink. 'You won't find the poker game anywhere, it's a private affair.'

The soap had stung my eyes and I'd cursed, only half-listening.

My husband had tapped on the glass. 'Did you hear me, babe? Don't tell anyone it's illegal…'

I was far too wrapped up in him leaving for work, to save me from more embarrassment.

I'm dragged back to the present and Greg's stare. Tears fall and my lip trembles. *This is all Susie's fault.* I'm right – she's had in for him from the get-go.

Greg gathers me in his arms. 'Babe, whatever is wrong?'

Even in the cold air, my face flames. Shamefully, I stand back to venture, 'Susie accused you of having an affair.' I look down and blurt out, 'And on our honeymoon, you said you hated gambling.'

He snorts. 'Oh, I see, the jealous Susie stirring up trouble again. Didn't I tell you before? She's a marriage breaker.' He pulls a packet of Silk Cut from his inside overcoat pocket. Cupping his hand around the lighter, he lights up. He scoffs, 'And you believed her – that's why you're here.' He blows smoke upwards, his expression faraway, then states, 'And I lied on our honeymoon only because I wanted to spend time with you.'

His words sink in with a heavy thud. I sniff, wiping under my eyes.

Greg locks his eyes onto mine. 'You didn't listen to me when I told you the game was private, did you?'

I step back a little like that is going to make everything okay.

Sarcastically he adds, 'And let me guess…you told Susie. She put two and two together and made five.' He nods to affirm this. 'I'm right… even though I told you the game was illegal.' He points his finger. 'You went against my wishes and dropped me in it.'

I see tears in his eyes. 'You're supposed to be my wife, Kate. The person I trust the most.'

I touch his arm. 'I'm…sorry.'

He brushes me off. 'But sorry really doesn't cut it,' he says harshly, crushing out his cigarette butt under his loafer shoe.

I face him squarely, pleading, 'Look, I got it wrong…okay.

But nothing bad has happened.' Well, nothing he knows about for now. But what if he found out about *Nick?* My marriage will be over. I'm the liar, not Greg. *He has every right to be angry.* Even more so *if* he knew.

His phone rings in his coat pocket; yanking it out, he states, 'It's Amy, the one I was just walking with.'

Amy. I go cold. I'd almost forgotten about her. Who is she anyway? And what is she doing with my husband?

He cuts the ringtone, shoving it back in his pocket. 'Don't look like that, Kate. She's the daughter of one of the guys I'm playing poker with.'

I breathe a little easier as he continues. 'They're from the States. She…Amy lost her mother last year – that's why she tagged along. Bill, her father, went to play earlier; he asked if I'd escort her over to the game. It's her first time over here, so he didn't want her getting lost.' He lights up another cigarette and inhales. 'They've asked both of us to visit them in the States after the game ends.'

I'm floored by a double dose of remorse; forcing a weak grin, I suggest, meekly, 'Perhaps you can invite them to dinner…sometime.' It's all I can think of to say sorry.

'After your rude outburst.' He sighs, disappointed. 'Look, just go home, Kate. I'll call you later.' He then seems to have an afterthought and his eyes bore into mine, adding, 'Or perhaps you'd like to say hello to Amy now.'

Catching a swift smell of sick off my jeans, I couldn't think of anything worse. 'Another time, perhaps,' I say lamely.

My husband strides off; his broad shoulders mingle with the crowds. I brush away tears, watching until he disappears out of sight. My footsteps are leaden, heading back to the car, and I hug my jacket tightly.

I slump onto the leather seat and do nothing. Through misted tears, cars drive off and park up. Even though the wind whistles outside, I make no attempt to start the engine. The bitter cold seeps into my skin like a punishment, one I think I deserve.

FIFTEEN

A dog barks in the distance; it triggers a thought of Timmy. I start the engine and exit the car park. Miserable, dirty clouds hog the sky. It's raining hard and the wipers flick with urgency across the windscreen. They're hypnotic, drawing me in, waiting for someone to let me out into the busy street. For the first time, I notice Christmas lights hung on lamp posts. Is it that time already? A horn blares behind me, making me jolt. To my left-hand side, a white Mercedes flashes for my car to exit. *Will my husband ever forgive me? Why did I have to blurt that out to Susie? What's wrong with me?*

I head towards the M5 and stick to the inside lane. *Should I even be driving with more spirit in my veins than blood?* The rain eases off just as the motorway lights glow on. Constantly I check the wing mirror. I read on the internet, after a heavy drinking session, the morning after you're still over the limit. But never mind that – how come I didn't remember what Greg said? He banged on the shower pane of glass.

I'm thrown from my thoughts when I spot the flash of blue lights in the overhead mirror. I panic and grip the steering wheel. *Keep calm, Kate.* Oh no, the police car speeds up, closer and closer. Now it's next to me. I hold my breath and focus ahead. I try not to draw unwanted attention. Out of the corner of my eye, the blue and white striped car edges forward. I go hot. *This is it...they're going pull me over.* Then it picks up speed and zooms in front on its way. I breathe out and tension seeps from my shoulders. Winding down the window, I welcome the blast of cold air. Further up I see a billboard. It displays a new drama, *Life as a Private Detective*. The actor's face presents me a with prickling sensation. I feel the sign is taunting *me*, then it's behind me.

I arrive home, and Timmy is on overdrive with his affection, which is to be expected. I bet if he could, he'd have dialled RSPCA. My guilt lies heavy in my heart at leaving him overnight.

I do my usual routine: let him out and guzzle Yellow. The smooth liquid enters my veins like a much-needed blood transfusion. I know, I was going to give it up, but after the previous night and day – well, I need it. Pretty much like the rain we need. I will give up, I promise, but not right now.

I linger under jets of hot water, chiding myself to get a grip. First off is to listen properly to my husband. Otherwise I could be heading for the divorce courts. I sigh and dry off. Why did Nick have to blurt that out to Susie? What was that about? *Why?* Wrapped in a towel, I reach for my glass and flop on the bed. Then I stand and curse Nick. What's he playing at, dropping me in it? *What does he want?* Could he be a friend of Jason's? Is this his way of revenge? What about Susie's meddling? I pour more Yellow and debate whether to call her.

She picks up on the first ring like she's been waiting. Before I can say anything, she butts in.

Her tone is curt. 'Where are you?'

'Home.'

'I presume that you didn't get killed then, speeding off pissed.'

I flinch and say in defence, 'I wasn't that drunk.'

'You could barely stand and you almost knocked that man over. I had to pay for another takeaway, being as he dropped his getting out your way. And what about the damage to your car? You gave it a right scrape on the wall.'

I grip the stem of my glass as she presses on hotly. 'I called you over and over, worried sick, out of my mind. But you... couldn't even bother to call me and tell me that you were okay. You're a fucking selfish cow, Kate.'

I flinch with shame when she cuts the call and I stare at the phone. Then I toss it on the bed like it's contaminated and pour out the remainder of Yellow. Tears well up and I bite down hard on my bottom lip. Well, I suppose she's sort of right. I wipe under my eyes and nervously wander over to the window. I tug the Roman blind up. Under the street lamp, in full view, is the damage to the passenger side of my Mercedes. I've no memory of it. I sigh and close the blind. *Looks like I'm in everyone's bad book.* Even Timmy hasn't bothered to come upstairs. I suppose I should buy Susie flowers as my way of saying sorry. I'm not sure what else to do. I guess if I'd have listened to my husband in the first place, then none of this mess would have happened. Perhaps I could pop back over and present Amy with flowers too.

Discarding the towel, I head for the dressing room with my mind made up. I select a wool dress and wonder what part of America Amy's from. Something niggles at me about her, but I can't quite catch it. I tie up my hair to apply foundation. This time I want to look presentable. I press my mouth edged with lipstick together on a tissue, stopping to think. I've no idea where the game is being played. I try Greg's phone, but it's switched off. I guess he's probably playing right now. But it doesn't matter because I'll just wait at the apartment as a surprise. Surely he won't be that long? The game can't go on all night, can it? Timmy has forgiven me because he is stretched out on the bed. I yawn. I'm tempted to join him. It's hardly a surprise, having hardly any sleep. I slip on a cashmere coat and descend the stairs. Timmy darts past, almost knocking me out the way. I call after him, 'Where are you racing off to?' Perhaps he thinks he's coming with me.

I'm surprised when the doorbell chimes. I wonder who it is as I cross the marble floor to open the door. 'What are you doing here?' Quickly I get over my shock as panic sets in. *What if someone sees him?* Without a thought, I yank him in and peer up and down the empty road. Before I have a chance to question him again, Timmy is at Nick's feet, wagging his tail like he is a long-lost buddy.

'He's a friendly little chap,' comments Nick, bending to ruffle his head. 'What's his name?'

I automatically respond, 'Timmy.' The scene is endearing but so wrong. 'No, he's not normally good with strangers.' What did I say that for? I then go cold. What if my husband had answered the door?

Nick scoops up Timmy, who licks his face. For a second I'm stunned until my senses kick in. I snatch Timmy back and demand again, 'What are you doing here?'

Nick grins like he has a right to be here. 'I wanted to see if you were okay?'

I widen my eyes. '*What?*' For an instant, I wonder if I'm having a nightmare.

'I was in the car park last night when you drove off in a drunken frenzy.'

I'm vexed and snap, 'I was not drunk…and anyhow, what's it to you?' Protectively I squeeze Timmy.

Nick strokes his head and states, candidly, 'My mother has Yorkshire terriers back in Greece.'

This is nuts, and I intend to put a stop to it. Bending down, I ease Timmy out of my arms. 'Actually, I'm just on my way out. And, as you can see, I'm fine, but thank you for your concern.' *He's got a nerve.* But then I have a horrible thought. *Is he out to wreck my marriage?* Perhaps I should humour him and find out his game plan.

'You are not driving, are you?'

'What?' Now I sound like a parrot.

'Look, your friend gave me your address, being as you have blocked me on your phone.'

'She did what?' *Why do that? What was she thinking? Has she gone mad?* I know she said to sort it out with Nick, but this is not what I had in mind.

I just want to forget I slept with him. But I can't help but feel a sudden flush remembering the vision of him on standing on his doorstep in boxer shorts. He's taller than Greg. More body hair too. *Stop.* I fan my face with the back of my hand, desperate to cool my flaming cheeks. I need a drink. I flinch when Timmy barks, darting towards the kitchen. He's after something outside; I bet it's that ginger cat, the new girl in the neighbourhood. She's a troublemaker, but what can I do? I can hardly complain to the neighbour, saying their pussy is taunting my dog. After letting Timmy out, I head straight for the wine rack. For once I struggle with the cork, and only out of frustration do I take up Nick's offer to help. I reach for a wine glass from the cupboard and think that perhaps now is a good time to discover Nick's true motives, so I grab him one too.

The smooth velvet liquid glides down my throat and I almost forget Nick is here. Quickly I step back to distance myself, removing my coat and draping it over the barstool. 'So how come Susie gave you my address?'

He takes a sip of wine before answering, 'I have not tried Yellow Tail. It is nice – a good choice, Kate.'

He's talking like we are best buddies, and I'm even more stunned when he lets Timmy back in. He then proceeds to inform me how worried and upset Susie was last night. Apparently, he left his phone in his car, hence him catching the scene in the car park. I pretend to flick off invisible bits off my dress and listen to how he invited her to join him and his friends being as she hadn't eaten. Literally, I want to cover my ears. As a distraction, I suggest we move to a more comfortable setting in the lounge. Nick heads for Greg's chair and Timmy jumps on his lap.

Timmy's behaviour leaves me speechless.

'Would you mind if I took off my overcoat?'

'I...err, yes, I guess.' Timmy is not budging, though. 'Wow, he's certainly taken a shine to you,' I state, scooping him up to plonk him on the carpet. Funny how he refuses to sit on Greg's knee.

Nick stands to remove his coat, then settles back down, almost like he's in for the night. I perch on the edge of the sofa and cradle my glass as Timmy dives back onto Nick's knees.

'Your friend mentioned the poker game that apparently was not taking place,' he says, stroking Timmy's head.

I turn crimson and splutter out my wine. 'What?' *What on earth has gotten into her? Why tell him that?* This is bang out of order, and I've got a good mind to call her now to demand an explanation. Instead, I dart from the room to grab the bottle of wine.

On my return, Nick confirms there's no game. I smile smugly. *It's private, that's why.* But I offer nothing.

'My brother Tony owns the Genting casino in Birmingham – he knows everything. In fact, his mate Rick runs illegal games and he knows nothing about this so-called card game either.'

A cold band tightens around my heart, visualising Greg being arrested. *I'm going to kill Susie.* But I never mentioned a private game and I stammer, 'I don't know what you're talking about.' I flop down, drowning wine, and fume, thinking my marriage must have been the topic of the night.

'It is okay, Kate. I am not here to cause trouble – I am here to help.'

'Help? Do I look like I need help?' Timmy gives me an odd stare, which I find bizarre. It's like he's siding with this stranger.

'Your friend is worried about you.' He pauses. 'Plus she is not entirely sure Greg is being honest either.' Before I have a chance to stand my ground, he presses on. 'Tell you what, I'll call Rick and you can listen in.'

It's as though my life has been bamboozled. But on the other hand, I'll get the address for the game and Nick and Susie will finally admit they're both wrong. However, I'm not happy with this situation. 'Okay, whatever.' And I'm less impressed with Timmy, soaking up Nick's affection.

'I take it you do not believe me then.'

'I never said that.' Why am I defending myself?

'But you thought it.'

I shrug my shoulders. I can't dispute that. 'But why do you want help? You must have a hundred other things to do, like running your restaurant.' *Why help? He hardly knows me.* There's something not quite right about him turning up.

He sips from his glass before answering, 'Can I not help a friend out?'

'We're hardly that,' I state sarcastically. Instantly I regret my words, knowing exactly what he's going to say next.

He raises his eyebrow in mock amusement. 'Lovers then.'

I scowl, feeling my cheeks burn. 'That was a mistake – besides, I was upset.' I want to add, *You took advantage of me,* but I want to forget this line of conversation, not add to it.

'Look, I am sorry. Let's forget that night.'

My hand tightens around the stem of the glass and I make my point. 'I love my husband, but foolishly that night I got all mixed up thinking he'd lied to me, but then you know that,' I say flippantly. 'I got it all wrong. Anyway, I thought you were going to call someone.'

He moves to pull his phone from his jean pocket and scrolls down with his thumb. Timmy is still not budging.

I hear it ringing out. After a while, Nick shrugs. 'I guess he is busy.'

I feel a spark of annoyance. How do I know who he's calling? I stand up, biting down on my lip before posing my question. 'Why are you really here?'

Nick sips from his glass leisurely.

I panic. What if Greg comes home for some reason? Striding over to the window I shove the curtain aside to peer out. A Tesco van trundles past, but that's it. Quickly, I straighten it and look down at Nick. *Why smile and not answer?*

I ask, more firmly this time, 'What would you have done if my husband had opened the door?'

Nick stares at me like he's thinking. It feels uncomfortable until he flaunts his charm. 'Like I said, to help a friend out.'

I'm unconvinced. And how did he know about the game being illegal? I cover my uneasiness and laugh, playing along. 'I suppose so.' I take a sip of wine. *I need to find out what he's up to.*

'I tell you what, let us go over there now, together in my car. Because if there is a private poker game taking place, Rick will be in on it – that, I can guarantee you. Besides, I need to pick something up from the casino. So in one way, you would be doing me a favour.' He holds his hands up. 'Just as friends.'

Alarm bells ring. *Pick something up.* I feel sick. Is he laundering money? Suddenly it sinks in. My *husband* is playing an *illegal* game. Why not play in a normal game, like ones I've seen on TV? They're above board. I bet this is about the debt Greg owes. My hand shakes, refilling my glass. Or is Nick setting me up for blackmail? Yellow tastes like acid. *It all makes sense now.* And I think of *Jason* again. Has this anything to do with him?

I gulp more Yellow to ease my fear. *Come on, Kate, you can do this – it's the only way.* 'I guess I could tag along.' A thought then flashes in my head. 'What if the game has finished and Greg is back at the apartment? How do I explain you giving me a lift?'

Nick frowns. 'What, has he moved out?'

I freeze. *What did he say it like for? Have I dropped my husband in more trouble?* I try to backtrack. 'No...er...I...er.' I shrug. 'He said he might stay near the game.' Flustered, I continue, 'I don't know, really. Anyway, I'll get another bottle – your glass is empty.'

'No, I am okay, I need to drive.'

'Fine,' I say tightly. 'But I want one.'

Before I have a chance to leave the room, Nick says, 'Look, let us go now. I will nip into the casino. Make a few enquiries about the game again. Which, to be fair, is best done in person anyway. And you can tell Greg you arrived by taxi.' He grins triumphantly.

He's got it all planned. I could always refuse to go. But I could lose my chance to find out his game plan. So I place my best grin forward. 'Okay then, just as friends.'

Nick bundles Timmy in his arms, easing out the chair. 'Tell you what; let us take Timmy with us.'

Timmy licks Nick's face. *And who says dogs don't understand?* Timmy is a traitor. But nevertheless, do I want my baby involved in any kind of danger? I'd rather him be with me, though, just in case anything bad should happen.

'Well, you've done it now.' I force a half-smirk, heading out for his lead, wishing I had something else to take for safety. I suppose a bottle of Yellow Tail is out of the question.

Outside there's only my motor parked up on the drive. I'm puzzled and ask, 'So where's your car then?'

'Oh, that.'

I'm confused as I change hands for Timmy's lead, strolling towards the open gates across the gravel drive behind Nick.

I catch his answer in the wind as he trots on. 'My bike is around the corner.'

I stop and gape. 'What! I'm not riding on the back of a bike.' Scooping Timmy up, I protectively crush him to my bosom. 'And neither is Timmy. Are you mad?'

Nick takes no notice, and I call after him, 'Where are you going?' I curse when the neighbour across the road takes his time emptying his rubbish in the bin. 'Wait, Nick, you can't be serious.' I follow, visualising a bike and sidecar parked up on the main road. I'm not getting in it…I'm not.

Nick turns around, laughing.

I stop. 'What's so funny?' *This is no joke.*

'You, when I said about the bike.' I'm more unnerved when he squeezes my shoulder, adding, 'I was joking.'

The neighbour is a witness, one I might need should anything happen to me and Timmy. He could be the last one to see us alive. Except, seeing a red Ferrari parked around the corner, I hardly think Nick's motive is murder in such a standout car. Plus if he was up to dodgy dealing, he is definitely driving the wrong motor.

Nick holds the door open for me and Timmy. He's well mannered, I give him that. However, I'll still reserve judgement.

The lights on the M5 pass in a blur as we speed along in the fast lane. We've agreed to go to Greg's apartment first just in case he's there. Maybe he's out in the game? Or on a quick break from it? Anyway, I'm still convinced the private poker game is still taking place. Plus heading over will prove I'm right, then this nonsense will stop once and for all.

As we approach the city, anxious nerves flutter in my tummy. I cuddle Timmy for comfort. Maybe it was the wrong decision to come over with Nick. What if my husband sees me? What if he happens to pull up at the same time?

Parked up at the entrance to the hotel apartments, I don't feel so confident. I turn to Nick. 'I don't suppose you've any mints?'

He's apologetic. 'Sorry.'

In the overhead mirror, I see bloodshot eyes. Nothing I can do about it now. I forgot to stop for flowers too. I fume inwardly. I should be doing this on my own. What was I thinking? I hardly know Nick. I scan around the car park. At least there appears to be no sign of Greg's motor, which I take as a good sign, I guess.

Nick reaches across for Timmy. 'I will have him while you go in.'

'But how am I going to explain you?' I cry feebly. 'Okay, I know… we discussed this, you're an old school buddy if my husband happens to see you.' That doesn't sound very convincing.

Nervously I smooth down my coat. At most I appear better than I did this morning. A hiccup escapes me. That's not good.

Outside reception, I turn around. Timmy is watching, along with Nick. I force on a brave face and enter. Everything is the same as it was this morning, only a different lady is behind the desk. She offers a warm welcome. My eyes dart around as I edge closer. Sweat lingers in the palms of my hands.

I clear my throat and say my prepared statement: 'My husband is staying here and… I wonder if you could let him know I'm here.' I continue hopelessly, 'I've no charge on my phone. It's where I stored his room number.' I shrug and offer a small chuckle. 'And silly me forgot it.' It sounds plausible, I guess.

Her name badge reads Linda; she's probably seen and heard every excuse there is. Her tone is surprisingly soft when she asks for his name.

'Greg Anderson.'

Her fingers fly across the keyboard. She pauses and stares at the computer screen. Her action is unnerving. It fills me with panic.

Linda is apologetic. 'I'm sorry, he appears to have checked out this morning.'

'What? That can't be right…I… was here then.'

She turns the computer around for me to see. Grateful for the gesture, I ask, hopefully, 'I know it's a silly question, but do you happen to know where he's gone?'

She shakes her head like she's genuinely disappointed when she replies, 'No, I'm sorry.'

'Oh, but thanks anyway.' *Checked out? Where to?*

'I wish I could have been of more help,' she offers with a small smile.

He never mentioned he was checking out earlier. Maybe he forgot to tell me – perhaps he did and I wasn't listening. But I know he didn't. Or is it because he can't trust me? I stumble outside and call his number. It's still off. The sound of a horn makes me jolt and I stare over at the Ferrari until I gradually remember Nick. He reaches over, pushing open the door. 'What happened? What is wrong?'

I slip inside, feeling dazed. 'My husband checked out this morning.'

'Oh, I see.'

Checked out? But where is he then? Wrapped up in my thoughts, I barely feel Timmy being transported back onto my lap. I bury my head into his fur and blink through misted eyes. The blur of shops and restaurants merge into one as we cruise along. Why is my husband doing this? *Why?* I reason that it has something to do with the game. *It must have.* I shiver; does *Nick* know something? He didn't seem surprised.

'I am going to pull up outside. I will try not to be long,' Nick says, checking for traffic as he exits the car.

I watch him stride towards the bright lights of Genting Casino. It's funny how my husband chose the apartments just around the corner in Chinatown. This is too much of a *coincidence.* Hang on, though; didn't Nick say he knew my husband? I sit up as my heart pounds in my chest, hearing loud shouts. It's just a crowd of drunken men jostling as they pass. The Ferrari is then spotted. Phone cameras light up and a string of faces peer in. Swiftly I lock my door and Timmy growls. Someone yells. I squeeze Timmy. The lads turn and bolt off.

Timmy and I both startled when the locks pop up as the passenger door is yanked open. Nick introduces Tony, his brother. He's an older version of Nick with a black shirt. It stretches across his portly belly as he puffs on a thick cigar. I produce a fearful half-grin. He's the perfect picture of a mafia boss. *Maybe he is for real?*

Tony pokes his head in. He confirms Nick's statement that there's no private poker game being held in Birmingham. I think Timmy is shaking, or is it me?

He straightens up. 'Trust me, I'd know.'

If Greg *is* playing a secret game. I reckon he's in big trouble by the looks of Tony, never mind his henchmen. Perhaps that's why my husband checked out? *Because he had to?* Perhaps that's why Nick wasn't surprised when I told him. Does Jason have something to do with this too? For all, I know he could be Nick and Tony's brother. I take a sneaky peak as they hug their goodbyes. *There's a resemblance alright.* Now I wish I'd never gone on online dating, and I whisper to Timmy, with confidence I don't feel, 'Hey, we'll be fine.'

Nick hops back in. 'Heard anything from Greg yet?'

I shake my head. I haven't checked my phone; I've been too busy working out what's going on – besides, the mobile would have pinged.

Nick starts the engine. 'I need to stop by my city apartment – perhaps you could do with a drop of brandy after your shock.'

I've never felt so grateful, and I croak, 'Fine.' Like I have a choice. Timmy is hugged to my chest like it's our last night together. *It could well be.*

The Ferrari attracts a lot of attention as we wait at the traffic lights just before the Mailbox residents' underground car park. Minutes later Nick reverses in between a Porsche and Aston Martin.

He remarks casually, 'I stay here occasionally amongst a few of the Birmingham City footballers, hence all the supercars.'

'Oh…' I thought he lived in a terrace house. Not that I'm keen to remember that night. Does it matter where he lives, though? It's all a bit confusing at the moment.

He turns to me. 'I thought a strong drink might help before I take you and Timmy home.'

Now I feel rather foolish. I'd hardly be in danger in a place like this, surrounded by security. Not to mention all the attention on a flash bright-red Ferrari. *Crimewatch* would have an easy job. I relax a little and say, 'Yes, that would be nice, thanks.' After all my shocks, I need it. And maybe I'll take this opportunity to ask him how he knows Greg. I reckon he knows more than he's letting on.

In silence, we stroll over to the elevator and wait. The doors flush open, but Timmy drags back on his lead. He's not budging, so I scoop him up and declare, 'I don't think he's been in a lift before.'

The glass box glides up smoothly and a river of city lights sparkle below. At another time, I'd be impressed with the view. Right now, though, all I feel is a sinking sensation in the pit of my tummy which has nothing to do with the lift shooting up. Timmy and I are escorted across the hall, leading to solid double doors.

Past the hall, through more double doors, I follow Nick into an open-plan room with a wrap-around balcony. Soft lighting edges from wooden borders. In front are two wicker sofas and chairs, surrounded by potted plants. It's very chic.

I flinch when Nick plucks Timmy from my arms. 'He is safe to go outside; I had to make sure of that before Mum came over with her two dogs.'

I slip off my coat to drape it over a white leather sofa. Outside Nick is keeping watch on Timmy, who wanders around, sniffing each plant pot.

He turns and calls out, 'Help yourself to a drink.'

I cast a glance around to the antique table to the right. A silver tray hosts a crystal decanter. Going over, I pour out a large measure of gold liquid. The burning sensation is welcome. Pouring another, I can't help being drawn to one of the framed photographs. The woman in the picture is beautiful: long, dark luscious hair, cupid lips. I pick up the frame. I know her – I'm sure of it. I take a closer inspection at her smile, her arms stretched out in a place which appears very like this balcony. No...I don't know her. I'm curious, though – perhaps she's Nick's wife? What's that to me? But why do I feel a hint of something? Nick then appears at my side and helps himself to a brandy. I flush and promptly replace the frame.

Nick strolls over to the white-grey flecked marble fire surround. He turns to face me, swirling the contents of his heavy crystal glass. 'It is my sister.'

His sister. Not his wife. There's certainly a resemblance, and I catch a hint of darkness clouding his eyes, then it's gone just as quick.

I perch on the edge of the sofa and Timmy settles at my feet. Nick seems preoccupied. I bite my lip and, to hide my nervousness, I offer, 'She's very beautiful.'

'Actually, this is her apartment.'

'Oh, will she mind us being here?' I ask, stroking Timmy's head.

He ignores my question and enquires instead, 'So what are you going to do now? Being there is no high-stakes game taking place and Greg has moved out?'

I stir uncomfortably and gulp my drink, then shrug feebly. 'But it might be for a select group, as in secretive...and the game may have moved to a different location.' Even I don't believe that, which is probably written all over my face.

Nick raises one eyebrow. 'And you think that?' He pauses for a drink before he adds, 'And for a million-pound stake. I find it strange that no one else in the casino business knows. And you heard what my brother said...come on... even you cannot be that naïve.'

I clutch my glass. I never mentioned the sum of money. I drain my drink as if to hide in it. *How does he know that? Dare I ask him?*

Nick crashes my thoughts. 'I had better take you and Timmy back home.'

I couldn't agree more.

SIXTEEN

I can't say I'm happy with my husband. He's left messages alright. But not the ones I want to read. I struggle to sit up and search the duvet for my phone. Could he have found out about Nick? Is he hurting me to make a point? Who could blame him? And how did Nick know the game was for one million? I curse for not asking. That was a week ago and, if I recall, all I wanted to do was get home fast and bolt the door. There was something not quite right about Nick and his brother. Something sinister – Tony for sure gave off that impression. I sigh and check my phone. Nothing. I think Greg is still annoyed with me. He phoned the night after he left the apartment to tell me the game had been moved to a secret place. As I can't be trusted, he refused to tell me the location. I guess in one way he's right. Plus I've had to wait the whole week for Susie to calm down even after I sent long sorry messages. Lucky for me she has relented and forgiven me. Thank God she has invited me around tonight, as it's been lonely on my own.

I plonk on the loo as Timmy pokes his head around the corner. 'I'm coming, don't worry.' He seems to understand and disappears off. I don't why, but I'm not keen for him to see me when I do my business, even though I watch him. Washing my hands, something nags at me. Then it hits me. With my heart thumping, I race downstairs and let Timmy out. Next, I bolt over to the calendar. It's the 15th December. *Oh my God.* I calculate the dates since my last period. I'm five weeks late. I suck in air. I can't believe it. My mind races back to when I slept with Nick and my husband. The date of the lunch with Susie silently screams from on the calendar: '9th November'. The impact hits me like a runaway train. I should be elated. *Fuck.* How did this happen? *What the hell do I do now?*

*

Later I drive over to Susie's cottage. I can hardly concentrate in the darkness of wet country lanes. How can I be pregnant? Parking up, I stare up at the stars shining from the velvet sky and finally the rain stops.

She flings open the door with a warm welcome. Sheepishly I thrust a bouquet of white lilies in her hand, her favourite flowers. We embrace and I breathe in her sweet perfume. She gestures for me to follow her to the sitting room. Logs burn and crackle with spit in the fire. It's cosy and warm, and in one corner sits a real Christmas tree, giving off a fresh pine smell. Its branches are hung with baubles that match the tartan theme. Presents are neatly piled underneath. I bite my lip and hold back tears with a sinking heart. Greg should be with me and not out playing bloody poker. We should be putting up our decorations.

Susie hands me a tumbler of Baileys. 'Martin's going out in a minute. Oops, I've just remembered I need him to pick something up. I'll be back in a tick.'

I place the drink on the side table. Now is the time to

give up and I wonder whether to tell her the latest news. I should be excited, but I'm not. I'm scared. I'd tried Greg again, but again his phone was switched off. I don't even know who the baby's father is – my husband or Nick? I can't believe my predicament. How I longed for this moment. I'm dragged back to reality by Susie's return, and Martin pops his head around the door. 'Have fun, see you later.'

'Where's he off to?' I ask, more for something to say as she eases into her shabby chic leather armchair.

'Old school reunion, he goes every year. Anyway, have you heard anymore from Greg?'

I shake my head with a sigh. 'No.'

She reaches out for a cigarette from the side table. She lights up and blows smoke upwards, asking, 'So are you going to put up with not knowing where he's staying? And have you called his work?'

'I don't want to make a fuss and cause trouble. Anyway, it's not been that long.' But it feels like forever.

She raises her eyebrows. 'I must say, you're taking it very well. I'd be going round the bend if I didn't know where Martin was.'

I give her a lame statement. 'Like I said, he's still out playing poker in a private game.'

Susie scoffs. 'Really! And do you think that young woman he was with is who he says she is? Come on.'

Something bugs me about Amy, but right now I have matters to contend with. I shrug hopelessly, not knowing what to think about my situation, and it's probably wise not to mention the game is illegal. God knows what she'd make of that.

Susie flicks ash into a silver pot and gently probes, 'How long do you intend to wait for him to come home? I mean, it is Christmas – your first, might I add.'

'What can I do? I'm at a loss.' And I mean it, adding, 'I'm not sure… I've never been in a situation like this before.'

I ought to confess about the baby. But I'm drawn to a book on the coffee table instead. It's a detective novel. Instantly I have a flashback to the billboard on the M5 about the new drama, *Life as a Private Detective*. It presents me with a niggling sensation, like I should hire one. Inwardly I dismiss the notion as daft. The prospect is unnerving. *Silly, in fact.*

'Hey, are you okay?' She sort of half smiles. 'Silly question I guess.'

I fiddle with my wedding ring unsure of what to say. The thought of a private detective has got me thinking. Aren't they for the rich and famous? But I remember reading somewhere about a woman who used one to catch out her cheating husband. She was from a council estate, a tattoo artist. Not much claim to fame there. But Greg is not out cheating? Susie is right, though – he should be here with me.

'You're very quiet – what are you thinking?'

The idea is madness. 'Nothing.' Could I? Dare I? I bite my lip. Greg needs to know my condition.

Susie is insistent. 'Come on, something's going on in your mind.'

'It's nothing, honestly,' I confirm.

She leans back and folds her arms, clearly unconvinced, waiting for my response. She knows me, and well.

I sigh. 'It's a stupid idea.'

'What is? Come on?'

I reach for my drink but make no attempt to drink it. 'It's silly, trust me.' But a tiny seed has been planted along with a nervous tingle. The thought has me on edge and Susie is right – how long do I wait for the bloody game to finish?

Susie smokes in silence. Her manner sends out uncomfortable waves. It forces me to blurt out my daft idea of engaging a private detective to find my husband. But I don't tell her the real reason why.

Susie perches forward. 'I think that's an excellent idea, because how else are you going to track him down?'

She has a point; however, I'm still uncertain. 'But I can't really go ahead and do that.'

'Come on, Kate, get a grip. What choice do you have?' She blows smoke in my direction, demanding, 'And how long do you intend to hang around and wait for him to turn up?'

I feel uneasy. 'Like I said, it's a daft idea. Anyhow, he might come back up any minute.' I sound lame and I know it.

She snubs out her cigarette. 'Really.' Her unimpressed sigh is loud. 'How long are you going to wait then – another day, a week? A month or years before you do something.'

I bite my lip, reluctantly admitting she's right. I pretend to take a sip of Baileys. Just because she's right, though, doesn't mean I have to use one. *Do I?*

She sounds smug. 'I know what you're thinking. I know you remember.'

I pout sourly and confess, 'Okay, you're right. I'll make an appointment.' I will. I just don't know when.

Then she reminds me, 'Just remember, you wouldn't be in this mess if it wasn't for Greg's actions.' She points her finger. 'You need to find out what he's up to.'

'Alright, I get the point.' The idea leaves me apprehensive and I mumble, 'I'll do it next week.' I suppose I've no choice, really, put like that.

'No, Kate, you will make the call first thing this Monday morning – this needs sorting out, and quickly.'

I purse my lips and wish I'd kept my big mouth shut. She's right, though – how long do I wait for my husband to appear? Plus there's another important factor: the *baby*, our baby. What if it's *Nick's*? What then? I lean back and wonder how the hell I got myself into such a mess? *Why get pregnant now?* There's a chance I'll never bump into Nick again, not if I can help it. What if the baby looks like him? Do I confess to Greg? And when do I tell Susie? Just at that moment my phone pings.

I rummage in my handbag and check the screen. My fingers shake and my heart races. 'It's Greg.'

Susie gushes. 'So he's alive then. What's he saying?'

I read the text out loud. 'Babe, can't talk right now. The game is heating up. Speak soon. Wish me luck.'

I call his number, but it's already switched off.

Susie pulls a face. 'He's not playing poker, more like shagging Amy; that's why he can't speak to you. He's afraid of dropping himself in it.'

Although her statement hurts, there's a ring of truth to it that I don't want to believe. She's right, though, as why can't he just pick up the fucking phone and talk to me?

'I hope his cheap text hasn't put you off,' she demands sharply.

I touch my belly and as tears roll, I say, 'No.'

SEVENTEEN

I can't tell you how embarrassed I was when I plucked up the courage to call Greg's work, only to be told he's on leave. I stumbled over my thank you to the receptionist, pretending to be a customer, and no, I didn't want to leave a message. That was this morning and I'm still in shock, which quickly turned to anger. Susie's right – I need answers pronto. So for the next hour, I search the internet for private detective agencies and the first available appointment. After six unsuccessful calls, I pace the kitchen floor. There's nothing for weeks. I can't wait that long. On one of the calls, someone suggested a new company that had just started up. I scramble through my notes for the phone number.

The next morning I fiddle with my wedding ring and check my watch for the hundredth time. I can't settle. I'm so tempted to pour Yellow; instead, I opt for another coffee. Dean Aston's appointed time is later this afternoon. I was dubious, being as he could fit me in so soon. But what choice did I have? I've polished, pumped up cushions and whizzed the hoover around, trying to rush the time. I check my phone again and again. There are no more messages from my husband. Why is his phone always still switched off? He can't be playing poker twenty-four seven. Why can't he return my calls? Why is he ignoring me? Susie's words taunt me. *Amy, I bet that's why.*

Rain pelts against the French doors. Timmy is seated in his basket licking his wet paws. I bend down and ruffle his head. He's such a dear old soul. He'd licked off my tears earlier when I'd woken this morning. I didn't even know it was possible to cry in your sleep until now. *Why is Greg doing this to me?* I only hope this private guy is worth the money. Under different circumstances, I should be celebrating. No, correction –*we* should be celebrating. *But we aren't, and I'm not.*

Later I smooth down my dress. I think it fits the occasion. Others out there are in the Christmas spirit but here I am dressed as the black widow, mourning for her lost husband. What shall I do or say when I eventually find him? My first thought is to black his eye…both of them. Do I have the right to be angry, though, with my guilty secret? Perhaps he already knows, hence his treatment. *Then what do I do?* My thoughts are broken into when I hear tyres crunch over the gravelled drive below. Nervously I pull back my sleeve and check the time on my watch. That's got to be Mr Aston. I slip on court shoes, head over to the window and peer out. A very shiny, clean silver Jaguar parks up next to my dented Mercedes. I step back slightly, not wanting to be caught out staring. I'm curious, though, what a real private detective looks like. I suppress the urge to laugh. I imagine an old bloke in a trilby hat and worn-out mackintosh. With caution, I gaze out again. The drives door swings open, followed by blue pinstriped suited legs. They belong to a rather tall silver-headed male. He reminds me of a TV presenter. I jolt back. I'd certainly not expected that vision when we'd spoken on the phone. I suppress a silly schoolgirl giggle. When the doorbell echoes in the hall I descend the stairs and bite my lip. I'm keen to appear a gracious host and fling open the front door with a flourish. Dean Aston is even more handsome close-up and shamefully I blush. Timmy, however, has other ideas and bares his teeth with a growl.

My good first impression is lost when I chase him down the hall into the kitchen. The last thing I need is an invoice for assault even before I've started. 'What's wrong with you?' I demand with a sigh, closing the door.

With haste, I return to shake Mr Aston's hand. 'Hi.' His smile is warm and I'm slightly convinced his hand lingers on mine.

'So nice to meet you, Mrs Anderson.'

'Please, call me Kate,' I say, pulling back my hand, trying hard not to be lured into his startling blue eyes. *Calm down, Kate, he's here to find your husband.*

I gesture for him to take a seat in the lounge and offer, 'Would you like a drink? Tea or coffee?' I'm tempted to add wine, but I refrain. It wouldn't be very professional for him and no good for me.

'No, thank you, Kate.'

He's a silver fox alright, and I hope my nervous smile is not too apparent as I perch on the edge of the sofa. The cloth of his suit is expensive and I catch a glimpse of gold diamond wedding band. If I'm honest, he's a bit flashy, and silently I question his empty diary. I wonder what I've let myself in for.

'So, Kate, would you like to tell me everything you know? And please, call me Dean.'

I move to stand; I guess it makes me feel more in control when I tell him what I know, which isn't much.

He opens his Louis Vuitton briefcase. I wonder if it's fake. He pulls out a notepad and pen before he asks politely, 'Do you have a recent photo of your husband? Also I'll need a few more details, like his place of business.'

I'm not sure I trust this guy. But what choice do I have? I try to convince myself his service will work. I could at least give him a chance now he's here, I suppose. Reluctantly I reel off Greg's business address. I then head off for the study. There's a single picture of Greg before we met. Carefully, I remove a photograph from the frame; the meeting feels surreal, like I am starring in a thriller. It's all very cloak and dagger, and I giggle nervously. It's rare I ever come in here, and I look around. There's a desk and leather chair – not much else. For some unknown reason, I pull out drawers. It's surprising, really, to find them empty. I can only guess my husband keeps his paperwork and bills at his office. But I'm intrigued to find the bottom right-hand drawer locked. That's strange. I promise to investigate further once the meeting with Dean has finished.

He studies Greg's picture without expression. Next, he opens his flash briefcase and shoves the photo in it, along with his notepad and pen. Closing it, he glances up and asks in a professional tone, 'Would you like the photograph back?'

I shrug; I hadn't thought of that. 'I guess so.' My old habit kicks in and I'm biting down on my lip before I pose the question, 'So what happens now then?'

'Well, I'll do my research and get an address for where your husband is staying.'

I run my hands over the sofa, impressed. 'Really, you can do that?' Just as quick, my spirit drops. What if he's with someone else? How do I act? More to the point, how will I react? Suddenly I don't feel so confident, and my mouth turns dry. 'Err… Dean, would you like a glass of wine?' I certainly feel like one.

He checks his gold watch and stands. 'I'd love to stay, Kate, but unfortunately, I have another engagement.'

This time I know his handshake lingers when he says, 'I'll call you in a few days.'

I nod and silently question, *Is he* flirting?

In the kitchen, I pour out a small Yellow. One won't hurt, surely. I relive the meeting and remember the locked drawer. With a glass in hand, I retreat back to the study. I question why I've hardly ever ventured in here. The antique desk probably cost a fortune, the same as the highly polished floor. I flood more light into the room from a gold lamp stand and cream shade. I place my glass on the desk and run my hand across the smooth wood. I wonder where the key is for the locked drawer. There isn't anywhere else to search. Behind the blinds is an empty windowsill. The pale walls are void of pictures. No cabinet, no bin. No nothing?

I flop down onto the leather armchair and cross my leg, swinging it in frustration. Fingers tap each side of both arms of the chair as I briefly scan the room again. I sigh and move to snatch up my drink, accidentally knocking the lamp over. It thuds onto the Persian rug. I curse and stand, then bend down to inspect the damage. It seems okay as I inspect it. But just as I'm about to put it back I spot something taped to the bottom. It's a small key. No guessing what that's for. I bite my lip. What am I going to find? I drain the contents of my glass. I then carefully insert the key and turn it. Slowly I slide out the drawer. A face in the photograph smiles up at me. She seems familiar. Where do I know her from? Then it hits me…and my fingers shake when I reach in for it. Maybe I'm wrong? I stare closely. No…It's definitely *her*. What's my *husband* doing with a picture of Nick's *sister*? Plus hidden in a locked drawer? *Why?* Unsure of what to do, I put the picture back. Taping up the key, her smiling face leaves an imprint on my mind.

EIGHTEEN

Spaghetti is swirled around a silver folk, and hopelessly I drop it again. I sigh, regretting my choice of order, and miserably seek out Susie's lasagne. I guess I don't have much of an appetite anyway.

I've updated her about the afternoon appointment I had with Dean. Purposely I've withheld finding the photograph. There's got be a reasonable explanation. Old school buddies, perhaps, or grew up in the same neighbourhood, maybe?

Her eyes laugh with mild amusement. 'Fancy Timmy going to bite him.'

I shrug. 'I know, how strange.' But what's most odd is how Timmy reacted to Nick. I guess some people have that effect on animals.

'So, it won't be long before you find out where Greg is?'

I nod nervously. Then what happens? The sort of not knowing is kind of safe in a funny way if that makes sense. I wonder at all the possibilities, but bad thoughts turn my tummy. I put down my knife and folk and push my plate away. Perhaps my dinner is too rich for the baby. I think of my husband and how much he longed for this moment. Next,

I consider Nick. Strange how he keeps turning up the way he does. There's something quite odd about that. What about the time he turned up at my house? Perhaps now's the time to question Susie about why she gave him my address. I suppose at some point I'll have to confess my sordid secret too. That will just have to wait because my first priority is to find my husband. I go cold at the prospect of Greg answering the door to Nick that night. What was Susie thinking? Well, there's only one way to find out.

'Oh, by the way, I had the shock of my life when Nick turned up on my doorstep… I can't imagine if Greg had opened the door to him.'

Just as I'm about to demand why she gave him my address, I'm distracted when the waiter appears. Apparently, someone has bumped into Susie's car in the car park below. She's up and out of the chair in a flash. As I watch her leave, I'm drawn to a couple with a toddler in a high chair. The woman's dark complexion reminds me of Nick's sister. There's a possibility she could be my child's auntie. I sip my wine, thinking of the consequences. I've certainly messed up alright.

Susie arrives back and slips back in her seat. Angrily she rips up her garlic bread. 'She's made a right dent, stupid cow.' Taking a bite, she pulls her face. 'Yuk…this is cold now.'

'Oh…do you want to order another?'

She pushes her plate away with a sigh. 'No…I've lost my appetite now.'

I offer, not sure what to say, 'So, did you get her details then?'

'Yes, I did, but that's not the point. I've only just bought that car. Then there was the robbery at the salon. Talk about bloody bad luck.'

Suddenly I'm shamed with guilt. I've been so wrapped up my problems I'd completely forgot about the robbery. The other reason why I wanted to meet up was to tell her about the baby. But now it doesn't appear that the timing is right. I wanted her advice on what to do. The secret can't be kept any longer; I need help. Right now I can't possibly burden her with more of my troubles.

NINETEEN

I fill the kettle with cold water and wait for it to boil. Then I run my fingers on the granite. Dean Aston called earlier to say he has Greg's new address. Before I could ask any questions, he cut the call. Said he'll drop by this afternoon. Steam evaporates from the kettle, but I do not attempt to make coffee. How can I settle?

Finally, the time arrives. On this occasion, I've dressed casually in jeans with a sloppy jumper. I've also taken the precaution of shutting Timmy safely in the kitchen. I'm not having a repeat of his last performance, no way. I check the lounge and catch yellow flames dancing in between the black coals. The soft lights glow from table lamps. Cushions have been pumped up and line the sofa. Touching the fabric on my husband's empty armchair, I bite my lip. *My perfect life is in bits.* How did it come to this? This should have been our first Christmas as man and wife. Miserably I take in Christmas decorations from the house across the road. Could there be a remote chance that when I have Greg's address then *perfect* will be back where it belongs? I taste a drop of Yellow Tail, grateful for the smooth liquid. There's also a possibility my husband doesn't want to see me. What do I do then?

I'm distracted when headlights bounce off the wallpaper. That will be Dean.

Again I think his handshake lingers and I fluster with a silly laugh. 'Hi.' What's wrong with me? Why am I acting like this? I put it down to nerves.

It's deja-vu, with Dean choosing Greg's armchair and putting his flash briefcase flat on pinstripe trouser legs. Only this time he accepts a glass of wine.

'Thank you, Kate.'

I drown mine in an attempt to kill my anticipation and edge on the sofa to ask, eagerly, 'So where's he staying?' I clench the stem of my glass while my heart thuds.

With deliberation, Dean places his glass on the side table. He then proceeds to open his briefcase. He takes his time to carefully rummage inside. I'm tempted to snatch the bloody thing off him and dump the contents over the carpet.

His tone is composed. 'Oh…here it is.'

I race up and my breath catches in my throat as I almost snatch the sheet of paper of him. I read the typed words with a frown. There must be a mistake. I'm not sure I understand. 'This is his business address, and I know he's not staying there.'

Dean is not so poised now when I snap, 'Is this sort of joke?' Admittedly I gave him the name of the business, not the address.

Hastily he stands, clearly embarrassed. 'I'm deeply apologetic; please forgive me, this has never happened before.'

I flop down on the sofa and drain Yellow Tail.

He clears his throat. 'But all is not lost.'

I give him a look and add despondently, 'Well, it is to me.' I knew this private detective stuff was a mistake. Why did I listen to Susie? Her intentions were good, but I should have trusted my instinct. What a complete waste of time, plus the strain on my battered nerves. No wonder his diary was free.

'I could put a tracker on his car,' he suddenly offers.

I'm unimpressed and vent sarcastically, 'Really. But what if it falls off?' What do I know about trackers? He could be rattling on about the Starship Enterprise for all I know.

Dean displays a knowing smile like he has a hidden gem up his sleeve. He slips back into the armchair and crosses his leg. 'It's a small, discreet magnetic, a GPS tracker that fits covertly underneath any vehicle and sends live updates to my computer.'

He has my interest, and I perk up and sit forward. 'Really, it can do that?' This sounds good, very good. The meeting now is taking a different turn altogether as I visualise the system working. But surely it can't be that easy? Can it?

Dean sips his drink before he explains more. 'The box has up to ten days' battery and is water-resistant with a 34kg pull magnet.' His smile is wide as he continues, 'So the tracker stays attached until I take it off. It also retains the full history of the locations visited and the duration of time spent there. So in effect, it provides me with all the information you require.'

I want to kiss him. I want to celebrate. This is great news, but then doubts slide in. It sounds too good to be true. 'You mean you just put it under his car and that's it?'

Dean is confident. 'Yes, I use it all the time.' Then he stalls. '...There is just one small problem.'

I knew it; I just knew it was too good to be true.

He winces and adds lamely, 'We just need to locate the car your husband is driving.'

'What?' Is he for real? Is this another one of his gags? I slump back, careful not to spill my wine. I wonder if Dean Aston is from this planet. First he gives, then he takes. The man is mad.

He, however, dazzles white teeth, shooting down my sulky expression. 'Don't be so disheartened, Kate, people are creatures of habit and that's what lets them down.'

It's his courtroom tone delivering his final speech. However, I'm unimpressed – really, I am.

'You told me he has a joined the gym; I presume he's paid for a twelve-month membership.'

So what? But the thought sinks in and Dean is greeted with my interest once more. Why would Greg stop using the gym? That fact, however, creates another problem, though. I stand to refill our glasses and venture, 'But that means you could be sitting around the car park at the gym for hours on end just waiting for him to turn up.' That's going to cost a fortune.

His grin is lazy. 'Kate, I like you, and I want to help you out, so, therefore, I can offer you another solution. That's, of course, if you agree.'

What? Is he serious? Don't get me wrong, I'm all for saving money for certain things, but really? Is this what I think it is?

TWENTY

A couple of days later I've arranged to meet Dean down a secluded county lane; this is certainly not what I had in mind. No way. Who'd have thought it? I check my watch. I'm early and in a lay-by with enough room for his car to park up behind. Outside, grey dismal clouds gather. I stare up and watch a flock of birds fly around in circles. The engine is running, blowing out warm air. I flick off the heated seat as it's making my bum itch. For the occasion, I'm wrapped up in a fake fur coat, wool jumper and fur-lined boots. It's a necessity since I'll be doing stuff outside, according to Dean. I check my phone and sigh. My husband has not called or left a message as promised. I've called and fired off texts. Soon, though, that could change. My fingers drum the leather steering wheel. Can I do this, spy on him? I imagine different scenarios. What if Susie is right about that Amy? Why would Greg lie? Why just abandon me, though, like I'm out-of-date food? Why did I sleep with Nick? Caught unaware, I jolt when Dean bangs the passenger window. Immediately I wind it down and curse, 'God, you scared me.' Fancy creeping up like that; how come I didn't hear him pull up behind me?

He rubs his hands together with a cheeky smile. 'So are you ready then?'

I'm mixed with a funny kind of excitement tinged with anticipation. Gliding out of the Mercedes, I laugh nervously, hanging onto the door. 'Yes, I guess… so shall we start?' Closing the door carefully, I coyly add, 'Give it a go, as you said.'

Dean holds the GPS tracker which at a guess is around six inches square. It reminds me of a big black magnet, but then it is one, I suppose. I glance up and down the narrow country lane and silently question Dean's choice of location again. His answer was because that there'll be no nosy sods around. I must admit I was rather dubious about his request. Truthfully I thought he was going to suggest something entirely different. I consider that I've watched too many romantic films. What was I thinking? After all, Dean's probably happily married; still, it didn't stop me. I push away the memory and pay attention.

Dean squats at the back wheel of my car, dishing out his order. 'Right, Kate, you need to see where I'm putting this because it's important you get it in the right place.'

I crouch down beside him like a spy in a *James Bond* film. I could be Kate, 007. But with Dean so serious I have to suppress the urge to giggle. I can't believe I'm doing this just to save money; the only consolation is, I guess, that it's not raining. What comfort that is, I have no idea.

Dean turns his face to me. 'Okay, Kate, remove the tracker and put it under the other side of the car, just where I've shown you.'

It looks easy, but it's not; the tracker is well glued on. 'Bloody hell, Dean, it's harder than it looks,' I moan. Should I even be doing this? I should be out celebrating, having a Christmas lunch. Not down a muddy country lane like a ruddy farmer. I do, however, complete my task and yank off the GPS tracker. Trudging over to the other side, I stoop down in an attempt to firmly fix the tracker underneath the car. Finally, after a few minutes, the mission is a success. And for some daft reason, I feel rather chuffed. It will also save a load of money. Standing up straight, I stretch my back. That was hard work, and I dust a fraction of dirt off my hands. Really, I should have worn gloves.

Dean appears pleased, nodding. 'Right then, off you go, and I'll speak to you later.'

I hop into my car, thinking we could have done this on my drive. A short while later I see the reason for Dean's choice of location. I've hit a pothole and I'm sure I hear a clatter. Glancing in the overhead mirror, I spot the tracker in the middle of the lane.

'Damn.' Instantly I hit the brakes. Before I have a chance to get out, a tractor hurls up behind me. A rosy-faced farmer indicates for me to move further down for him to get past. I fume at his timing; however, I'm in no position to argue. I edge forward to where the lane widens and hold my breath when he edges past, far too close for my liking. He waves a cheerful thank you and gives a toot of his horn. I move forward a little so I can exit the car and retrieve the tracker. It now resembles a flat piece of cardboard. *Unbelievable.* Five minutes and already I'm out of pocket. I kick the mashed-up box. I'll need to call Dean for a £500 replacement. Never mind that, though. I groan inwardly, knowing the Mercedes' suspension is low. The Audi R8 is even worse. How many trackers can I afford to lose?

TWENTY-ONE

This is it. The night we planned to put the tracker on. I'm doubled up in knots. My trainers pace the marble-tiled hall, sipping Yellow. Countless times I've pulled back my black polo sweater sleeve to check the time on my watch, waiting for Susie. She's offered her support for the latest mission – hopefully the one to locate Greg's car to shove the *new* tracker on. As per Dean's suggestion, our stakeout is taking place at Hartwell's Hotel and gym. It sounds so surreal, like I'm starring in a thriller. I sigh. This is for real, and the only consolation is that my heartache has been replaced with apprehension. Not that that's much better. Will my husband even turn up? How long do we give the mission? It could be hit and miss for weeks – months, even. What then? What if he's with that *Amy*? The list goes on and on…suddenly I stop. I hear music. *We wish you a Merry Christmas…* I race to the lounge and slightly part the curtains to peer out. On any other occasion, I would greet the sight with a welcome warm grin. Tonight, however, I sour my lips. A sleigh with a reindeer has been hoisted onto a trailer pulled by a Land Rover. Of course next door's brood mingle with the small crowd. They surround the relic of Father Christmas, his red tunic stretched across his potbelly.

Susie was supposed to be going Christmas shopping with Martin. However, she was adamant that I didn't conduct the mission solo. A kind gesture indeed, and I'm very grateful. Because left up to me I might have chickened out. The idea and thoughts about the task sort of felt okay, but in the here and now, I don't feel so confident. I take one last look before I straighten the silk fabric. My *husband* and I should be out Christmas shopping – no, correction: buying baby stuff. I place a hand on my tummy and consider the tiny seed growing. Is it a boy? Will he look like Greg? Then dark thoughts sneak in. Will he suspect the baby might not be his? My inner demons fight: *Tell him. No, don't.* Do I confront him if he parks up? What if he doesn't? What then? What if the tracker falls off again? The Audi R8 is going to be useless, a nightmare. I'm startled when a horn blasts.

Opening the door, I'm pleased to see that the Santa show has now moved on. The security lights shine on Susie's new red BMW. It's one of Martin's early Christmas gifts to cheer her up regarding her bump and the salon's robbery. Tears lurk behind my eyes. Funny how my husband accused Susie of being jealous, whereas now I'm full of it. She has a supportive husband whereas I have not. I bet if Susie slept with someone else, good old-natured Martin wouldn't abandon her – oh no. He'd probably want to discuss the matter. He doesn't seem so boring and dependable now, does he?

From her white leather seat, Susie turns to face me. 'God, I bet you're nervous because I know I am.'

I smell cigarette smoke on her breath and I nod silently, not trusting myself to not break out in tears. Christmas is an emotional time, but blended with this it's even worse. Everywhere I look on Stourbridge Road, Christmas decorations taunt and tease me. We stop at traffic lights and the car's indicator ticks in the silence. Susie breaks it with a tender pat on my leg. 'Hey, it will be okay, don't worry.'

I force a grim smile as my nerves knot with tension. I'm unable to settle, and I shift for a more comfortable position, except it's useless. I then lean my head back and close my eyes, but that's just as bad.

As we approach the hotel, Susie slows down. On the curved brick wall to the entrance, a granite black and gold sign reads 'Hartwell's Hotel & Exclusive Gym'. The high wrought-iron gates are already open as we pull into the car park. She chooses a spot at the far end with a good view of the entrance, even though Greg won't recognise her convertible. I slink down into the leather seat and attempt to slow my rapid heartbeat by watching cars leave and enter. A gold Lexus parks nearby. A man in a tuxedo clambers out and heads for the passenger side. He assists a pregnant woman while another man emerges from the back seat. I wonder if she is in the same predicament as me, with the father unknown.

The need to blurt out my secret is strong and I turn to face Susie but lose my nerve. Instead, I give her a grateful nod. 'Thanks for coming; I could never have done this on my own.'

She reassures me, 'Hey, what are friends for?'

I return my gaze to the three people. The woman in a gold maternity dress has linked both her arms with her male escorts. For a second I flash to the same scene, with me, Greg and Nick. I'm distracted from my thoughts when Susie slips outside for a cigarette. The clock on the dashboard reads 5.30pm. We've been here one hour, and I drum my fingers on the leather seat. I wonder if my husband will turn up. How come his phone is still switched off? If he broke it, then surely he'd call me from his new one. None of it makes any sense, unless he's found about Nick. Surely, though, he'd want to confront me to find out the truth. The almost full car park stretches ahead. I sigh. *This is a waste of time.* I sit up. *Except, didn't Dean say people are creatures of habit? Maybe there's some truth in that, I guess.* So I decide to give it one more hour. Idly I turn my attention to a white Range Rover entering the car park. The face is familiar. I gasp, realising it's my *husband*. It seems such an age since I last saw his handsome, smooth face. There's a flash of our wedding day.

His smile…

His kiss after we'd pledged our vows…

Tears loiter now.

How could he do this to me?

Why?

Then, just as quickly, I feel anger, noting that he is alive and well. He couldn't be bothered to call me or just bloody return home. And, judging by his expression, he certainly doesn't come across as a wronged *husband*. He appears quite happy – content, even.

Susie yanks the door open. She dives in and exclaims, 'He's here…did you see him?'

Instantly I remember why I'm here. Quickly I slither down with just enough room to spy on him as he drives around for a free parking spot. I bite down hard on my bottom lip, wanting to draw blood – not mine, *Greg's*. I wrestle with my raging anger. How dare he ignore me? *Why?* Is this some sort of punishment?

Finally, the Range Rover parks up and my husband hops out, swinging his gym bag. He struts off, then abruptly stops like he's forgotten something. I freeze and hold my breath, waiting. He turns and faces our direction.

Susie thumps me and whispers urgently, 'Get down.'

My heart thuds in my chest; I'm convinced he's spotted us. Any second I expect him to bang on the window; instead, to my surprise, Susie sits up.

I hiss, 'What are you doing? Get back down.'

Susie scoffs defiantly. 'I haven't got to hide.'

She's right, she doesn't. 'But what if he sees you and walks over?'

My question is ignored. 'So he's still alive then? And don't worry, he's gone.'

I panic. 'What! You mean he's left?'

Her tone is reassuring. 'No. He's gone inside.' Nodding, she adds, 'So the private detective was right about creatures of habit. I must admit, I was rather dubious.' She states, more to herself, staring out the windscreen, 'But why is his phone permanently off? That's extremely odd, unless he's hiding something, of course.'

The shock of seeing my husband sinks in and I struggle to sit up. I wonder at his reaction if I were to sneak up behind and tap his shoulder. Would he be surprised or point an accusing finger at me? For a second I close my eyes and wish I had my perfect life back. This should have been the moment where we headed inside for a romantic candlelit dinner. The time of excitement, telling him of my wonderful news. The vision blurs as I imagine his smile of joy.

I'm drawn back to the present when Susie asks, 'Are you okay? Silly question, I know.'

My sigh is heavy. 'The situation seems surreal.' *A nightmare, more like.*

Susie touches my arm encouragingly. 'Come on, you can do it.' She also backs up her statement with an effective smile. 'It's the only way to find out what's he's up to.'

I reflect, 'Now he's here, surely it makes sense to have it out with him?'

'What! You can't be serious. Then what are you going to do if he tells you to do one, then dashes off?' She shakes her head. 'Come on... he's left you high and dry, a text here a call there… You're going to stick to the plan and that's the end of it.'

I fold my arms with a sigh. She might be right. But she's no idea of the mess I'm in and how I feel. There's a possibility Greg could act differently if he knew I was pregnant. Except, like she said, I can't take that chance. She's right – I have to do it. I can do it. I will. However, I make no move. Instead, I circle my first finger on the seat, gazing at Greg's car. *Come on, Kate, at least he's in the Range Rover, not the low Audi.* I agree with my friend: more information is needed regarding his movements and to find out exactly what he's playing at. Whatever it is my husband can't ignore me forever.

Susie nudges me, demanding, 'Come on, he might not be in there for long.'

I take a deep breath and look down at my handbag in the footwell. Something's wrong. Then it hits me, and I struggle for breath. .

'What's the matter?' Susie exclaims.

I bite my lip and stare at her.

'What?'

'I left the tracker at home.'

'What? You're joking, right?'

I raise my eyebrows, wincing with a shake of my head. 'I wish I was.'

She blows out a long sigh.

The drive back home is silent and I curse my forgetfulness. But I do have a lot on my mind. With the key in my hand at the ready, I rush into the hall just as Timmy darts from the lounge. He bolts straight outside. Immediately I turn to race after him and scream, 'Timmy…Timmy.'

He is on the road in seconds. I freeze and watch hopelessly when he disappears under the wheels of a white van. I feel like I've been hit by a train and I struggle to breathe. The van trundles on and lights blur, disappearing down the road.

Susie urgently shakes my arm. 'He didn't get hit. He almost did, though.'

I'm confused and sniff, wiping my face. 'What?' I'm sure he went under the van. A dog barks in the distance and I strain to listen; it's Timmy's distinctive yap. *It's him. He's alive.* I gulp in cold air and dart across the road down to the wooded coppice. There, a short distance away, is Timmy jumping around. He's barking up at a tree. I stop and bend to catch my breath.

'What's got into him?' Susie asks.

I stare up to scan the tree and curl my lips. Just as I thought; the arched ginger cat is balanced on a branch, hissing down at Timmy. 'Oh, yes… I can guess what's gone on alright. That thing up there probably strutted her bony ass across the windowsill, gloating at Timmy like she's always doing.' I turn to her and snap, 'And you can guess the rest.'

She appears partly amused. 'Well, at least he's alright.'

'No thanks to her. I knew that minx was trouble when she moved in.'

I scoop Timmy up and march him back home, shoving him in the hall. 'I'll deal with you later.'

Diving into the car, I moan, 'What if Greg's gone?' Clicking on my seatbelt, I add miserably, 'Then what? We can't be on permanent surveillance forever.'

Susie screeches off the drive, sending gravel everywhere. 'Let's hope he's still there.'

Turning into the car park, I breathe easy. The Range Rover is still parked up and we resume our position. I stare down at the footwell and freeze. I want to smack my dumbass head when I blurt out, 'You're not going to believe this.'

'Tell me you're joking, right?'

I wince again. 'Sorry. I forgot with all the commotion of Timmy.'

This time when we arrive back on my drive Susie insists I show her the tracker before we depart. Ten minutes later my nerves are stretched more than ever as we resume our position once again. If ever I needed a drink it's now, and after the deed is done I'm heading straight to the hotel bar. Call it a medicinal purpose.

Then, as if the night couldn't get any worse, my husband suddenly strides out, swinging his gym bag once more. I whisper in alarm, 'Shit…now what?'

Susie gapes, silently.

Grabbing the tracker, I nudge her. 'Quick, do something.'

'What…what?'

I yank the door open and hiss, 'Think of…something, anything to slow him down.'

Darting out I duck between cars and race towards the Range Rover. Blood pounds in my ears, spying Greg getting closer and closer. Silently I beg, *Come on, Susie, hurry up. He'll be gone…soon…*

I reach his car and crouch down beside it. I tremble, thinking I'm going to miss my chance. Somehow the tracker slips from my grasp. Its clang echoes in the car park. I freeze, expecting my husband to appear and demand to know what's going on. I stare down at the black box, too scared to pick it up. I hold my breath when I hear a female voice call out, 'Mr Anderson…You've left your membership card.'

My heart beats erratically as I take a chance and peer through the Range Rover passenger side window. Greg strolls back towards the entrance. It's the diversion I need, and I almost fall to my knees to grab the tracker. My fingers shake as I attempt to fix it under by the back wheel. When I spot Greg's shoes aimed my way, I pray he'll approach the front of the car and not the back. A silent thank you is sent when he does and I slither around to hide behind the next car. I'm startled when a voice asks behind me, 'Are you okay?'

I glare up to a security guard and stutter, 'I...er, lost my earring.' Next, I run my fingers over the tarmac. 'Ah...here it is, under the car.' I can't see Greg's shoes and I pray he's in his motor, ready to leave. I spot a small stone and I reach out for it. It's bunched in my hand as I crawl backwards, pretending to shove it in my jacket pocket. As the Range Rover's engine starts up, I half bend, dusting off my jeans as I glimpse my *husband* drive off. The bored guard drifts off too.

Feeling a little safer, I turn around.

Susie makes her way over. 'Phew...that was close.'

'You can say that again – I've never felt so stressed in all my life,' I state, wiping mist off my upper lip.

She nods. 'You managed to put the tracker on didn't you?'

I smirk. *Oh, yes.*

'I think we both need a strong drink at the bar,' she suggests.

'I'm not even going to answer that,' I retort back.

At the entrance, I breathe in fresh pine from the Christmas trees planted each side. In reception, a fire burns in the lion stone surround. It's decorated with hanging Santa socks. Susie offers to fetch the drinks, which allows me time to catch my breath and resume some sanity. I scan the crowded bar for vacant seats. I guess everyone is having pre-drinks before celebrating in the ballroom next door. A couple rises from a table near the window. I push past the crowd to grab it and sink into a velvet armchair. I sigh, sensing tears lurking behind my eyes as the reality of what just happened unfolds. Was he the loving man I married? He seemed unfazed – happy, almost. Not someone who's abandoned his wife, a *pregnant* one. I then flush with the shame of my misconduct. I wriggle out of my jacket and drape it over the back of the chair.

Gratefully I accept a crystal glass of brandy from Susie. The liquid glides down into my tummy and the slight burning sensation is a welcome warmth as it eases into my veins, smoothing them out.

Susie pulls her chair closer to me. 'I tell you what, I never thought you'd get the tracker on.'

I agree with her in a measured tone. 'Me neither.'

Susie leans back and crosses her leg. 'I can't understand what Greg's up to?' She shakes her head. 'And what's with his phone being permanently off? From where I'm sitting, it looks like he's dumped you.' She then perches forward, adding. 'You haven't got to put up with this. I mean, you still have your inhertiage and the money from your house, you can start again.'

I'm going to have to come clean and tell her about the baby. 'I…err… need to confess something.' I cringe, but press on. 'But I think you'd better get another round in first.' I'm sure two brandies won't hurt the baby.

She signals a waiter over to place our order. She then leans back in her chair and folds her arms as she listens. I'm only interrupted by the arrival of our drinks.

Susie gulps hers down, as she needs it. After, she states, 'Pregnant…wow…I wasn't expecting that. And I have to say, Greg could have found out somehow, hence the cold treatment.'

Reluctantly I agree as I nurse my glass.

She leans forward, asking, 'Does Nick know?'

'Hey, Susie, what I should know?' questions Nick, who suddenly appears with a mischievous grin.

My jaw drops and crimson creeps up my neck. *How much did he hear?*

Susie appears as stunned as me but manages to fake a tight smile. 'Fancy seeing you here.'

My eyes are averted when a glamorous brunette calls out, strutting over, 'Ah, there you are, Nicky.' She purrs and links her arm with his in his tailored tuxedo.

I force a grin and clench my drink. I can hardly breathe not knowing *if* he heard or not?

Nick makes introductions. But all I want is for them to leave. *Cynthia*, his date, tightens her grip on Nick. She gives us a brief, distasteful glance.

Susie hastily says, 'We've just come from the gym.' She stands up. 'And we really must dash now.'

I'm grateful and scrambling to get up, I deliberately avoid Nick's stare and focus on a non-existent stain on my trainers.

Susie adds, 'Kate wanted to say thank you for helping her out the other night.' I imagine her fake smile when she presses on. 'That's what she wanted you to know, Nick.'

Susie grabs my arm to rush us both forward through the crowd to the exit. *Fancy him being here.*

Outside, the cold air does nothing to chill my bright cheeks, even when Susie affirms that Nick heard nothing significant. Somehow I don't feel her confidence. *He's not to be trusted.*

TWENTY-TWO

Days later I lean on the bedroom windowsill and idly watch snowflakes gather on the gravel drive below. I burn at the thought of Nick overhearing us the other night. I've been unable to sleep. I half expected him to turn up and bang his fists on the front door, demanding to know whose baby it was. Plus, to make matters worse, Susie insists that I tell him. How do I do that after one foolish drunken night? I sigh hard, thinking about it. I then cast my eyes to the flashing lights on the tree in the neighbour's house across the road. This is a Christmas nightmare. With my dressing robe sleeve, I dab the corners of my eyes. Should I even bother trying my husband's mobile again? Then I'm surprised when a text arrives, as though I've willed it:

Babe still playing

DON'T CALL WORK DON'T WANT THEM
TO KNOW

I read the text over and over. I try to call back, but of course it's already off. I sniff, dragging a tissue from its box, and slump on the unmade bed. Not knowing what to think, I idly ruffle Timmy's head. He's in no rush to get up and rolls on his back. I tickle his warm tummy. I'm at a loss. I am.

The only consolation is that Dean has promised me Greg's address later. Tears fall and mingle with Timmy's fur. Surely when I tell my husband I'm pregnant he'll want to pack in the poker and come home. *If it means me lying, then so be it.* How do I convince Susie to keep her mouth shut? I pace the bedroom. Why did I tell her. How was I to know, that she'd insist I do the honourable thing and tell Nick? *Tell both of them…and move on, she said.* Don't live a lie…Easy for her to rant. And I don't want to even consider the implications if she's right about that Amy.

I'd love a glass of wine but force myself to make coffee instead. Filling the kettle, I gaze outside as a stampede of thoughts demand my attention. I'm shaken back as the kettle grows heavy in my hand with overflowing water.

Seated at the island with my hands cupped around a mug of coffee, my heart sinks, realising my Christmas could be spent alone. I take a sip coffee then instantly spit out the cold liquid. If there's one thing I hate, it's cold coffee. When my phone vibrates on the granite worktop there is a feeling of trepidation seeing Dean's number.

His voice is friendly like he's on a social call. 'Good morning, Kate, how are you?'

What a daft question. 'Yes, fine,' I say, holding in my sarcasm. But then again, he's not privy to the full, messed-up story.

'Well, good news. The computer has uploaded information from the GPS tracker, displaying the address where the Range Rover has stayed overnight for the last couple of days. This would indicate your husband's new place of residence.'

I stand and can't help but reach out for Yellow Tail; the shock is too much for me to digest his update. I should be elated, but I'm not. I'm scared and grip the worktop with my free hand, whispering, 'Where?'

'It's an apartment in King Edwards Wharf, Birmingham. I must say, they're very expensive – I checked out the prices.'

His tone is upbeat like an estate agent's. 'And I've already driven over to have a look around.' When he pauses, I clench the phone harder. 'But… I'm afraid I don't have the actual apartment your husband is staying at, but it's definitely the white Range Rover in the underground communal car park.'

Confusion creeps in. Is this good news or not? How much more of this can I take? Yes, we have it, then we don't. This isn't how it happens in the movies. Then again, they have their answers on a script and not the crap service of Dean Aston. I drain my glass. I don't give a damn how early it is. 'So what happens now?'

'Well, I could monitor when the vehicle is on the move again.'

I guzzle the wine frustratedly.

'You still there, Kate?'

I wipe my mouth and mumble, 'I'll call you back.' Okay, so he's located the car, but no Greg, and by the time he arrives back, he'll have vanished into what apartment? This is no use to me at all – useless, in fact. It's clear now that Dean Aston's business is shoddy, and I wished I'd used another reputable company.

Susie's name flashes across the screen. 'Well, did you get the address then?'

I pause and sigh before answering, 'Yes…and…no.'

'I don't understand.'

So I explain.

Her tone sounds as deflated as mine. 'Oh.'

'So basically, I'm back to square one, as they say.'

I hear her inhale on a cigarette. 'Well, I have to say I wasn't expecting that.'

'Me neither. And before you ask, I've decided I need to tell Greg first. After all, he's still my husband.' *I think?*

I imagine her one eyebrow curved with displeasure as she snorts, 'In paper only. And as I've said, there's no need for him to treat you like he has, no matter what you've done.'

I choose to ignore her remark, but I can't help but silently agree with his childish behaviour, because he can't ignore me forever. Plus if he hadn't lied in the first place I wouldn't be in this mess. No, correction: we wouldn't be in this mess. *He has to see that, surely.* But then I remember I'm keeping that a secret. I'm sure I'm not the only woman to have made a mistake and I won't be the last either.

Her tone softens. 'Look, I'm sorry, but you know my thoughts on Greg.'

I sigh. 'I know.'

She adds, 'Just because you don't know the apartment, what's stopping you from going over there to hang around for a while? You might even catch him; after all, he's supposed to be staying there, isn't he?'

I think, do I want to hang around another car park? 'I'm not sure.'

'I could try and get time off to come with you?' she offers kindly.

But we both know that's impossible with it being her busiest time of year. 'Thanks, but you can't let customers down.'

'Okay, so I'll come after work then?'

Guilt creeps in for taking up her time when I have nothing else to do.

'Anyway, I've just thought, isn't the tracker still on Greg's car?'

'Yes, of course it is, why?'

'Well, you're missing the point.'

I shrug, confused. 'What?'

Her tone changes down the line like I'm a child. 'If the tracker is still on the car, then you'll know if he's there or when he arrives. Track his movements, like if he's gone back to the gym, that will give you plenty of time to drive over and wait for him.'

Why didn't I think of that? More to the point, why didn't Dean suggest it? I cut the call, and punch in his number.

TWENTY-THREE

For the tenth time, I've called Dean. It's now late afternoon, and I toss the mobile on the bed. I fume. Why is he not picking up? I apply lip gloss with shaky fingers. I'm determined to drive to Greg's address today, and I polish off Yellow Tail for courage. I've tried to cut down, I have.

After slipping on a cashmere coat over my charcoal wool dress, I check my phone again just in case for some reason I didn't hear it. How long do I wait for Dean to return my call? I check my reflection in the dressing-room mirror and sigh. I'm more suited for a funeral than a hopeful encounter with my husband – that's if I can locate him. Maybe this is the death of our marriage? I slump on the bed and force back tears, stroking Timmy's head, wishing I could stay here. I wish this wasn't happening. I wish I could turn time back. Eventually I gather myself up and stand, shoving my handbag across my shoulder. Heading for the front door, I hesitate outside Greg's office, remembering the photograph locked inside the drawer. My hand lingers on the cold handle and I bite my lip. What is he doing with it? And what's the connection to Nick? I decide to leave it for now; I have enough to deal with at the moment.

I can always ask him when I see him, that's if he'll speak to me. He has to, one way or another. How else can we move forward?

For once the M5 is clear with no sign of rain and I cut across to the outside lane. As a distraction, I press on the radio. 'Jingle Bells' belts out; automatically I switch it off. Then panic sets in. It's Christmas, a time when the police are out in force for festive drivers. But I've only drank to settle my nerves; it's not like I'm celebrating the season. I glance at the overhead mirror and freeze. Blue flashing lights are several cars behind. Gripping the steering wheel, I attempt to change lanes, but I have to swerve back when the harsh sound of a horn blasts out. *Shit.* This time I indicate when I manoeuvre the Mercedes to the inside lane. My eyes dart back and forth in the mirror, spying the panda lights move into the middle lane. It's creeping up, and a cold sweat mists on my upper lip. I hold my breath, watching when a black BMW is flagged down instead of me. The relief is welcomed by a long, thankful sigh. The next exit is taken, just to get off the motorway. With my nerves shot to pieces, I head straight for a sign to McDonald's for a cappuccino.

One hour later I feel a touch more with it. Trepidation is heavy in my heart, and mounts as I cruise towards Five Way Island. I have a good idea where the King Edwards apartments are situated. Street lights flick on and enhance Christmas lights hung off every lamp post. Any other time, the sight would bring out my smile. I glance down at my phone on the passenger seat. Dean has still not returned my calls.

Finally, I reach my destination and bite my lip. I cruise slowly and briefly glance at the canal-side apartments. Some have balconies decorated with Christmas trees, lights flashing. Who would Greg know here? I wonder if Dean has the right address. No, this is it, because he claims he checked it out and monitored my husband's motor in the underground car park.

There's a free parking bay further up. Quickly I reverse in

before someone else does. Cutting the engine, I stare out and drum my fingers on the steering wheel. I wonder what to do next. Grabbing my mobile off the passenger's seat, I try Dean again. It goes straight to answer machine and angrily I toss it into my handbag. Some professional he turned out to be. I don't care for being stuck here all night, waiting. Slipping out the warm comfort of my car, I lock the car and stand at the kerb. Cars rush past, all in a mad panic to get home from work, I guess. My head turns left then right a couple of times before I'm able to race across. Standing at the kerb, I can't believe I've forgotten my handbag; the bag I don't need, the phone I do. I drag out an agitated sigh and attempt to cross the road once more to my car. Several minutes later, I'm back to where I started, only this time with my phone firmly tucked in my coat pocket. Suddenly I stand still. What if Greg has changed cars again? He could have easily done so, as he often does.

A young woman in high heels and skinny jeans startles me when she asks, 'Hey, are you okay?'

'Er… yes…fine,' I say, forcing a limp smile. I bet she thinks I'm a nutcase, just staring into space. Quickly I think of a suitable answer and add, 'I'm thinking about buying an apartment here.'

'It's the place to be, that's for sure. The apartments are very expensive.' I'm sure she smirks when she pouts smugly with oversized lips. 'No point wishing for one of the penthouses because my boyfriend – you know, Tom Ryan – and I bought the last one.'

'Who?' I shrug. How would I know him?

She glares at me like I'm an idiot. 'The famous footballer.'

I shake my head. I've no idea who she's talking about.

She cocks her head to one side. 'You've never heard of him? He plays for Birmingham City.' She flicks her blonde extensions.

'How nice.' But I'm more concerned by the fact that she may know my husband. She might have spotted him. Before I can ask, her mobile rings in her hand. Long, pink, diamond talons tap the screen and she engages in conversation, strutting off like I don't exist. It appears I have been forgotten, what she's wearing tonight being more important. Off she goes to the security door of the apartments, and she taps in a code. She enters, with the door automatically closing after her. *Shit.* I could have gone in with her. But is my husband staying here?

When drops of rain fall, I turn and search for cover. A blue BMW waits for the underground car park barrier to rise. Idly I watch it enter. Suppose I could shelter in there for a minute. Perhaps there's a chance the Range Rover might be parked up? The first car I encounter is layered in dust like it's been abandoned or stolen or just forgotten. Other spaces are filled with high-end sports cars, which somehow I expected. With cold feet, I stamp my boots and button up my cashmere coat. I decide to venture further into the heart of the car park and have a quick scan around. An overhead light flickers; its buzz fills me with unease. That sense of being watched is back. I'm being silly again. But when the dodgy light suddenly pops off, I flinch. Who'd hear me if I was attacked? Stepping backwards, I jolt when a car door slams. Instantly I spin around and bolt towards the exit. I'm taking no chances. Silly or not.

TWENTY-FOUR

The next morning there's still no response from Dean's mobile. What's he playing at? Timmy barks to be let out into the garden. I leave the French door open for him and open up the laptop. Somebody at his office must know where he is. I locate the web page for the landline. It rings out but then switches to the answering service. I fume, shaking my head. 'Dean... it's Kate Anderson, can you please return my call?' What a bloody waste of time he is.

After Timmy wanders back in, I close the door and snap the kettle on. What use is his service if I can't get hold of him? My fingers tap on the granite island, wondering what to do next. First of all, is Greg using the Range Rover? I know what his text said, but I'm sick of this charade. I'm calling his business. What if he answers? Well, I'll bloody drive over, that's what. I could pretend to be a customer interested in buying the Range Rover. Say, I'm on my way for a test drive. What if they have more than one white one for sale? I try to recall the plate, but it's useless. It's new, that's all I know. Tapping the company name into the laptop, I scan their stock list. At last, something is in my favour. There's only one white Range Rover on their site – that's got be it. I feel jittery thinking about making the call. Instead, I pace the kitchen. Dean should be doing this, not me. *Just call them.* Before I lose my nerve, I punch in the numbers; I then cut the call. *Come on, get a grip, Kate.* I try again but panic when I recognise the salesman's voice. *Dave.* He was the one I spoke to when I was last there.

I disguise my voice, lowering it to a whisper. 'I, er...' Clearing my throat with a cough, I venture, 'I'm on my way over to look at the white Range Rover you have for sale.'

'Yes, of course, and may I please take your details?'

Damn, I hadn't thought of that. I scan the kitchen for ideas. The brand Morphy Richards on the kettle stands out, so I say, with confidence I don't feel, 'Mrs Richards.'

'So, Mrs Richards, can I start by taking your phone number please?'

I freeze, feeling uncomfortable. 'Why, what for?' This is not going to plan, and I think hard. 'Look... I can't because it's a surprise buy for my husband, and I don't want him picking up a call from your firm. It would spoil the present.' I have to admit, I sound convincing, even to the point that I believe my wild tale.

'Ah, I see your point, Mrs Richards, please hold the line.'

I relax a little and wait.

Dave is back online. 'Sorry to have kept you. But the Range Rover is out on a test drive.'

'Oh... so what time will it be back? Maybe in about half an hour?'

Dave pauses like he's considering what to say next. 'The thing is, the test drive is taking place in London. But when the vehicle arrives back I could get Pat, our receptionist, to call you. She could perhaps say, if your husband picks the call up, she's your hairdresser or something like that.'

I wonder if he's telling the truth and whether Greg might

be there. After all, he's supposed to be one of the directors. I lower my voice to a whisper once more. 'Er…that could work, yes… But is Greg there? My husband and I came in a while back. He was very helpful.'

'Yes, he's here. Would you like to speak to him?'

My heart speeds up. *Greg is there*. Not at the apartment. I grab my car keys and race to the door, blood pounding in my ears. *He has to talk to me*. I can't stand the wait any longer. This needs sorting now.

'Hang on, Mrs Richards, I just want to check some details, as we do have two Gregs here.'

I stop, gripping the phone, and splutter, 'Twwwwo Gregs…?'

'Yes, Greg Tranter the director, he's here. But, unfortunately, the salesman Greg Anderson is on leave.'

Salesman. Greg? That can't be right? I don't bother disguising my voice this time and blurt out, 'I thought Greg Anderson was a director?'

He appears not to notice the change in my tone as he confirms that he is a salesman for a second time. The statement hits me like a smack in the face. I reach out to the wall for support and murmur, 'Sorry, I have an urgent call. I have to go.'

Why would Dave lie? For what purpose? I think back to the time when I was in the showroom. He meant Greg Tranter. He thought I was Mrs Tranter. Greg must have known that. A cold band of fear tightens around my heart. From day one Greg told me he was a director. I didn't mishear that, no way. I go back to Susie's warnings. *What's the rush? You hardly know him.*

I help myself to a very large wine. If Greg is only a salesman, how can he afford this house? I refill my glass as further panic sets in while I recall his words. *I didn't want to worry you about the debt.* I sense fear. *Where's my money then?* Has he gambled it? I race to the office in search of bank statements and the high-interest account where Greg transferred my cash. Instead, I just stare at the antique desk, knowing the drawers are empty apart from the locked one. Frantically I still try just in case, then reluctantly I give up. I pace the study, bunch my hands and bang the desk with my fists. He must have something somewhere. I bolt upstairs to our bedroom and rip out drawers. I open wardrobe doors and search. I feel icy sweat, finding nothing of interest. Standing on my tiptoes, I hesitate. The shoebox is still neatly placed at the back.

I carried it into the hall the day I officially moved in with Greg; it was the last of my belongings, the most precious. It tells the tale of my real mum, the one before whisky claimed her. It contains letters from her lover, Billy. Every time we moved she'd hide them in there, pretending to Dad that it was filled with my childhood trinkets. Nothing was ever the same after that one horrific night.

I stumble backwards. A flashback of stale cigar breath crushing my small mouth. I sway and reach out for the wall for support. The dark memory haunts me. Only when I hear a bark in the distance does it snap my mind to the here and now. Timmy jumps up to my leg, but my heart still hammers in my chest. I take in deep breaths…I'm *safe*…it's okay…calm down. No one can *hurt* me now. It's almost like he senses my terror.

I slump on the bed and the past rages up again. After what happened with my dad, he then spent more nights out, boozing with his army buddies. I'd imagined he tried to run away from his demons. A winter night stationed in Germany flashes up in my mind. Mum stabbed the fire with a poker, a glass of whisky loosely in her other hand.

'That's what you get when you mix colour.' Her tear-stained face had turned to me. 'My family disowned me for getting pregnant with you.' She'd knocked back her drink and poured another.

I'd known what came next. The tale had been spat out so many times. In the morning when she woke, her memory of the night was lost in her blackout. At fourteen, I was the one who made her bed. I tided up. I cooked. I cleaned. I made sure where we lived was always pristine, just the way that man, who I was supposed to call *Dad*, liked it.

I cast around now and think how funny it is that he shares his trait of tidiness with my husband. But I can't think of *him* now as I'm dragged back in time once more. Seeing the box has opened up a Pandora's box inside me. I wonder if Mum ever remembered telling me about her so-called friend, my dad, who'd raped *her*. A rushed marriage had followed as I was in her belly, the product of his dreadful deed. After their wedding in London, they fled for life in the army. Billy, her boyfriend at the time, was working away on the oil rigs. Mum knew Billy would have killed Dad if he'd ever found out the real truth. But there was no way she was going to let him go to prison over her. So she'd lied to Billy's mother. Told her she'd fallen in love with Dad. Billy never gave up, though. In the end, he killed himself. That letter sent from his mother to my mum was her death warrant in the name of whisky. Mum also claimed that Dad had threatened to kill Billy if she ever left him.

There's an itch on my head. I scratch it and feel my blonde hair. Dad would turn in his grave if he could see the colour now. He was proud of his Sikh roots. He was also a hypocrite. Unbeknown to Susie, she sided with him, not wanting to colour my dark hair. Perhaps if had she known my dad she'd have nodded in approval. I changed my name too. I wanted to erase the past. But I can never wipe out when Dad tried to drown me in the ocean in India. He blamed *me*. *I was thirteen when I miscarried his child.* Mum had dragged him off me as I coughed up sea salt, trying to catch my breath. I told my husband my fear of water was because of a childhood prank.

I fiddle with my wedding ring from the man who claims to love *me*. Mum's words haunt me. *Lies don't kill a marriage; the truth does.* My origin is rape and I'm the product of misery. I place a hand on my tummy and vow to love and protect the tiny seed inside me. I will not allow *he* or *she* the same horrors of my childhood. In one way, I suppose I have inherited the Sikh's code of the warrior. How else did I survive? I draw on that strength now; I fear I might well need it.

TWENTY-FIVE

I arrive back to the underground car park of the apartments, determined to find my husband. How else do I uncover the truth? Is he a director? Or not? And what the hell did he use my money for? Surprisingly, the dust-covered car is still here. I stamp my feet and rub my hands together to warm up. I've circled the whole area four times in search of the white Range Rover. The broken light has been fixed, which is pretty quick – not that's important.

I check my mobile again. There's still nothing from Dean. Probably due to the cold I have the urge to pee and I sigh, frustrated. I'd be useless on a real stakeout. Now, I'll have to leave to find somewhere to go. In the time wasted I could well miss Greg. With no choice, I march over the entrance and hover. The sky has unleashed a heavy downpour. The sight is depressing and even more so when street lamps light up, displaying festive decorations. Tears blur my vision. How did I end up in a damp, cold car park trying to find my *husband*? My *perfect* life has certainly shattered. This is not how I visualised married life. I sort of figured we'd have a few bumps but with lots fun of making up after. I most definitely hadn't expected this.

With no umbrella, I stand under cover for a while, peering left to right in the hope that a pub or cafe will magically appear. When the rain eventually eases up, I take a chance and turn left. I dodge puddles and pass glass-fronted office blocks each side of the road as I hurry along. After a while I wonder whether I should have turned right instead. I decide to turn back if there's nothing at the end of the crossroads. Then, as I plough on, I curve a relieved smile, spotting a pub just around the corner. It's sign swings above: 'The Golden Goose'. I wrinkle up my nose at the chipped black-painted filthy windows. It's a dismal choice, but I can't hold on any longer.

I shove open the door and enter a small, quarry-tiled hall; it stinks of stale cigarette smoke. The door marked snug is chosen over the one labelled bar. Inside is just what I expected. The place is trapped in time, with yellow-stained Artex walls separating oak beams. The warmth of a real log fire is very welcome, though. An elderly man stares at his half a pint of Guinness on the round table in front of him. A collie dog sleeps at his feet, most likely his only mate. Lights on the small Christmas tree flash on and off. I ask the blonde barmaid if I can use the ladies.

The toilets are freezing. Quickly I use the loo, then hurry back to the warm snug. I linger at the bar and thank the woman. Behind her, a bottle of red wine stands out. It's a Shiraz. A good brand, not the kind you'd expect in an old pub like this. They normally serve cheap vinegar wine, the one most suited for chips.

The barmaid has obviously seen my curious expression because she offers, 'It's a gift from one of the locals from her holiday in Spain.' She tosses her head back and gives out a throaty laugh. 'The landlord hates the crap.' She folds her arms and continues, 'Nora's got the hots for him. But she's got no chance.' She nods. 'Now there's a tale I could tell you. Anyway, the Shiraz is for sale. So what do you fancy, love? A small or large one?'

I should head back, but the temptation is so strong. Surely one wouldn't hurt to thaw me out for a bit? One half of me reasons, *You could miss your husband.* I'm tempted; however, I manage to drag myself back out into the cold, damp footpaths. Besides, I can't leave Timmy too long.

I'm almost at the barrier when I spot something that wasn't there before. Although I slow down, my heart speeds up. A white Range Ranger has landed in one of the vacant spaces. *It has to be Greg's.* It's too much of a coincidence. Gingerly, I approach it. Holding my breath, I peer inside. There's no indication it's his. *But it has to be?* What now? Call him? Why will he answer now? I have to do something, and I rip the phone from my pocket. Urgently I stab the black screen until I realise it's blank because I forgot to charge *it.* I sigh, shoving it back into my jean pocket. *Now what?* When a car door slams and I dart to the side of Range Rover so as not to be seen – not yet, anyway. Through the window, I spy a Chinese kid engrossed on his phone as he strolls to the key-coded security door. Before he has a chance to punch the numbers in, the door opens. I freeze when Greg strides out; he too has his head bent over a mobile.

A phone! One he could have easily called me on! What the hell is he playing at? I'm floored with anger and step away from the car just as he looks up and our eyes connect.

He's shaken. 'Kate, what are you doing here?'

What am I doing here? I can hardly get my words out, shaking my head. 'I see your phone works then, but you can't call me?' I jab my finger at him. 'I've called you over and over.'

He butts in. 'Calm down, I can explain. I lost my phone and all the numbers.'

I exclaim, hotly, 'You are joking, right?' But he's not listening. His eyes are focused on something behind me.

My anger steps up. What the hell is more important than *me*? I spin around to find out what has captured his attention. A firework of fear explodes inside me as Nick approaches us. *What's he doing here?* He *must* have overheard my confession with Susie, the one with father *unknown*. He's come to confront *me*. Why else is he here? I want to *run*. I want to *hide*. I want to race back to the pub to down that bottle of Shiraz. I hold my breath, not daring to breathe. I dart a sly glance at Greg to gauge his reaction. He is as shocked as me. But then I remember that Nick claims to know Greg.

Nick's tone is sarcastic when he greets Greg. 'Fancy seeing you here.'

I search Nick's face, then Greg's. *What's going on?* Unexpectedly I get the impression this is not about *me*. There's an undercurrent between them. I can feel it. Almost touch it.

Greg angrily snaps, 'What are you doing here?'

Nick ignores him and turns his attention to me. My legs turn to jelly. I was wrong. It is about *me*. Silently I plead, *Please don't blurt out anything*. I try to think of something to say to separate them. But my brain is dead. *Useless*.

However, I'm more stunned when Nick turns on his charm and says, flippantly, 'See you around, Kate.'

And just like that, he strolls off like he's just asked for directions. I'm confused; what the hell was that all about? But thank God he didn't say anything. That's something I have to be thankful for at least. What did he mean? *See you around?*

My thoughts are shattered when Greg demands, harshly, 'How do you know him?'

I flinch at his sharp tone and blurt out the first thing I can think of. 'I, erm… went to school with him.' Why is he having a go at me? *Unless* he does know? Perhaps this is his way of prising the dirty deed out into the open?

His eyes narrow as he accuses me. 'You never said you went to a Greek school.'

I feel on trial, but secretly I realise something reassuring. Greg can't possibly know because he wouldn't be asking these questions if he knew I'd slept with Nick. Why the attack on me. Should it not be me accusing him – well, sort of? Then I recall when I first came across Nick. Automatically I say, 'No…no, I forgot, I met him when I was out with Susie.' How come he's asking this?

Greg frowns so I quickly explain, 'The fortieth birthday party I went to not long back.' That bit is true at least.

His blue eyes harden. 'He was there? Why didn't you say?'

I'm caught off guard and quickly stammer, 'I…forgot.' Instantly a memory flashes. *Me naked in bed with Nick.* I go hot. As a distraction, I stamp my feet and stare down at the concrete floor, wanting it to open up.

'He's the reason why I had to leave. I couldn't let him find out where we lived. I had to protect you too.'

Puzzled with his poignant tone change, I gaze up in surprise. 'I don't understand.'

He drags a packet of Silk Cut cigarettes from his overcoat pocket. Lighting up, he inhales a long, slow drag before he continues, 'He's a nasty, vicious bloke. I'm warning you.'

Our situation right now can wait. I need to know exactly what's going on. 'I'm not with you.'

Greg blows smoke into the cold air. 'He's connected. That says it all.'

I frown. 'What do you mean, connected?' *Connected to what?*

Greg states, like I'm stupid, 'To the mafia, Kate, what else would I mean?'

I murmur, uncertain, 'You mean like a hitman?' *Surely he's joking? He has to be.*

He stamps out the cigarette butt with his black loafer shoe. 'He's the one who broke my phone. He's the reason why I had to lie low.' He grips my shoulders to affirm this. 'He's why I couldn't come home, babe. Now do you understand?'

This must have something to with that *private illegal game* and a heavy dose of fear glides down my back like a broken tap. *Nick is in the mafia?* Somewhere in my fuddled brain, it rings true, because gambling and mafia go hand in hand. I've watched plenty of gangster films to know that. *Money.* It's always about paper gold. Plus Nick's connected to the casino. *The one his brother owns.* What about *me? Did I sleep with a murderer?* I could be *pregnant with a killer's baby?* How was I supposed to know? I was drunk; he took advantage. But Nick didn't come across as a villain… What does a *real* one look like? One thing is for certain. I can never confess to Greg now. *Not ever.*

As the poker game is pushed forward in my mind, I step back nervously. I need to confirm this. 'This is about the private game, isn't it?' The one Nick and his brother flatly denied. I hold my breath, waiting for confirmation of what I suspect.

Greg's shoulders slump like he's defeated and he nods. 'I lost all my money to him and more.' His blue eyes fill with tears. 'I've let you down, babe, I'm sorry.'

My thoughts turn to the baby. The one I desperately want to be *ours. I've let him down too.* Only I can't let on. My fear escalates as I consider the outcome if Nick ever discovered I might be having *his* baby. My mind flashes to me embroiled with gangsters and a gun shoved into my mouth if I tried to take his child away.

Greg is concerned. 'Babe, you've gone very pale. Are you okay?' His sigh sounds deflated, adding ruefully, 'But that's a daft question, after what I've just told you.'

My mind runs on overtime. If Nick is a hitman, he must have followed me here. He's the one I bet is watching me, not Jason. Nick knows where we live. I ball my hands into fists. What have I done? What if Jason happened to be Nick's brother and this his way of revenge?

Greg gathers me up in his arms. He thinks he's to blame. Tears mingle on his coat as he whispers in my hair over and over how sorry he is. I'm the guilty one. *It's me who should be sorry.* I've lead Nick to Greg. *Now we're both in danger.* I need to think, and fast. I'm partly to blame.

I can't think now because Nick could return any second. 'Greg,' I say, edging out of his arms. 'Come on, let's go somewhere and get a drink.' I know I'm desperate for one as I wipe under my eyes. I hook my arm through his, more to support my unsteady legs. 'There's a pub just around the corner – let's go there and talk.'

Our stroll is silent along the moist footpath. A round moon shines bright in a blacked-out sky. Office workers fly past on their way to get home, probably after a long, hard day. We must look like an ordinary couple out for an early dinner, or perhaps on our way to the theatre. Not fugitives planning to escape from the mafia. I speed up our pace as we approach the corner of the crossroads. Something bugs me, but I can't quite catch it. The thought is then lost as we enter the pub. I spot a vacant table with two stools close to the fire. I'm frozen more from shock than cold, rubbing my hands towards the welcome flames. Unlike earlier, the snug is popular with city types. I welcome the large Shiraz from my husband; the barmaid must have remembered me.

Greg plonks down opposite with a pint, wearing a sorry

expression. I feel the urge to reach out to reassure him, but I have to remind myself that had he not started playing poker, we'd not be in this mess. Yes, I'm partly responsible, but he still has some explaining to do.

First, I need to know exactly what is going on. So I whisper, uncertain, 'Do you still owe money?' I'm too scared at this point to mention Nick's name aloud. I nod to affirm. 'You know who to.'

Greg sighs wearily. 'He wants me to transfer the deeds to the house over to him.'

'What?' *He can't do that.* My voice trembles.' He can do that?'

Greg states, his tone flat, 'As I said before, I lost to him in the game. And now he wants his money back.'

But I was with Nick when he was supposed to be playing. How can that be right? I have to ask, so I do, 'Did you play in the evenings or daytime?'

Greg sounds perplexed. 'What difference does that make? We played whenever the game was on.'

I sigh, inwardly. Why do I even doubt my *husband?* But hang on, what about what Dave said? That will have to wait.

Greg wipes the froth from around his mouth and volunteers, 'We played in the day and late into the nights, if you must know.'

I have an uneasy feeling. *Is this a lie too?* My hand shakes as I reach for my glass.

I flinch when he asks, like he's just remembered something, 'Did you tell Nick where I was?' Before I have a chance to reply, he presses on. 'You were drunk that night at the party; did you talk about me to him?' He leans forward, his tone more accusing with his suspicion. 'Is there something going on between you and Nick?'

I go hot as guilt flares across my face like a rocket while my mind scrambles for words that won't come, ones I don't have. My heart thuds in *fear* of the consequences. Will he demand a *divorce*? I don't want to be a *single* parent.

He's on a roll, not waiting for a response as he continues, with narrowed eyes, 'Why else would he say, "See you around, Kate"?' He then demands, 'Did you tell him I was here? But, more to the point, how did *you* find me?'

I stammer, 'I…err…' I shrug and fan my face with the back of my hand as a distraction. My mind is blank. I can't think fast enough. I'm only saved when a man in a suit accidentally bumps into Greg's shoulder. For a brief second, I have respite when the guy repeatedly apologises.

I think fast. Greg must be surmising; he can't possibly know about me and Nick, otherwise he'd have said something more concrete earlier. Although now is not the right time to tell him about the baby, I see no other choice. I feel guilty using Dean's services, but Greg has to see I had no other way of finding out where he'd disappeared to. Suddenly I feel sad. This is not what I'd planned. I wanted the moment to be romantic. Not in a dump like this. I wanted us to be alone with rose petals and soft music. Plus not with so many unanswered questions that will just have to wait.

Greg tries to wave off the guy's insistence to buy us a round of drinks. I wish he'd just shut up and bugger off. I feel quite desperate now to confess my secret. I glare up at the man, hoping my irritated expression will make its mark and he'll go. But now he's spilling his story about being promoted. He's drunk, and when he eventually turns to me I force a small grin for his offer of a glass of wine. Hopefully that will get rid of him.

What's unbelievable now, though, is that Greg is engaging in conversation, offering to help him at the bar. I find the situation surreal. Maybe my husband is masking his thoughts? Perhaps he's hiding his true feelings at the thought of me with someone else. It's natural to feel hurt when you suspect the one you love might have let you down. I've been so wrapped up in myself, I never even considered he could be heartbroken. Jealous, even? I know I'd be inconsolable. *Devastated, in fact.* Beyond repair. I dismiss the idea. It's far too painful. Anyway, I convince myself I didn't go off and I'm not in the process of having an affair either. What happened on that dreadful night was a mistake. I don't want to dwell on that, so with Greg still at the bar, I distract myself and silently play a game. The baby is *ours.* Greg's the father. *He has to be.* Can I do the unspeakable? Carry out the lie and tell Greg the baby is his, even when I don't know for sure who the real father is? *Can I do that?* I imagine a scene with me propped up in a hospital bed, my *husband* at my side, cradling our baby, his smile radiating love. *It's Greg's – it has to be.*

As he sits down I remove my jacket, giving the impression I'm hot from the fire, which would explain my flushed complexion. I gather my thoughts and take a deep breath. 'Look…I…I…can explain.' I pause when my drink arrives; Greg thanks the guy who at last thankfully makes his way outside for a smoke. I do wonder why Greg didn't bring over my drink with his. However, I dismiss the thought as useless. I have far more serious business to conduct.

Greg turns back to me and exclaims, 'Oh God, Kate… what have you done?'

His accusing statement sets of my fear, producing an uncomfortable sinking feeling in the pit of my tummy. I convince myself he'll understand why I hired Dean. I take another deep breath and reach out for his arm. 'Greg… I'm pregnant… I needed to know where you were.'

At first, he sounds confused. 'Pregnant?' As he shakes off my hand, I catch a flash of something across his face, then it's gone before he states slowly, 'You're having a baby?'

I dismiss his action as being down to shock. Now I've officially told my secret, I relax a little. The episode with Nick is well and truly behind me now. He's in the past. I assure myself, *It never happened.* I fudge a happy face and grab his hand. 'Yes, just like we planned.' For the minute I'm back in my *perfect* world, gazing into my *husband's* eyes with all our troubles fading. I glance around with a shrug. 'It's not where I wanted to tell you.'

Greg's tone sounds breathless. 'No, I can't argue with that.' He stands up. 'I guess we both need another drink to celebrate. But first I need a cigarette.'

Watching him leave, I bite my lip and fiddle with my wedding ring. Shouldn't he be hugging and kissing me? Not shooting outside like a bullet from a gun. I reach for my glass. Perhaps the timing is wrong, especially with my embroilment with Nick and the possibility of losing our home. Not an ideal situation, I admit. I suppose in one way I can understand my husband not jumping around with joy. Yes, the moment is wrong, I convince myself. We still have my money, though – well, I hope we do. We could move, start over again. Get as far away from mafia Nick as possible. The wine suddenly turns bitter in my mouth at the thought of me having slept with a murderer. I imagine he could have washed the blood off his hands before he came to my house. I flash back to when Timmy was happy to sit on his lap. Fear swirls and snaps at my insides. Could Nick have secretly slipped Timmy something while I wasn't looking? *A treat that somehow calmed him, and made him like Nick?* My mind runs on over time.

Is it possible he gave Timmy something like a human finger from someone he murdered? When the room is thrown into darkness, I drop my glass with a scream.

In an instant, phone lights flash on and a male voice shouts out, 'Sorry, folks, we've had a powercut.'

My heart hammers. *Is this Nick's doing? And where the hell is my husband?* Quickly I turn around to scan the room, searching for him. A sea of phone torches give out an eerie glow. It adds to my already crushed nerves. *What's keeping Greg? Where is he?* I reach out for my drink and realise I dropped it. I bend down and slam the glass on the table, almost breaking it. Greg must still be outside smoking. Did he not see the pub plunged into darkness? Is he not worried about me? I grab my handbag and make for the door. It's a tight squeeze as I pass a woman in an office suit, the cold radiating from her.

Outside there's no Greg, only the guy who bought us the drinks. He's smoking, chatting gibberish into his phone. Maybe he knows where Greg is? I bite my lip and wait for him to finish his call. 'Do you know where my husband is? We're the couple you bought drinks for.'

He slurs words I can't catch. Then he disappears inside the pub. I jump when someone taps my shoulder. I spin around and sigh with relief. 'Where have you been? I was worried.'

'What are you doing out here? I told you I was going for a smoke.'

'I panicked when the lights went out and I came out to look for you.' Wasn't he concerned about me? And why is he in a mood?

'Well, there's not much point going back inside. No power, no till. So we might as well leave.'

Before I can comment, there's a flash of lights from inside the pub. Greg grabs my hand and we end up in the queue at the bar. For a second I'm stunned by his actions. But more so that he hasn't even mentioned the news of our baby like it's of no consequence. He could have at least said something before dragging me back in here. I'm just about to launch into a discussion regarding our *baby*, but he cuts in, asking how I found him again. Although I guess I owe him an explanation,

I'm slightly perplexed why that's important right now. Still, I confess to hiring a private investigator. I think it sounds slightly softer than a private detective. I justify my action and stress, 'Your phone was permanently off.' I press on urgently. 'What was I supposed to do?' I'll mention his work later.

Greg gathers me up in his arms. 'I see your point, babe, but I explained that.'

My worries vanish when a safe, protected feeling claws its way in. I breathe in his aromatic-wood aftershave. *The past can be put behind us.* We can move forward. Plan the birth of our first child. We can get through this. Our child must have two loving parents. Okay, I admit, there are issues to sort out.

'Nick must have followed you. Because how else did he know where I was?' he declares, releasing me from his arms.

My safe mode evaporates and I can hardly get my words out. 'Do you think so?' What if he's right? Because Nick did trick me into bed. He got me drunk. It was probably all part of a set-up to stitch Greg up. I've watched plenty of gangster films to know how they operate. I bite my lip. Fear tingles down my spine. I could be his next victim of *blackmail*.

Bile rises, and I feel hot. I make my excuse and bolt to the toilets. I bang the cubical door open just in time to heave out a red mass of vomit. After I stand up straight and drag tissues from the dispenser. My finger shakes, wiping my mouth. The coldness of the room seeps into my bones. Nick's words haunt me. *See you around, Kate.* That's what he said. What did he mean? In an instant, I imagine Timmy's slaughtered head on my pillow in my bedroom. I'm over-reacting; I have to be. What if I'm not? Susie said Nick had asked questions about me on that night with the curry. She might have let slip about my money. The only other person I told that to was in a message to Jason, only after he opened up to me. I didn't even tell my husband until after we were married. I wanted to prove to Susie he wasn't after my money. I know she never actually said anything, but she implied it. I stare in the mirror – like it can help me. We have to leave. We must get back to Timmy. Will we be safe at home. How do I tell Greg that Nick has been to our house, even sat on his chair? *How do I explain that?*

My legs feel heavy as I return to Greg. What do we do when we get Timmy? Where do we go? I decide to deal with it when we get home. Greg can follow in his car. I'll just have to take the chance that Nick won't come around. If he does, hopefully we'll be safe inside. If he tries to force entry, I'll call the police. I'll deny all knowledge to Greg of how Nick found us. Not the best of plans, but what else can I do? Of course, if Nick does show up we could pack up and leave. I bite my lip hard; if Nick does appear, the mafia doesn't take kindly to being snitched on. *Why did Greg put us in this predicament?* What was he thinking, playing poker with someone so deadly?

TWENTY-SIX

want to get home as fast as possible to Timmy, but every traffic light turns to amber on my approach. It's a bad omen. Is the universe is attempting to slow down my frantic journey? The longer it takes, the more fear I breathe in. What if Nick is so angry over the money Greg owes that he wants payback? His kind wouldn't think twice to torch the house as a warning. I picture *Timmy's* cries of torment, trapped inside the burning house, his fur melting. I wipe off tears and curse Greg. *Why did he start the game?* How did I not see all the trouble it would cause? How was I supposed to know? I'm hardly a mystic Meg with a crystal ball with an insight to predict the future. A thought is triggered in my head. Is this what the clairvoyant meant?

Right this minute, I forget her words because finally, I'm almost home. I grip the steering wheel and my heart flips with dread. Turning into my road, I hold my breath. I expect to see harsh lights from fire engines and a firefighter cradling Timmy's dead, limp body. I sigh with relief at the quiet, peaceful setting. No fire engine, no police. Just as a precaution, I cruise past my house. It's the only one in darkness, soulless without Christmas decorations. It's a sorry scene behind the closed wrought-iron gates. Everything else is normal, with cars parked on their respective drives. There is no indication that Nick or his cronies have been there. Nevertheless, I'm unsettled until I visibly see my baby. After all, Nick could have easily broken in around the back.

Turning the car around, I drive back and press the gate fob. The heavy gates slowly swing open. I drum my fingers on the steering wheel and beg them to hurry up. Edging onto the drive, I waste no time darting over the gravel to the front door. My fingers shake and I almost drop the keys. I flick a table lamp on, flooding the spacious hall with a soft light, expecting to see Timmy's wagging tail. He's not here, and my panic escalates. *Where is he?* Why is he not waiting? I fear the worst and reach out to the bannister for support. Do I wait for Greg?

I jump when a horn blares. Automatically I race to the lounge to peer out the window. A taxi has pulled up opposite; the neighbours come out. Nervously, I scan up and down the road for Greg's car, but there's nothing. How long can I wait? Timmy could need medical help. I'm wasting bloody time, hanging around, doing nothing. Adrenaline fuels my urgency. I decide on the bedroom first. Bolting upstairs, I stop at my bedroom door. I take a deep breath and say a silent prayer before I cautiously ease the door further ajar. Moonlight lands on Timmy's body. His breathing is peaceful. I let out a long sigh; my anxiety melts like a weeping snowman. Creeping across the carpet, I slip onto the bed next to him.

I allow myself a small chuckle; perhaps I over-reacted, making a mountain out of a molehill. I guess that's part of my DNA, my mad tendency to overthink. *Paranoia*, some would say. Then I silently question why Timmy was not waiting at the front door like he usually does. Fear strikes up again. *Is he ill?* Is this the after effect of if Nick had slipped him something?

Gently I stroke Timmy's head. At first he appears dazed, confused. Then, in an instant, I'm covered in wet kisses and my panic turns to dust. This calls for champagne. It is, after all, Christmas. As we descend the stairs, I plan a romantic meal for my husband's return. I brush aside the episode with Nick for the time being. Besides, if he was going to come over, I'm sure he'd be here already, I'm convinced and mentally I prepare for one night where we can celebrate the up-and-coming birth of our *baby*. Should I even be drinking in my condition? A couple won't hurt, surely? Tomorrow I'll make an appointment with the doctor to gain his or her advice. Despite all that's gone on, I feel a flutter of excitement, knowing my *husband* is on his way home, even if it's only for one night of peace until we can sort out our troubles. The confusion nags at me, though; I mean, is he a director?

Timmy shoots back in from the garden and shakes his coat. I put my flute of bubbles on the granite worktop to lace ham with Cesar dog food. Idly, I glance up at the clock and wonder what's keeping Greg so long. After placing Timmy's dish on the tiled floor, I lean on the island. My mobile rings. It must be Greg, saying he's on his way. His name flashes across the screen. I must admit, it's a nice surprise.

'Hey, babe, did you get home okay?'

'Yes, but where are you?' I ask, not overly concerned.

I hear him blow out smoke before he pleads, 'Look, don't panic.'

But I do as he presses on. 'Just as I was shoving my suitcase in the boot, Nick showed up again.'

My breath catches in my throat. Did he purposely wait to catch Greg alone to confess about our one-night stand? I stumble over my words. 'Whaaat...did he...er...say?'

Greg grunts sharply. 'He wants his money.'

I sort of breathe easy. 'What did you say?' Not that that's a better answer.

He ignores my question and lowers his tone. 'He knows where we live, babe…'

I grip the phone. Nick must have told him. This is it. Greg might never forgive me; perhaps in one way, with my secret exposed I won't have to lie again. No more being afraid. Plus if Nick had planned to blackmail me, then that will fail too. So all in all, the truth is best out, I guess. It still, however, doesn't prevent my dry mouth sounding hoarse. 'Oh…how…' I leave the question open. Laced with high-end tension, I wait for his explosion. *How could you do it, Kate? Why? Don't you love me?* Sorry tears fall; I brush them away. There will be time for plenty of those later.

'He said he followed you home.'

Tears stop. My mouth gapes. *What?* There's a sting of unease. Something's very wrong with that statement. Why would Nick follow me home when he already knows where we live?

Greg sounds urgent. 'Babe, you still there?'

Confused, I mumble, 'Yes.' There's an urge to ask how he followed me and then race back to Birmingham; first off, the timing is wrong. Doubts set off silent alarms and I feel my world go off-kilter once again. *Why would Nick lie? There's no need.* Abruptly I know my husband is going to use Nick as an excuse to not come home. I hope I'm wrong, I do.

His voice carries annoyance. 'He's a conniving bastard and I'll have to move to another safe place.'

My heart thuds in my ribcage, but I manage to steady my tone. 'You're coming home still.' Instinct tells me he's not, and not for the reason he's giving either. I gulp down my drink and, with a shaking hand, pour out another.

'Damn, babe…I have to go, he's back.'

I glare at the phone as the line goes dead. I ring him back only to get the answering service; somehow, I expected that.

Instead of feeling afraid of Nick, I fear I'm in a much worse position with my husband. *His lies are building up.* In the warm kitchen, I shiver. There's a sense of dread that I've uncovered another Pandora's box. One that was so cleverly hidden. Why lie about being a director? Then there was the lie of the poker game, and how that came about. Also, Nick didn't follow me. That's the most dangerous lie of all. It triggers off a whole new set of thoughts. Nick is probably not in the mafia. My only escape tonight is in bottles of Moet Chandon. How else can I settle the fear that's rising inside me? Again, no mention of the baby, like my husband is in denial. *What's all that about?* And if he is scared of Nick, where the hell does that leave me?

TWENTY-SEVEN

You can tell I haven't slept well. There are dark circles under my eyes as they glare back at me from the bathroom mirror. Harsh lines have appeared overnight and all I feel like doing is crashing on the toilet seat to sob. I drop the idea as time-wasting. There were numerous occasions when I'd watched my mother perform that wasted duty. *Trapped in her tears.* Only to take herself back to her buddy. The one who'd understood her, the one who'd helped diminish her pain at the loss of Billy? I used to joke to my mates that she was out with an old friend, Mr Walker. What I kept hidden was *her* Mr Walker was whisky. In one way I guessed she was with Billy in spirit. I used to laugh at my pun, only because it masked the hurt of having to cover up for an alcoholic mother.

I sigh despondently. Never mind her, with her shitty ways – what am *I* supposed to do at this time? Help and advice is needed. When my phone bleeps, I race to the bed where I left it. There's a vague possibility it might be my husband, returning my calls. From the depth of my sinking heart, somehow I know it's not him. Susie must have read my mind as her text reads:

Sorry, haven't been in touch so busy. Any news
from Greg? Let's catch up later for dinner 7.30
at Thatcher's x I'll book a table... love ya xx

Tears sting; grateful for my friend, immediately I text back;

Fab...see you lata sweet X

*

Later that evening I pay the cab driver. Then I navigate across
the cobbled pavement to the eighteenth-century oak-beamed
restaurant. The gothic door is heavy, and I breathe in the heady
scent of pine from the Christmas tree. Laughter mingles with
party poppers from a crowd seated at a long table to the right.
The scene is very festive and I have a happy expression, wanting
to blend in. On the outside I probably look the part, dressed in
a ruby wool dress and jacket edged with gilt buttons.

Joe, the manager, rushes across the flagstone floor, his grin
wide and welcome with a reindeer jumper stretched over his
belly. His mouth flutters a brief kiss across my hand. 'You look
wonderful.' His eyes then dart behind me. 'Is Greg parking
up?' It's amazing what make-up can cover up. I stick with my
forced mask covering up my heartache. 'No, it's just Susie and
me tonight.'

We weave our way over to a round table next to a leaded
sash window. I thank Joe and order a bottle of rose Moet
Chandon. The place is crammed with jolliness, all enjoying
the Christmas spirit. As my bottom lip trembles, I bite my
lip and tilt back my head up to hold back tears. Earlier my
husband had sent a text, stating he'd be in touch when he'd
found a new safe place. I fiddle with my wedding ring. He's
out there somewhere, supposedly in hiding, with no thought

of the *danger* I could be in. That notion earlier had made my blood boil. I'd switched from tears to being livid, almost like I've no control over my senses. I'd punched in his name only to hear that damn answering service. So I left several messages for him to call me, each one harsher than the last. In the end I'd snapped and texted:

Fuck you Greg.

Dean has not returned any of my calls either. It's like I'm a leper. *Well, fuck you too Dean.* Instead of leaving that message, I'd decided to be just as evasive as him when he hands me my bill.

My nails drum on the table and I have a good mind to yank the tracker off and shove it up for sale on eBay. But with my *husband* absconding yet again, it's going to prove difficult. I grab my handbag from the chair and rummage for my phone. If only Dean would pick up, then I'd know my husband's whereabouts. His name is stabbed in. It rings out and the answering service picks up. I sigh and shake my head, cursing myself for rushing in to use his company, one I now know is dodgy. It's my fault. I had reservations about using him. I slump in my chair and guess this will be the time that Susie vents, 'I did warn you about Greg.' I don't know what to think anymore; it's all such a bloody mess.

My thoughts are disturbed when I spot her hovering at the entrance. I wave half-heartedly to catch her attention. She bobs over, dodging waiters. We air kiss and I take in the faint aroma of cigarettes on her breath. I perch forward and bite my lip. I'm not looking forward to unloading the latest episode on her. What choice do I have? I'm at a loss at what to do next. She wriggles out of her fawn coat as the waiter arrives. I thank him as he sets down two flutes with an ice bucket of champagne.

'Would you like me to pour, madam?'

'It's okay, I can do it, thanks,' I offer. Then I turn to my friend, 'Sorry, did you want a gin and tonic?'

'No, that's fine.'

My hand shakes as I hand her flute and fill her in.

She almost chokes on her drink. 'What?'

I express a sad face and wait for the *told-you-so* saga.

Her eyes narrow and bore into mine. 'You know I never trusted him.' She holds her hand up, adding, 'Don't worry, I'm not going to say I told you so.' She slumps back with a long, hard sigh. 'What a bastard.'

I venture uncertainly, 'Do you think Nick is part of the mafia?'

She huffs. 'Are you kidding?' She then states, quite firmly, 'Of course he's not.'

I quiz her, unconvinced, 'How do you know that for certain?' I take a sip and say, 'I suppose it is another lie of Greg's.'

She arches an eyebrow. 'It certainly is. Because I forgot to tell you, I went to school with Jim – he was one of the guys with Nick on the night I joined them for a curry. At the time I didn't think I needed to mention the fact that Jim is a *detective*. So, I hardly think the force would take kindly to him dining out with a gangster.'

I gulp bubbles to settle the sharp bolts of disbelief. The air I breathe seems to have disappeared. This is worse than I can imagine. *Jesus.* What the fuck?! My only consolation is that my life is not in danger from Nick... But my husband is a different matter entirely. My hand shakes, pouring out another glass of fizz. *What a lie...* How did I not see?

Susie reaches for my hand, giving it a reassuring squeeze. 'Are you okay? Can I get you anything?'

A gun springs to mind, to blast off Greg's fucking head. 'I'm fine,' I say with assurance I don't possess. It's just one bloody lie after another. I turn away and sigh. That drunken night flashes up in my head with Nick and how he just appears like a magician. It triggers a thought, and I pose a question, 'Why did you give Nick my address?'

She's confused, her tone mildly defensive. 'I didn't. Why would I?'

'Then how did he know where I lived then?'

She shrugs. 'Maybe you told him when you went for that drink, and kind of forgot.'

What she means is when I was drunk, but she's too polite to say it. She could be right, of course, and I mutter, 'Maybe.' After all, most of that evening is in a black hole somewhere in my head.

'I'm going outside for a cigarette, I think I need one.'

I'm tempted to join her.

'Look,' she reasons, standing over me, 'I think you should go back to the apartment.' She affirms this with an effective nod. 'I have got a funny feeling Greg is still there. And if you want my opinion, I'd bet he's shacked up with that Amy. This is just a simple case of having his cake and eating it.'

A sinking sensation rolls to the pit of my boots and trickles out to the flagstone tiles as her words sink in. 'It certainly looks that way.'

'Back in a tick,' utters Susie forlornly.

Left alone with my thoughts, I bite my lip and try my best not to cry. She can't know that for certain. There's still a tiny chance she's wrong. I clutch on to that like a buoy tossed out to sea; it's the only hope I have. I'm nudged from my thoughts when a drunk man asks, 'Is that chair taken?'

Perplexed, I glare at him. *Do I look like I'm sitting on my own?* My husband may have deserted me, but my friend hasn't. Before I can snap out my retort, Susie excuses her way to her seat.

182

The guy in a Christmas jumper stumbles off without a word. 'What a bloody nerve,' I vent.

She sips her drink. 'That's men for you.'

I fume and watch him go back to his crowd of friends. With nowhere to sit, he pulls out his phone and snaps away. A girl joins him and snatches his phone, squealing, 'I look terrible.'

Her actions remind me of the picture I found locked in Greg's drawer, and I enlighten Susie, adding,

'But I don't understand the connection with Nick.'

'Didn't you say that he knew Greg? Maybe he dated his sister before you? Or went to the same school? The list is endless.'

I pick up my drink. 'I guess so. I wonder if you can contact Jim and ask about Nick's sister? She might know where Greg is. Do you think you could him call now?'

She is apologetic. 'I would normally, but it's Christmas Eve – you know, family time.'

Christmas Eve! How did that pass me by? No wonder she asked to see me. Probably ranting to Martin what a bastard Greg is with his disappearing act at *Christmas*. How did I not see? Yes, all the decorations were there, but I was more concerned with finding my *husband*.

TWENTY-EIGHT

I wake up in a panic. Where's my husband? I touch his side of the bed, confused. Then it all floods back, inviting pain. I brush off tears and stare hopelessly at the glow of street lights shadowing the bedroom walls. I'm fully clothed on top of the bed. A bottle of Moet is on its side with a damp patch on the carpet. Timmy is curled up asleep at the bottom of the bed. My head is banging and my mouth is like a desert. I reach out to drain the flat bubbles and scramble for bits of last night.

There's me seated at the table with Susie in the restaurant, then nothing. I dig deeper but give up on the wasted search. My mind has destroyed the memories – never to return, like so many before. Fresh tears fall, they roll down my face and trickle into my ears, but I'm not laughing. I touch my belly and say a silent sorry. I've no excuse for my drinking. I just feel so desperate. You could say now I understand what my mother felt, why she felt the need for her addiction. It's the comfort that it brings, if only for a short while. It's the escape, blocking everything out. The one pretending all is well. That's the illusion of the allure of alcohol, its claim to cure the damage inside you. *But who I am kidding?* Just me, the fool. Next, I question what I did to my husband for him to treat me like this. When Nick's naked body appears, I flush with shame and regret. *I guess that's why.*

The clock on the side reads 6.30am. I go over what bits surface of last night. So if yesterday was *Christmas Eve,* today is *Christmas Day. This was supposed to be my first Christmas with my husband.* I struggle to sit up and rearrange the pillows behind me. *Nick is not a mafia hitman.* For a second I close my eyes and bewildered thoughts attack me. I feel soulless and drained. Tossed out, used up, like garbage. Like I don't matter.

*

I have must have drifted off, because the next time I wake up it's 12.30. As soon as I move my leg, Timmy is up and over, licking my face. His love and affection brings on a small rush of gratitude; just as quick, though, it disappears as I remember my situation.

Before I shower and remove the dredges of last night's make-up, Timmy is let out. More tears flow and mingle under the hot jets of water. My memory fudges a small thought of Susie, insisting I spend Christmas day with her and Martin. A nice gesture, but food is not something I need right now.

I tighten my dressing robe and head downstairs. My handbag is on the island. Idly I rummage in it for my phone. I expect to see nothing from my husband and I'm right. I stroll through all the shitty messages I sent. You'd think he'd at least respond to something, even just to swear back. Just then a text arrives from Susie:

I'll pick you up at 3xxx

I'm too depressed to respond; instead, I select one of the rows of Moet from the American fridge. Which, I guess, were stacked by me last night with intentions to drown the whole lot in my drunken state. I know I shouldn't drink. But my need is too great. Perhaps I don't deserve to be pregnant anyway. *What kind of a person am I?* Father unknown? How could I have so stupid? So crazy to sleep with Nick. What was I thinking?

When the mobile pings with another message, I'm in no rush to pick it up. What's the point? I tighten my robe and down the bubbles. There's a sense building up in me that I should refuse Susie's offer. How can I go around there, pretending to be jolly Kate? I'd choke on the turkey, that's for sure. I snatch up the flute and the nearly empty bottle and drift into the lounge. There's morbid fascination when I stand at the window. I sniff and watch the cars park up across the road; guests are loaded with Christmas presents. I drain the dregs of my glass before it slips from my hand when tears blur my vision. Waves of emotions crash together, ripping and tearing up my heart. I slump down in Greg's chair, bury my head on the arm and sob. I know what I said about my mother, but I don't care, because my soul bleeds from pain.

*

Nick shouts,'Run, Kate...run...' I turn and see him in an underground car park...his arms carrying a small buddle wrapped in a blanket...

A phone rings...I wake with a jolt, heart thudding in my chest. At first, I'm confused, then everything falls back into place. The phone's tone from the kitchen sounds urgent. I sniff and lean back. I'm in no hurry to get it, and I wipe my face with the sleeve of my dressing robe. Timmy is asleep on the sofa. He's what keeps me going. I sigh and struggle to sit up. The time on my watch is 2pm. I'm guilty of not returning Susie's messages. I bet that was her call too. She must be worried; the least I can do is phone her, even if it is only to refuse her kind offer. Then I realise I've not fed Timmy. I catch my breath and wonder if I fed him yesterday. I must get a grip. Or there's a chance I could end up like my mother, slumped in a chair with a bottle of whisky. And yet here I am, the one who vowed never to end up like her. There was never a day that I could understand why she didn't leave Dad after Billy died. It was like she'd given up and accepted her fate. Have I done the same?

I move slowly and wander into the hall. Idly I trace my fingers along the bland walls to the kitchen. How did I end up in this situation? How did I not see through Greg's lies? The fridge is opened and I locate ham and dog food. A fresh bottle of bubbly is popped open. I suppose I'd better return Susie's messages. I pick up the mobile and hiccup. I squint; I don't understand her texts.

> I've let you down I'm sorry

> I can't live without you

> I'm going to kill myself if I can't have you

I read them again. *She hasn't let me down, what is she going on about?* Gradually Greg's name comes into focus. Fear bites at my insides, as I read again...*I'm going to kill myself if I can't have you.*

Another is sent, like an afterthought: *and our baby.*

My fingers tremble, punching in his name. No matter what he's done, nothing is worth taking your own life. Yes, I'm still angry and upset with him. But I can't just simply turn off the love button and press delete. Emotions don't work like that. The ringtone seems to last forever and my mind sprints into overdrive. *Greg hanging from a tree.*

I grip the stem of the glass. He must have read the vicious texts I sent. I imagine the headlines of the papers: 'A man pushed to the edge by a deranged drunken wife'. I cut the call and frantically ring again. I pace the tiled floor. *Shall I call the police?* I freeze when the doorbell sounds; its urgency slices my nerves. For support, I grab the granite worktop to steady myself. I bite my lip. *It's the police.* Loud bangs thump the door. *Greg is dead.* I struggle to breathe. The banging is insistent, the voice demanding, 'Kate… are you in there? Kate… open up.'

It's Susie. *They must have sent her to tell me first.* I shove my phone in my pocket and force my jelly legs to the door.

She exclaims, 'Kate, are you okay? And what's happened now?'

I can't get my words out. Automatically she gathers me in her arms. Between sobs, I muffle out my words.

As she pushes me away, her grip is firm, holding both my arms. Her tone sounds sharp with a hint of anger. '*He threatened to kill himself?*'

I sniff and nod, wiping my nose with the back of my hand.

Susie shakes her head; her expression smacks of disbelief. 'I never expected that.'

She then appears to gather up her thoughts, taking action like someone has to, which can't be me. She settles me on the sofa. I refuse her offer of coffee. That won't even make a dent on my broken nerves. I hear her speaking to Martin in the kitchen. Then nothing, like the door has shut.

I try and call my husband again. No answer. I stand up and cry, 'He's not answering his phone.' I peer up and down the road, expecting to see a flash of blue lights. *I don't know what to do.*

Susie hovers at my side and Timmy jumps up at me for attention.

I confess about the vicious texts I sent to Greg.

She places her mug on the side table. 'I don't understand why he won't pick up his phone, unless...'

Her empty words echo in my head. Unless he's already killed himself...

I tremble and mutter, 'Do you think he has done something bad? Oh my God, shall I call the police?'

'Kate, I don't know what to say.'

I flinch when a text arrives.

Please babe can I come home...

My fingers shake so much I can hardly text back.

Yes come now xxxxx

I whisper, 'That was him.' I blink, staring at nothing, and add, 'He's coming home. He's okay.'

Susie gives me a quick hug. 'At least that's good news.'

At that moment I have a dreadful thought and stare into her eyes. 'Do you think he's hurt Nick?' Panic explodes. 'How else can he come home?' I grip the chair. 'Or he's sorted out the money. Yes, of course, that's got to be why; maybe he won at poker and paid Nick off?' I reason with myself that this is the case. 'But why threaten suicide?'

I don't quite catch her expression when she turns to get her handbag off the carpet. 'I'd better call Martin and tell him not to come over.'

I nod and wonder at her change of tone, like she's not concerned now. 'Okay.' Next, I catch my reflection in the mirror over the fireplace. I flinch and panic. 'God, I must look a mess.'

I need to hurry and get ready to look nice for my husband. There's no reason to pile on more worry with my dishevelled appearance.

Susie's tone now appears rattled for some strange reason. 'Right then, I'll leave you to it.' She dangles her car keys, adding curtly, 'Call me if you need me.'

Abruptly I'm embarrassed at my situation. I avert my eyes and glance across the road at the neighbours; the lights on their Christmas tree flash in the front window. In an instant, I understand her mood swing. 'Thanks.' I touch her arm. 'Sorry I ruined yours and Martin's Christmas Day.' I bet they don't know if they're coming or going. *Not that I know myself.*

After she's left, I race around and puff up cushions. I load the dishwasher and wipe the granite worktops. Jasmine air freshener is sprayed everywhere. As an afterthought, frozen steaks are pulled from the freezer – at some point we will need to eat. It might not be a stuffed turkey, but I can lay the dining table like it is and with scented candles, just how Greg likes it.

Heated rollers are plugged in and I carefully apply make-up. I finish off with a rich red lip gloss. Nervous of what to wear, I rummage through the wardrobe in a fit of hiccups. Perhaps I should slow down on the bubbles; instead, I take a small sip to calm my nerves. *What do I say to Greg?* How will the conversation start? Will he still be suicidal? I must be the one to calm my husband, and I stand back, fiddling with my wedding ring, remembering our vows. *For better or for worse.* We were so happy that day. There's a small sense of duty to take care of my husband. I don't want to be a single parent. When he's more settled, we can discuss our situation, bring everything into the open – well, maybe not quite everything.

TWENTY-NINE

With both hands, I smooth down my emerald-green wool dress. I pick up the crystal flute and take a mouthful of fresh bubbles. Next, I check the dining table. The chandelier is dimmed, which gives off a soft glow. I'll leave the candles for a minute. My watch reads 4.30. And I wonder what's keeping Greg. Unexpectedly there's a bad sense of deja-vu. Do I call and ask where he is? He could be driving, stuck in traffic. Hardly likely on Christmas Day. I wander into the kitchen for a top-up. I hiccup and struggle to twist the cork out. When I finally do, bubbles spill and drip down the ivory unit. I clean up and drain my flute, drumming my nails on the island. Another glass is poured and I pace the kitchen. This is ridiculous. *What's keeping him?* I glare at the phone on the worktop. Just as I reach out for it, there's a sound of a key the front door. *Greg.* I sigh, relieved, coupled with a hiccup.

He smiles from the hall. I gasp inwardly. He looks so well – happy, in fact. I'd sort of expected him to be unshaven, red-eyed from crying. I sneak a glance in the mirror at my reflection. I guess you could say I scrubbed up from earlier too. I feel giddy, like a schoolgirl on her first date, and my head feels light.

'So,' I gesture as if my husband is a guest, 'are you going to come in, so we can sit and talk?' I want to giggle, which I put down to too many bubbles. At least it's taken the edge off my nerves and I promise after today I will stop.

His sigh is happy. 'It's good to be home, babe.'

His tone melts my heart. His handsome, winning smile cranks up my love; no matter what's gone on, he's still my husband, and I feel a sexy tingle. I can't remember when we made love, the last time his lips crushed mine.

He steps forward and gently strokes my face. 'I've missed you, babe.'

His for finger trails down my neck. My breath catches in my throat; releasing a small groan, he whispers in my ear, 'Have you missed me, babe?'

I'm lost in the moment until the doorbell urgently sounds. I drag myself away, cursing whoever had come around now. If it's Nick, then perhaps now is the time to have everything out in the open. Fuelled with Moet, I don't care about the consequences, yanking open the door. I've had enough of this cat-and-dog drama. At first, I'm confused by the young woman stood there. Then I remember it's Amy, the American. *What's she doing here on Christmas Day?* I stammer, 'Oh hello.'

'Is Greg here?' she demands sharply, barging her way in past me.

I stare after her. 'What?' For a minute I can't think straight. Subsequently, her accent triggers a thought. That's *Brummy*, clear as day, and certainly not *American. What's that all about?*

Greg's tone is measured when he states, 'I thought I told you not to come over?'

I gape at him, then at her, confused. What does he mean? And what does she want? What's going on?

She snarls, 'I know what you fucking said, Greg. That *you* were going to get madam here.' She jerks her thumb in my direction, emphasising the point. 'So pissed like always, then you'd come back to me.' She rushes forward, stabbing her finger in his chest. 'But after you left, the whore you're also fucking came around looking for you.'

What? Is this some sort of joke? Amy, my husband and someone else?

Greg's eyes blaze as he hisses, 'Shut up, Amy.' Marching over, he slams the front door, almost taking it off its hinges.

I flinch and step backwards against the wall. I've never seen this side of my husband; it's like I don't know *him*. And Susie's words echo in my head: *You hardly know him.*

Abruptly Greg turns and pushes Amy. She stumbles backwards and he snaps, 'I can't control what that silly bitch Jane does. I can't get her off my fucking back. And *you* are going to wreck the plan.'

My mind screams silently, *What plan?* I bit my lip hard and uneasiness filters in my veins. Who the hell is *Jane*?

Amy yells, poking Greg's chest again, 'Don't you dare fucking push me.'

Suddenly they are strangely silent, weighing each other up. I can hardly take in what's happening. My husband, who vowed to love me, is having an affair with *Amy* and someone called *Jane* too.

'Have you calmed down now, Amy?' Greg asks, as if nothing happened.

Is this for real? Am I dreaming? Anger explodes from me, probably caused by the initial shock wearing off. 'What's going on, Greg?'

He's silent watching Amy, who is back in control. Shrugging

her shoulders, she heads for the door with a couldn't-care-less attitude. Her hand lingers on the handle; turning to Greg, she scoffs, 'Do you want to tell her, or should I?'

A curl of dread swirls in my tummy and I try to control the wobble in my voice. 'Tell me what?' What more can they say that I can't already work out for myself?

Amy sneers in my direction, 'He's not interested in you – it was your money he was after.'

I struggle for breath, too shocked to speak. I don't want to believe her. But truthfully, with all that's gone on, it makes sense.

Greg is over in an instant, towering over her small, child-like frame, demanding, 'What the hell is wrong with you?'

She yells, 'That fucking Jane coming around, that's what.' She points her finger in my direction. 'She might have fallen for your cunning lies and charm,' aggressively she taps her chest, adding, 'but I know you. Don't ever forget that, and to be quite honest, I'm sick of waiting for the plan to work.'

I tremble. *The plan?* What could be worse than this?

I recoil when Greg snarls, 'Shut up, you don't know what you're talking about.'

I want to hurt them both, so I blurt out, aiming my statement at *her*, 'Did *he* tell you I was pregnant?'

She's stunned for a second, possibly digesting the information. As she is *fucking* my husband, she needs to know he's still sleeping with *me*. Am I just as bad? No, mine was a one-off, a mistake. This is *different* altogether.

I hide a small, perverse amount of satisfaction, knowing she didn't know. But that still doesn't stop me feeling hurt and betrayed.

I'm shaken when she screams, jabbing her finger at Greg. 'You told me you'd moved to the spare room because you couldn't stand her touching you.'

I take a sharp intake of air and glare at Greg. *He said that?* I step forward, hardly able to get out my words. 'You said that about me?'

Amy smirks and speaks for him. 'You stupid cow, you know nothing—'

Greg sharply cuts her short. 'Amy, watch what you're saying.'

Amy then changes tack, like she feels sorry for me, shaking her head. 'You've no idea what's going on, do you? If you did, you'd have an abortion.' Her mask quickly turns to a mocking face, adding, 'Your baby's fucked anyway, with how much you drink. A woman like you is unfit to be a mother.'

Rage erupts and I slap her hard across her face. What right has she to come in my house, insulting *me* after sleeping with my husband? *How fucking dare she say that?*

She recovers in instant, grabbing my hair. I try to duck her punches as I wriggle around, yelling, 'Let go of me.'

She rages, 'You drunken bitch, I'm going to fucking batter you.'

I'm an easy target, laced with so much Moet, as her fists connect with the side of my head. I see stars and collide with the hall table. I end up on the marble floor with a thud. The lamp is smashed and Greg has his arms around her waist, trying his best to drag her off me. The hands free phone is next to me and I grab it, punching in 999, screaming, 'Help me.'

The action stops Amy and Greg snaps at her, 'Now look what you've fucking done.' Quickly he escorts her outside and demands she goes home; he says he'll deal with the police when they arrive. He must be whispering now because I can't hear what else is being said.

My hand shakes as I replace the handset on its cradle. I'm dazed and lean back against the wall. When the landline rings I jolt; its sound jars with the throbbing in my head. The noise needs to stop, so I rip the cord from its socket.

I can't believe what just happened.

Greg and Amy? How long has it been going on? What more lies will I uncover? *He married me for my money.* I'm too stunned to cry, reliving what happened, over and over.

I shake my head in disbelief. How did I not see? How could I have been so blind? And who the hell is Jane?

Susie's words echo in my head again: *You hardly know him.* She was right.

What do I do now? What am I supposed to do? I don't know...

It's very quiet outside and I wonder if they've both gone. Do I care? I feel like I'm stuck, trapped in this moment. How do I get through this? My finger swirls the marble floor. I see something, a strand of fur – Timmy's. It's then that I think of him. He's probably terrified, hiding somewhere upstairs. I have to get up to see if he's okay. It's the only thing I can think of doing. With the support of the wall, I manage to stand up. My head hurts and I feel dizzy. That cow Amy might be small, but she packed some right hard punches. There's a small clump of my hair on the floor. I sniff and wipe my nose with the back of my hand, closing the door. I've no fight left in me. I just wished I'd listened to Susie's warning. But I didn't, did I? I knew best, didn't I?

I hardly recognise the shocked, gaunt reflection in the hall mirror. Slowly I turn my head from left to right; I expect bruises will appear tomorrow. Smudged mascara is wiped from under my eyes with shaking fingers. *How could she attack a pregnant woman?* Admittedly I only slapped her because she deserved it. I'm the victim, not her. What about my husband, sleeping with *Amy* and *Jane*?

And me.

What if Amy and Jane also fall pregnant? They could be now. Sickness washes over me, thinking I could be expecting that bastard's child. Did he even want a baby? Was that a lie too? He wasn't exactly thrilled when I told him. My heart feels as if it's been ripped out and shredded into nothing. It hurts too much to even cry.

Heavy feet drag upstairs, and I cling to the bannister for support. My marriage is over. Did Greg even love me? I trusted him. Did he even play poker? I shake my head, going over all the lies. Amy the American. Was anything he said truthful? He lied with such ease, as though he was born a liar. Everything fucking word that came out of his mouth was a lie.

Susie was right when she insinuated he was after my money. He must have laughed all the way to the building society. He said he'd look after my money. Stupidly I offered it to him for the business, all half a million pounds. *How did I not see?* How could I have been so brainless to have fallen for his shit? And what did they mean about the plan? It seems obvious to me. Marry me then abscond with my cash. I stop at the top of the stairs; but that's the puzzle. Greg didn't know about the money until after we were married. When a thought pops up I dismiss it, then I move on to the fact that he doesn't even own the bloody business. To say I've been conned is an understatement. This person I fell in love with and married is a conman, plain and simple. Plus Amy, the bitch, must have been in on it too. I wished I'd smacked her harder now and I wish I'd have thumped Greg as well.

What can I do on Christmas Day? In the safety of my bedroom, I close the door and wince as a searing pain shoots across my eye. With a glance out the window, I see that cow Amy has her arms folded, listening to the person I married. *The conmerchant.* I want to sling something hard at both their heads; instead, I turn away before I do.

Timmy is cowering in the corner of the en-suite and I scoop him up to cradle him in my arms. My tears blend with his fur as I nuzzle my head with his. *How could he do this to me? Did he ever love me?*

The doorbell rings and I freeze. *Why is he ringing the bell? He has a key.* Then I remember the call to the police. That pair must have left because otherwise he would have opened the door. Shoving Timmy on the bed, I dart over to the window. No, they are still outside, and I can't help but fudge a satisfied smile, watching as she is questioned by a female police officer. *That will teach her to attack me.* Serves her right if she gets banged up; that should knock the smug smile off her face. It's a pity they can't lock up my husband and throw away the bloody key.

The bell rings again, only longer this time, its tone urgent. Why isn't Greg opening the door? What are they doing? Shouldn't that bitch be cuffed and carted off?

I hover near the door and prise it open a fraction. I hear Greg and a jangle of words regarding an emergency call made from this address. He reassures the two constables that everything is okay. *What's he playing at?* Instinct tells me to keep quiet. They seem unconvinced and the male officer sounds firmer than the other, asking to come in. Anxiously I edge further into the hall for a better view.

Greg's voice is loaded with embarrassment as he apologises. 'My friend's daughter Amy and my wife had a little misunderstanding, that's all.'

My blood curdles. *What?* However, I keep quiet.

The female constable fires her question: 'Where is your wife, Kate Anderson?'

I stumble back into the bedroom and close the door carefully. What a *bastard. A little misunderstanding?* My heart beats furiously as I wait for the police to leave so I can give Greg a piece of my mind. What I don't expect to hear next is a thunder of footsteps ascending the stairs. The female officer calls out my name, flinging the door open wide.

I'm startled and I stagger backwards, stumbling over a shoe. I steady myself as Timmy starts to growl.

The tall male police officer addresses me with authority: 'Are you Kate Anderson?'

I feel like a criminal and stammer, 'Er… yes.'

'Did you make a 999 call and scream for help?' he asks with the same official tone.

I begin to feel uncomfortable and, too afraid to trust my voice, I nod instead. I dart a glance at Timmy, who is still baring his teeth. For once I wish he'd shut up, as I fear he's not helping the situation. The two constables don't appear fazed by him; however, they don't seem too happy with my silence either. My confidence fails because I slapped Amy first. How can I lie to the police when they ask? I feel drained and more tearful. They should be consoling me, the victim, instead of giving me the dead-eye. Feeling deflated, I flop down next to Timmy on the bed. Thankfully he stops growling to lick my face. My fingers shake when I accept a tissue handed to me from the policewoman.

Her soft tone now sounds reassuring when she questions lightly, 'Kate, would you like to tell me exactly what happened earlier that prompted you to dial 999?'

The tissue is used to blow my nose and wipe off tears. I'm going to sound like a woman scorned the old proverb. How I wished I'd never called the police, but at the time I was scared. What if they arrest me and not Amy? No, they'd never do that. I'm pregnant, after all.

She slips on the bed next to me, patting my arm for encouragement. 'Take your time, Kate.'

I study the violet duvet, still hopeful they will cart Amy off. I clasp my hands and dig my fingernails in. Preparing myself, I look into her brown eyes. Her smile is warm. *She's on my side; she'll understand my actions.*

I open my mouth. 'My… er… husband brought his mistress home… and… I… er… slapped her… and—'

Before I have a chance to finish Greg appears in the door frame. I bet he was hovering, waiting to see what I said.

He stares at me and snaps, 'She's my friend's daughter, and it's Amy who should have called the police, not you.'

In a more controlled manner, he addresses them both in turn. 'This is what I have to put with.' Nodding, he carries on. 'She's constantly drunk – I mean, God only knows how many bottles of champagne she's polished off today. So far I've counted four bottles in the bin.'

The policewoman stands up; the softness of earlier has vanished. 'You are drunk, Kate, that is evident.'

Blood drains from my face.

Greg butts in. 'Of course she is, and if you'd like to follow me I'll show you the mark on my friend's daughter's face – God knows what I'm going to say to him. Poor Amy's displaying delayed shock, sobbing downstairs.' He shakes his head. 'Christmas Day ruined by her constant drinking and mad accusations.' He runs a hand over his cropped hair. 'I swear her behaviour caused my hair loss.'

I stare, not quite grasping his words. I want to defend myself, but from the policeman's expression he appears to agree with Greg, probably due to all the aggressive drunks they have to deal with. So I think it's best to keep quiet for now.

'Huh, not screaming and shouting abuse now, are you, Kate?' Greg states in affirmation.

The policewoman asks, 'Does Amy require an ambulance?'

Greg seems to consider this for a moment before saying, 'You'd better see for yourself.'

The female constable gives me a withering glance before she departs. She addresses her colleague. 'You keep an eye on her while I check on Amy downstairs.'

Didn't they see her when they came in? I don't understand. I then do myself no favours when I hiccup. The policeman raises his eyebrows, unimpressed. Then I have a fit of hiccups. For a distraction, I stroke Timmy and pray the police will leave soon; I need a drink, and fast. How dare Greg talk about me like that…after what he's done?

Minutes tick by slowly. What's keeping them downstairs? Unable to stand the suspense any longer, I get up just as the policewoman enters. Inwardly I sigh, relieved. *At last, they're going to go.* Silently I watch her whisper to her colleague. He's staring at me, nodding. Instantly, I feel uneasy.

The policewoman speaks. 'You need to come to the station with us to sober up.'

To say I'm speechless is an understatement.

Greg hovers in the door frame, pretending to be shocked. 'Are…you sure—'

The policeman butts in. 'Sir, your wife is drunk and she's also used violent, threatening behaviour—'

I interrupt, my voice raised, 'Hang on, it was Amy's fault.' I shake my head. 'You can't take me in – what about her?' I want to add, 'What about Greg?' but he did nothing.

'Kate, for your protection and our peace of mind, we are going to remove you from this situation until you sober up.'

The policeman takes a step towards me. 'And, lucky for you, Amy is not going to press charges.'

'What…you can't do this,' I argue. *They can't.*

I realise this is no joke. They are deadly serious, but I still plead anyway, 'Are you sure about this? Please, I beg you.'

They've had enough, and when one of them grabs my arm, I start to cry. *This can't be happening.* And I demand, 'Can I change out of this dress…?And… I need the loo.'

'You have five minutes while we wait in the hall.'

What? I stand stuck to the carpet. My mouth gapes. I'm

not drunk; I don't feel it. I hiccup again. Maybe a little, surely not enough to get arrested for slapping a face, one that needed it.

I force on a brave face, stroking Timmy. I don't want him to be upset. 'Don't worry, baby, I won't be long.' Or will I? I have no idea. I've never been inside a police cell before.

THIRTY

I slip off my dress and drop it on the carpet. I can't believe this is happening. Quickly I shove on jeans and drag on my boots. With legs that wobble, I face the police officers on the landing. It's like I'm having an out-of-body experience. Descending the stairs, the house is quiet. The lounge door is closed; no doubt Amy and Greg are hiding in there. I feel I'm walking the plank with sharks swimming underneath. My legs plod one in front of the other as if on autopilot. The male policeman opens the front door, sending in a draft of cold air. I shiver and grab my fake fur off the bannister.

Escorted to the back seat of the panda car, I shuffle in while someone holds my head down. The PCs clamber in front and automatically the back doors lock with a click. *What? Who do they think they have in here?* I sit bolt straight and dig my nails into my hands. How is this happening? Greg appears at the door. He watches when we drive off. *This is so wrong.* I'd like to stick up two fingers at him, but I fear I'll get into more trouble so I don't.

Christmas Day and I'm on my way to a police cell. Never having had the pleasure before, I don't know what to expect.

Dread curdles in the pit of my tummy. I conjure up scenes from blockbuster films, with murderers and rapists locked up together. I could be banged up with prostitutes, women who kill. I allow a tiny smirk at that thought. Perhaps I'll get some tips. I being stupid, I know. For a second I close my eyes and imagine I'm on my way to the airport; it's the only thing I can think of to calm my nerves. I feel like smoking.

When the car jerks to a halt, I peer outside and blow out the longest sigh ever. We've stopped at traffic lights. An inflated Santa sways in one of the front lawns. White and blue lights flash from the window from the semi-detached house next door. Tears lurk behind my eyes and I close them once more. My mind goes over what Greg has done. I picture the scene with Amy. To think I'm in this situation because of them; my blood begins to simmer. If they imagine they are going to get the better of me, then they can think again. How dare he treat me like this? Who do they think they are?

A short while later we stop once more. Bleakly I stare out at the blue and white neon sign. *Police station*. I tremble; surely they have made a mistake?

When the back doors of the panda car unlock, I tremble. I'm told to get out and follow. I shiver, pulling my fake fur coat together. The velvet sky is littered with stars; I could be anywhere but here. It's bitterly cold nights like this that make me think of the fated Titanic. Its survivors praying they will be plucked from the deadly icy Atlantic Ocean. Why I am even thinking that? Maybe I'm going mad? Perhaps I feel the fear of their unexpected fate – hardly the same, I know. It still, however, is a daunting prospect, an unknown territory, a foreign place which I stand before, shivering. The gated car park is full of police cars neatly lined up. I suppose I should be grateful I've not been cuffed. I'm hardly on Britain's most-wanted list.

Entering the building, I find small comfort in the warmth. At least it blanks out the cold cell, not that that makes me feel any better. We walk down a long, greenish corridor with closed doors each side. Up ahead I see a high counter with a male officer grinning, like he's expecting me. He reminds me of a gypsy with his unruly mass of curled hair. I manage a fake grin only because I have no desire to find myself in any more trouble. I gather from the PCs that he's the desk sergeant. Well, I know he's not the barman. I'm desperate for a real drink, and I wonder if I cut myself and guzzle my blood if it might help. Get the fix I so desperately need to block all this out.

The desk sergeant asks for my name and address. I guess he's adding it to Britain's most-wanted list as he scribbles it down in a book. I'm even less impressed when I'm told to remove my coat. What do they want with that?

He appears friendly and I notice his white even teeth when he questions, 'So, Mrs Kate Anderson, what brings a lady like you to us?'

Where do I start? I wonder. I manage a tiny smirk. 'I got drunk.' That bit is true. And I feebly add, 'Do I have to stay here?' And I'm guessing he already knows about the assault on Amy, but I'm certainly not bringing it up.

'Yes, Kate, you do have to stay here.'

It's not what I wanted to hear, but I agree with a tight smile, nodding.

'Drink is the cause of why most people end up here, Kate. Not until I see fit are you able to leave.'

I'm glad I forced a smile now at my gatekeeper. It's probably best if I comply and keep quiet too. There's no point saying anything else which might keep me here longer. I experience a nagging thought. *He must know I slapped Amy. What if I end up in court?* I convince myself they'd have said something earlier – I'm sure of it. I'm torn from my reverie when I'm ordered to remove all my jewellery. Easing off my wedding band and engagement ring, I shove both of them across the counter, asking, 'What do you need those for?'

'It's part of our procedures,' he says, offering nothing else as he jots down the items before bagging them up. As an afterthought, he asks, 'Would you like a drink, Kate?'

I'd love a Moet or Yellow, or...but I guess that's out the question, so instead I say, 'Cup of coffee, please, one sugar.'

'Okay, but now, Kate, I'm going to ask you to take your top off.'

'What?'

He laughs at my expression then explains, 'Kate, when the bow on your jumper is untied it leaves a clear opportunity for you to hang yourself with it.'

I blink and exclaim, 'I can assure you I will not be hanging myself with it.' *Is he mad?* I wish now I had kept on my dress.

'Procedure, Kate.'

I protest, 'But what am I going to wear?' I take a glance around. 'And where do I take it off? Because I'm not stripping off in a corridor or whatever you call it.' I don't care how I sound.

I notice the female officer has conveniently disappeared when her colleague offers, 'We have some black T-shirts in the back office.'

I'm sure he's enjoying this. And I'm unable to hide my sarcasm when, a minute later, he hands me one. 'Thanks, it's what I've always wanted.' *Is this for real?*

He shows me the office where I can change and I ask, 'Do you mind if I close the door?'

'Be my guest, Kate.'

I'm sure he's laughing. The windowless room is small with an empty desk and two chairs on either side of it. I sigh, shaking my head. Do I have to do this? I sniff the cold T-shirt and wrinkle my nose. Has this even been washed? The more concerning question is, who the hell wore it last? I dread to think. I jump when someone bangs the door. 'Come on, we haven't got all night.'

In a flash, I ease out of my top and shove on the T-shirt, pulling it down – not that it makes any difference. I look at my jumper, unable to see how the flimsy bow ties could hold my weight.

All too soon I'm shown my bedroom for the night. I take in the most dreadful green-coloured metal door I've ever seen. One I vow never to come across again. Before I can enter I'm told to remove my ankle boots and leave them at the side of the door.

'You're kidding, right?'

The constable shakes his head. 'I'm afraid not, Kate.'

'You are joking.' *He has to be.*

He says nothing, like he's heard it all before.

I close my eyes for a second before I bend to unzip my boots. I flinch when my feet connect with the cold concrete floor and I try my hardest not to imagine what has ended up on it. The constable unlocks the door and hands me a plastic cup of coffee before I'm ushered in. It's worse than I could envisage. I stand still, taking in the cell. I blink. I think I might faint. I wobble slightly and reach out to the wall for support. Instinctively I recoil my hand from the damp, clammy paint. Disinfectant lingers from the metal toilet in one corner. I wonder how long I can go without using it. Next, I focus on the stacked bricks until I realise there's a plastic mattress on top. That's the bed? It's disgusting – I don't even want to bother searching for a pillow. Acting as a blanket is some sort sackcloth; I cringe. The compact window is lined with bars. I consider foolishly that they are for stopping anyone breaking in. Never in the whole of my life did I want to be somewhere else, even being at home with Greg would do.

My anger rises quickly, thinking about him in luxury. He should be here, after what he's done, not me. I shiver; the room is far from warm. But the cold is probably down to shock. I pull one arm of my coat which I was thankfully handed back. I transfer the coffee to my other hand, taking a quick sip; instantly I spit out the putrid liquid. That's got to be the worst coffee ever. I want to cry. How long is it going to be before I sober up according to the desk sergeant? I don't dwell on the fact that I'll be here all night. I'll take a rain check on the porridge breakfast in the morning. I glare at the bed; it's either that or the floor. It's rock hard, but with no choice, I climb on top to lean my head against the damp wall. It's not the most comfortable position, but I see I don't have much choice, really. On the opposite wall, I read, '*Tom waz ere*'.

Lucky him. Next, I notice a deliberate statement in black ink on the ceiling: '*Why are you here? Is it because you have taken drugs or you are drunk?*' Did they know I was coming? I wonder irrationally.

The hard wall is beginning to hurt the back of my head and I move it slightly. Now I wish I'd thumped Amy harder, maybe blacked her eye or busted her nose. One tiny slap and I'm the one banged up in here. There's no logic in that. I rest my tired eyes. Hopefully, when I wake, I'll be free to leave.

But if I thought I was in for a quiet night, I'm very much mistaken. First I'm unable to sleep as my arms start to itch. It's very annoying and very uncomfortable as I scratch furiously. But far worse is to come, when I discover I've been bitten by *fleas*. I count seven mammoth bites, three on one arm and four on the other. I have an urge to complain. To think they have supplied me with a flea-infested T-shirt is utterly *unbelievable*. I scratch again with infuriating speed until I hear a drunk male shouting out obscenities. Instantly I bolt up with unease, almost forgetting the bites. What if all the cells are full and they throw him in here with me? I've seen it done on the telly – a crowded cell, mixed with men and woman. I dangle my legs over the side, waiting with dreaded apprehension. *I'll complain, I will…I will.* I hold my breath, listening to a cell door clanging like he's being shoved in next door. I imagine him kicking and punching because I can damn well hear it. He's going mental as his door is finally closed and bolted. But does that stop him? Oh no. The racket is horrendous, his choice of language…

*

I must have drifted off because when I open my eyes the station is strangely quiet. Outside through the bars, the sky has turned dark blue; it's got to be early morning. I sigh, satisfied that I made it through the night. This hopefully means I can leave. I yawn and go to check my watch. I panic. Where is it? Then I remember it's locked up with the rest of my jewellery. I jerk when I hear the bolt prised open. I hold my breath, waiting, watching in trepidation as the metal door is flung open by the desk sergeant. He's smiling like he's pleased for me. 'You're free to go, Kate.'

I don't need to be told twice as I swing my legs down. I wince when my bare feet hit the cold concrete and reluctantly I use my coat to wipe them before shoving on my boots.

At the counter, I'm asked to check and sign for my jewellery. I'm hesitant to put on my wedding ring, but I do. I've no desire to stay here longer than necessary. I smirk inwardly when I'm handed back my jumper, the one I could have hanged myself with. *As if.*

'Right then, Kate, I never want to see you in here again.'

I shake my head. Ditto that.

'Okay then, but there's a condition that you must abide by.' His busy eyebrows arch. 'You have to stay with someone else until noon today. And only then can you go home. Do you understand?'

I agree quickly and sigh. I'm going to have to call Susie. The clock on the wall reads 5am. She's not going to be very pleased. What choice do I have? Who else can I call? And while I'm at it, I'll tell her of the gruesome tale of how I ended up here.

THIRTY-ONE

I shiver in front of the police station, clutching my jumper – I wasn't going to waste time any time changing back into that. Sarcastically I think how lucky it was that I got to keep the black T-shirt as a souvenir, the one I'm going to burn or wrap around Amy's neck, or Greg's. With all that's happened, I've hardly had time to digest last night. I slump on a low wall and wait for Susie to pick me up. The street is empty apart from Christmas decorations swaying from every lamp post. The icy wind blows an empty crisp packet to my feet and my tummy rumbles. I don't remember the last time I ate a decent meal. I stamp my feet, folding my arms tightly in an attempt to keep warm, and pray Susie will appear soon. A lager can rolls across the road; the sound echoes loudly. Next, I hear a car's engine in the distance. I strain to listen and sigh gratefully when Susie's BMW screeches up. I waste no time in rushing over to clamber inside the warm car.

Her expression is murderous as she slates Greg. 'He's going to get a piece of my mind – I can tell you that for nothing.'

Even though her driving is aggressive, I relax back and close my eyes, breathing in the soft smell of the luxury of leather.

The heated seat warms my tired, aching bones. I feel dirty and smelly. My head pounds when Susie shrieks, 'That bastard… I knew he was after your money. I warned you at the time…'

She never lets up, but gradually her voice fades as I drift off from pure exhaustion.

*

I wake up when the car stops. At first I'm confused, until the awful events flood back. I stumble out and stare at Susie's white thatched cottage, which has never looked so appealing.

Martin is at the door, displaying a sad expression. 'God, you look awful.'

I'm too knackered to care or comment but manage the words, 'Bed, please.'

I'm shown to the guest room and I collapse on the double bed with its white linen cover. Fully clothed, I pull the duvet on top of me.

*

At some point I must have undressed, for when I open my eyes I'm naked. Idly I watch the sun filtering through, but then I'm confused at the open curtains instead of Roman blinds. I panic. Where am I? A memory floats back and I sigh. As a distraction, I take in the white ceiling. Then I study the patterned blue Mintonesque paper; the effect is tranquil, but there's no sense of that inside me. The cover is pulled up to my chin and I want to stay here forever. Tears sting as I recall the scene with Amy and Greg until I can no longer stand the painful memory. My watch reads 11.30. It's another half an hour before I can go home. *Do I still have one?* My thoughts are distracted as I hear a soft tap on the latched door.

Susie pokes her head in and steams curls from a mug.

I'm startled at her appearance. Dark circles seemed to have suddenly appeared overnight under her eyes. I feel a wave of guilt, knowing her obvious worry is down to me. The phone call to pick me up must have been a shock to receive in the early hours of Boxing Day. God knows what she thought when I told her what had happened after she left.

She averts her eyes when she questions lightly, 'Did you sleep okay? And how do you feel?' She places the coffee on a coaster on the side cabinet, adding, 'Silly question, I know.'

I don't know if it is my imagination, but she seems on edge. I grin weakly and struggle to sit up. 'I feel exhausted, and it wasn't an experience I could recommend, I can tell you that for nothing.' And I don't want to even start on about my husband. That's just too painful.

She rests on the bed and takes my hand. 'Well, I think you were very brave.' She shudders. 'I can't imagine being locked up in a police cell.' Shaking her head, she affirms, 'I don't know how you coped, I don't.' Her hand squeezes mine. 'You are stronger than you think, and last night proved it.'

I'm grateful she hasn't mentioned Greg or Amy. I guess my bruised face tells the tale anyway. Susie seems as shocked as me. She isn't her normal self. There's no sparkle in her eyes. My night in the cell seems to have taken its toll on her too. I try to reassure her, 'Look, I'll cope somehow.' *I'll have to. I don't have any other choice.* I don't know how though.

She looks uncertain. 'Yes…I…er…guess…you will.'

Her eyes moisten, but quickly she gathers herself and stands up. 'Martin's cooking breakfast and I'll drop in a clean tracksuit – save you putting on the clothes from last night.'

It's a thoughtful gesture and I thank her, reaching for my drink. She seems more upset than me. She probably wishes she tried harder to stop me from marrying Greg. That's my stupid fault for not bloody listening. How I'd love to turn back time. I cup the mug with both hands and sip the sweet coffee. The smell of the cell lingers and I tighten my fingers, feeling anger twisting around like poison ivy. I want revenge for what that *bastard* has put me through. I want my money back too. *What if he's spent it all?* Well, I know he hasn't gambled it, because it was Amy he was poking, not gambling. And don't forget Jane too, whoever she is. *How could he? He said he loved me.* How did I not see? I trusted *him*. I brush away a tear. What I thought I had is gone –I never had it, if I'm honest. There's a chance of his seed growing. Gently, I rub my tummy. I'll bring up the baby on my own. I don't want anything to do with him. He didn't seem bothered anyway. Did he even want a child? Or was that part of his scheme too? Everything he said must have been a *lie*. Do I confess to Nick now? Suddenly I feel foolish. Susie's right – he's not part of the mafia; that was another lie. What about the photograph of Nick's sister? Well, as my marriage is over, I can solve that mystery by simply asking Nick directly. No point in asking my lying husband. But what was the plan? What did that mean? And why did he want to come back? Why send those texts? No, none of that makes any sense. According to Amy, he was after my money, and with his cunning ways, he's got that. What else can he want from me?

As I stand under a jet of hot water, it washes off last night's grim smell. I scrub furiously using a rose gel, lathering the sweet, soft texture. Susie's words linger in my head. She's right. I am strong. I will get through what Greg's done. *I've been in worse situations and survived.* And the bruises will fade in time. Searching my reflection in the mirror, they don't appear that bad, and nothing a touch of make-up can't sort out. I brush away a tear and sigh. On the outside I look normal, but it's not how I feel.

I slip on the tracksuit and use the hairdryer Susie left. I dump my dirty clothes on the unmade bed and stare at them until I can gather myself up enough to venture downstairs. The aroma of bacon greets me. Given any other time, I'd be rubbing my hands together; right now, I've no appetite. I pause on the landing and grip the bannister. Why did *Greg* choose me? Am I the type to fall for a conman? Was I such an easy target?

Martin is frying bacon and eggs. Gingerly I sit down at the oak table next to Susie. I take in the pine kitchen and the warmth radiating off the Aga cooker. A radio hums in the background. Strangely, though, in the relaxed setting, I sense a tense atmosphere.

Susie offers, 'Do you fancy another coffee?'

'Yes, please.' I nod gratefully.

'Morning, Kate,' says Martin, without turning around.

I offer a weak greeting back. Then bite my lip and sigh inwardly. *I've ruined their Christmas.* I feel a flood of guilt.

Martin places a plate in front of me but avoids my glance when I humbly thank him. 'It looks very nice.' Now he's gone to the trouble I should at least make an effort to eat it. I take a nibble bite of crusty bread and wipe off egg that has dribbled down my chin. The sandwich is very tasty and I devour it. Thinking about it, I decide to refuse an offer of a lift home. I'll call a cab to save them the trouble. I can't possibly impose on their hospitality any longer; I've already spoiled their Christmas. But what if Greg and Amy are still at the house? I suppose I've got no choice but to ask Susie to check for me. That's not a prospect I look forward to. What else can I do? As I wash down the rest of the bacon and eggs with coffee I suddenly remember Timmy. God, I hope he's okay. Those pair had better not have hurt *him*.

A bark from the utility room makes me look up in surprise.

That can't be right. But then I catch an odd exchange of looks between Martin and Susie. I wonder if they've secretly bought a dog. Surely not with their cat Flo…unless.

No, I'm being silly, but I venture anyway, 'Was that Timmy barking?'

Martin sighs. 'I think it's time to tell her.'

There's a sense of dread and I cry, 'It's him in there, isn't it?' I don't wait for an answer and, leaping up, I scramble to the door, raging, 'That bastard better not have hurt him.' I imagine Timmy's limp body and I vow to kill Greg and Amy.

I yank open the door and fall to my knees, hugging Timmy. He jumps around and I'm smothered in wet kisses like I've been gone for years, and my tears mingle with his fur. After a minute or two we both calm down. Next, I take the time to carefully check him over. He'd better not be harmed. Quickly I'm reassured; he seems okay. Scooping him up, I carry him into the kitchen.

Susie appears anxious with Martin stood behind her, his hands resting on her shoulders.

I feel uneasy and question nervously, 'What's going on? And why didn't you tell me Timmy was here?'

Martin squeezes her shoulders. 'It might be best if I left you to it.'

Susie turns, appearing unsure when she glances up at him.

I tighten my arms around Timmy and plead, 'Can someone tell me what's going on?' Has Greg had an accident? It's the only idea that jumps to mind. For a second my heart sinks. Just as quickly the feeling disappears when I harshly remind myself of what he's done. So if something has happened to him then it's his own fault. I believe the term is *karma*. I pose the question anyway: 'Did something happen to Greg?'

Susie stands to turn to Martin like she's considered his idea. 'Maybe you're right.'

He suggests, 'Tell you what, I'll walk Timmy around the block. I could do with some fresh air.'

Timmy's ears prick up and he wriggles to be put down. The word walk did it. On any other occasion I'd be delighted, but now I'm not sure.

Susie pats my arm with reassurance. 'He'll be fine with Martin.' Reaching for my hand, she offers, 'Come on, let's go to another room where we can talk more comfortably.'

I follow her down the hall to the sitting room. She guides me over to a brown leather Chesterfield sofa, and I perch on the edge and nervously ask, 'Well?' My heart thuds in my ribcage. This must have something to do with Greg; maybe he's had an accident and he's dead. What would I care after what he's done?

'I'll get us a another coffee first.' She sort of grins half-heartedly. 'Because I know I need one.'

I nod and cast my eyes around. The wait is unnerving. I just wish she'd blurt out whatever she has to say. Flames dance in the grate; they crackle and spit. Santa stockings dangle from the wooden beam surround. I realise again with a sinking heart that it's Christmas. I glance at discarded wrapping paper and neatly stacked presents under the tree. Fleetingly I recall Susie telling me they exchanged gifts on Christmas Eve. Newspapers lay uneven on the coffee table next to a full ashtray. For a second I can't remember if Martin smokes. I guess I'm trying to distract myself as I wait.

I take the mug from her but settle it on the table in front of me. I'm far too worried about what she has to tell me first.

Susie perches on a high-backed armchair and a grandfather clock ticks in the silence. Rain pelts against the patio doors, sending the room darker than it already is. I shiver despite the warmth from the fire.

Susie's sigh sounds deflated. 'I don't know where to start –

I don't.' She then takes a brief sip of coffee before setting it on the side table next to her. 'Nick called Martin this morning.'

I arch my eyebrow in surprise. *What does he want?* And why call on Boxing Day morning? I reach for my drink because I have a suspicion I might need it.

'Apparently he knows Greg very well.' She pauses. 'Erm… he says he needs to warn you about him.'

'What!' I slam down my mug. 'It's a bit late now, don't you think? And why the hell didn't he say anything before?'

'He wasn't sure if you'd believe him.'

I demand, 'How can he say that?' *Did he even try?*

She shrugs. 'I don't know, if I'm really honest.'

'Okay, so if he felt like that, why didn't he say something to you when you had that curry together?'

'I don't know, maybe because his friends were there and he couldn't.' She picks up a packet of cigarettes and lights one up.

I look away for a second, then ask, 'So what else did he say?'

'He said he was coming over to see you.'

'What's he doing that for?'

She avoids my question and stares out the window. Her action is unnerving, and I question, anxiously, 'Is there something you're not telling me?'

'No.'

Her answer is far too quick. It's suspicious, and I bite my lip. I sip my drink and stare at her accusingly. Something is wrong; I can feel it. But what is it?

She relents. 'He wants to come over and talk to you. He said it was important.'

'And you didn't ask what it was all about?'

Her glance is guilty as she expresses her no, then blows smoke away from my direction.

I don't believe her. She'd have demanded to know; it's in her nature.

Susie snubs out her cigarette, changing the subject. 'Looks like your bruises are beginning to show slightly.'

Instantly I touch my face and remember why I'm here. 'Yes, although she was small, she packed a right few punches.'

Thinking about Amy brings up the memory of my husband. I look away. I don't want to be reminded. But I am when my eyes land on Susie and Martin's wedding photo hung on the wall. Our day was bathed in sunshine. The afternoon was so perfect. I blink, returning to stare at the rain outside. Something bugs me and I say, 'I wonder why Greg married me. We could have just lived together. I don't understand. And if he was only after my money, how did he know about it? I'm positive I didn't mention it until months after our wedding.'

Susie's tone sounds forgivable, offering, 'Maybe you let it slip out when you'd had a few too many?'

I appreciative her politeness instead of using the harsh term 'drunk'. I sigh, knowing that fact rings true; sadly I have to agree. 'Most likely I did.' *Because how else did he find out?* I drain the contents of my mug like it's going to burn out my stupidity. How could I be taken in by his cunning, charming lies? I revisit the sunny day in my garden and go over Susie's *warning*. If only I'd have listened. But for now, I must force away hindsight and focus on what to do next. No matter how much I'd like to reverse the situation, I can't.

Next, I plead, 'Nick must have said more – come on, think.' Secretly I'm certain he did, and it could well explain the atmosphere earlier. I almost laugh, thinking she was going to tell me Greg was dead. *I wish he was.* I add, more to myself, 'I still don't understand the link between Nick and Greg.'

She shrugs and offers, 'I guess he'll tell you that when he gets here.'

'I suppose. But why does he want to help me?' I lean my head back and sigh loudly. 'Do I tell him I'm pregnant?' This changes everything now. What if it is his and he wants nothing to do with the baby? Greg's intentions have been made very clear. Money, that's all he was after. Suddenly I shoot forward, daring to ask, 'Do you think I've lost all my money?'

Susie produces a weak expression. 'I wouldn't like to guess, if I'm honest.'

I mumble, shamefully, 'I can't even bloody remember the bank Greg put it in either.' I rub my eye, feeling incredibly stupid. 'I trusted him.' Lamely I add, 'After I sort of forgot to ask him, I didn't think I needed to.'

Susie attempts to hide her disbelief and I turn to watch the flames dancing in the grate. *How did I not see? Why did I act so dumb? And what else is Nick going to unravel about Greg? What could be worse than this?*

'Nick did sort of mention… that… it's probably best if you didn't go home just yet.'

I scoff, sharply, 'Greg's pissed off to have an affair. He's not a mass murderer.' I stand in order to compose my point. 'I think he sounds paranoid.' I sigh, frustrated. 'I appreciate his concern, but what gives him the right to dictate for me not to go home?' Quite quickly I understand the connection with his sister. Greg probably conned her too, and Nick, the angry brother, wants revenge, hence the help. There's no other reason. And why didn't they tell me that Nick called earlier? But hang on, how did he know I was here? Unless he called at the house and found it empty. Something doesn't quite add up, so I ask, cautiously, 'Is that why you picked up Timmy, because of what Nick said? Come on, Susie, what's going on?'

She averts her eyes like she's holding something back. She stands up to leave. 'I'll be back in a minute.'

I edge over to the fire and bite my lip. What's keeping Martin and Timmy? Surely they should have returned by now? I glance outside and stare at the sodden grass. I suppose they're sheltering under a tree from the rain. That makes sense, but nothing else does. Plus how did Susie gain access to my house? She doesn't have a key. More importantly, why did he insist I don't go home? .*Unless Greg has moved in Amy.*

When Susie returns, I stare in surprise at *my* suitcase she's holding, along with my hand bag.

'What are you doing with those?'

'After what Nick said, Martin and I agreed we had no choice but to fetch some of your things and, of course, Timmy.' She nods curtly to affirm this. 'And yes, I took the keys from your pocket while you slept.'

Before I can get over my shock and speak, she drops the suitcase and urgently presses on. 'I didn't tell you earlier because I wanted you more settled and with something in your belly. I know you, remember?' She states, 'You probably haven't eaten for days.'

I appreciate her concern, but after the episode with Greg and Amy, then being locked up, plus discovering I married a conman, it's as though I'm losing control over my own life. And I'm not surprised when a touch of irritation creeps in. 'Can you please explain exactly what is going on?'

A commotion sounds from the kitchen. Timmy bounds in, all cold and wet. He stops at my feet, shaking off the rain. I shield my face as Martin rushes in with a towel. His wet clothes drip on the carpet. 'Bad time for a walk, I guess,' he offers.

I kneel and set about rubbing Timmy's fur. Martin disappears to get changed with Susie behind him.

I suppose the only way I'm going to get the truth is to wait for Nick. But if Greg's not at the house, I don't care what anyone has to say, I'm off home. All this cloak-and-dagger stuff is over the top. At least then I can make some sort of sense of what to do next. I'll also ransack every cupboard and drawer; there's got to be paperwork somewhere of the bank account with my money in it.

I look up when Susie returns, followed by Nick and Martin.

I ease up carefully. 'At last, this mystery can be revealed.'

Susie gestures for Nick to take a seat and without any prompting, Timmy jumps on his knee. Nick fusses him like an long-lost buddy.

Susie remarks candidly, 'He's certainly taken a liking to you.'

I bite down my irritation; yes, I'm pleased for Timmy, but this is not a tea party. Before I can ask, Martin's parents arrive. Grudgingly I force on a welcoming face.

Susie bustles off to prepare lunch. Martin, the gracious host, offers drinks and introduces Nick.

I feel guilty lying to Margaret and Tom when they ask after Greg. 'Yes, he's at home, and I only popped in.' I glance at my suitcase, adding quickly, 'I just needed to pick this up.'

Margaret smiles politely and enquires, 'Going somewhere nice, dear?'

I force a grin. 'I'm not sure.' I head over to the door and graciously add, 'Anyway, nice to have seen you both again, and enjoy your lunch.'

Nick is up off the sofa offering his goodbyes, grabbing my case. 'I'll give you a hand while you get Timmy.'

In the kitchen, I clip on Timmy's lead. Susie is adding Christmas crackers to side plates on the table. She's flustered and opens a window to let out steam from boiling pans on the hob. 'Sorry, I forgot to say Martin's parents were coming.'

I'm the guilty one. 'No, I'm the one who's sorry; I've ruined your Boxing Day.'

She gives me a brief hug. 'Hey, it's okay.' Her tone changes; it sounds serious as she holds both my arms. 'You need to go with Nick – trust me. He's got something really important to tell you about Greg.' Her gaze drops. 'I wish you could stay here, I really do.'

There's a sense of unease and I bite my lip. Before I can comment, Margaret strolls in to offer her assistance.

THIRTY-TWO

Nick shuts the boot of the Bentley. It's probably another car of his. Reluctantly I slide in with Timmy. It seems daft to call a cab when he's offering a lift.

He climbs in the driver's side and I turn to face him. 'Look, I appreciate your concern, but I can go home, and you're welcome to say whatever you have to about Greg there.'

He fires up the engine. 'I wish it was as simple as that, Kate.' He then adds, as an afterthought, 'Look, I'll cut you a deal – if you still want to be dropped off home after what I tell you, I'll bring you straight back.' He gestures with his hands. 'How does that sound?'

I breathe in slowly and consider the option; however, I still can't understand what's so important that he can't just tell me at my house. What could be so bad? I can conclude from his response that Greg and Amy have not moved in. That doesn't answer any of my niggling questions, though. So I shrug and say, 'Okay.' I slip on my belt and think, *I didn't have a choice really, what with my bag already packed and in the boot.* Another thought strikes as we weave around the country lanes. Susie didn't give me my front-door key, unless she shoved it in my handbag. With it being in the boot, I'll check later.

Leaning back, I concede that I might as well make use of the journey and ask questions. Surely Nick can tell me something regarding what's going on? Before I can, the car phone rings. Nick's smile is regretful. 'Sorry, I have to take this, it's work.'

I switch off to a conversation about a reservation that wasn't booked in for today. Six people have arrived at one of his restaurants and there's no available table. The M5 is quiet and the rain has finally stopped. Flooded fields whizz past and merge with a graveyard. I steal a sly glance at Nick. He's talking calmly on his hands free phone. I never noticed the diamond ring on his left hand, the pinky. It's elegant, not flashy; it goes well with his Cartier watch. He has tiny hairs on the backs of his fingers; without a strong glance, you'd hardly notice them. I bite down on my lip in an attempt to curb my hot flush when I recall the morning I left him half-naked on the doorstep.

I return my gaze to open fields and factories whizzing past. Rolling down the window, I welcome a blast of cold air. I wonder whether to mention the baby. The thought needs to be considered. *Suppose I ought to, really.* Only after he's dropped me at home; that way there'll be no awkwardness. Do I still have a home to go to? I'll have to get a solicitor. Do I want a divorce? Do I have a choice? My chest tightens. *What if my money has all gone?* How will I live? Can I involve the police? But Greg hasn't stolen it; I permitted him. I went with him to the bank to add his name on my account. *How could I have been so bloody damn trusting?* Surely, I can claim half the house? And who owns the apartment Greg's staying at? Why did it happen at Christmas? A bloody time when I can do absolutely nothing.

On the Quinton Expressway we stop at traffic lights. Nick turns his head. 'Sorry about that.'

I shrug. 'It's your business, you have to deal with it.'

We arrive back at his sister's apartment. I perch on the edge of a white sofa. The scene has a deja-vu feeling to it as Nick escorts Timmy out onto the balcony. I touch the soft leather as a distraction and wonder what Nick has to say that I don't know already. When he panders to Timmy, offering him food and water in the kitchen, I get frustrated. Although I love my dog to bits, how much longer do I have to wait? I'm about to stand up to ask when he appears with a bottle of red wine and two glasses.

I take up his offer and take a sip. He sits on the opposite sofa. His expression appears regretful. 'There's no other way to say this, so I'll make it short and simple.'

My heart sinks with a sense of dread and I sit up straight and glide my glass down on the low table that separates us.

His eyes seem isolated, like he's drifted off somewhere, when he quietly says, 'Greg killed my sister, pushed her off the balcony in Greece.'

My muscles tense. *This is some sort of joke.* I never expected this.

He blinks back from where he was and locks his eyes on mine. 'The police deemed it an accident; they could not prove it was murder. But the family and I know *he* did it.'

My eyes bulge. *Murder?* I'm unable to process the fact. It won't sink in.

I stay quiet. Is this a personal vendetta? How would he know better than the police? Why would they lie? I go hot, then cold and gape at him.

'You are probably wondering how I came to that conclusion.' He reaches for his glass and takes a small sip before continuing. 'Voleta was the baby of the family. With three brothers, including me, we doted on her.' He places his glass down. 'She met Greg two years ago. It was love at first sight, so she claimed, and a rushed marriage followed.'

I almost choke on my wine. *Married before?* He never told me that.

His eyes narrow, his tone harsh. 'I hated him on sight.' He shrugs hopelessly. 'But what could I do? Her heart was dead set on him.'

I have to ask; I have to know for certain. 'You said murder?' I babble on; surely he's wrong about that. *He has to be.* 'But you say the police didn't think so?'

'What man gets married and insists on life insurance straight away?'

Is he telling me or asking? 'I…er—'

His smile is unpleasant as he cuts in. 'Five hundred thousand – that's what my sister was worth.'

The room fades and I find my breathing becomes shallow. I'm transported back to me sat on Greg's lap in the office at our home. I'd laughed at something he had said. He'd guided a glass from my hand and I'd hiccupped. We'd had a lazy, long lunch, I remember that. He'd nuzzled my neck. Was it then that he'd shown me his silver pen? Some of the memory is hazy. There was a document he'd wanted me to sign – that bit is clear. I'd knocked over the bottle of wine, then nothing. I'd not given the night another thought. Greg must have cleaned up because the next day, when I'd peered into the study, it was spotless. What did I sign? I'm sure I saw life written…somewhere.

Nick's face comes back into focus. His penetrating eyes lock onto mine, almost like he was there with me just now. His head moves slowly up and down, guessing. 'I bet he has taken out life cover on you too – that's his game plan.'

My breath catches in my throat as his words sink in. *Greg planned to kill me too.* The room blurs and swiftly I feel myself being crushed in Nick's arms. 'It's okay, Kate, I'm here. He cannot hurt you now.'

Huge tears splatter on the sofa as I take in the full implication. Greg had murder in mind, not love. He must have planned it from the start. Susie's warning echoes in my head. I move from Nick's embrace and gulp wine like it's going to save me.

Nick stands up, offering another glass from his hand. 'A brandy will probably be better.'

The burning sensation does nothing to thaw my frozen heart and I welcome a refill, not trusting my voice. The bottle is left on the table and I pour out a large measure again and again. I want to drown in the gold liquid and lose myself.

*

I close my eyes and rest my head back. I'm on the terrace, looking down. There's no railing to hold onto as I edge forward. The city lights plunge into darkness when I'm pushed forward. I snap my eyes open. My heart races and I blink in confusion until I recall where I am. There's a blanket on top of me; I must have drifted off to sleep. The conversation from earlier tumbles back like an out-of-control turbulent nightmare. Timmy is curled up at my feet, snoring. The lights of the city shimmer across the horizon below. There's no drone from the traffic we're so high up – there's only the silence. I want to wake up again and reverse back to the night I met Greg. I form a vision of me refusing the offer of a drink. Then I find a seat far away from him in the corner and wait for Jason. He arrives with a bunch of roses, heading over with a happy face. The scene blurs and if onlys play over and over. I struggle up and reach over for the wine. The velvet Shiraz is room temperature, but nothing can melt the ice in my heart. Is it true the man

I married murdered Nick's sister? Is that my fate too? I'm sure the lamp in the corner flickers like it agrees. I shiver and wonder where Nick is. Throwing off the fluffy blanket, I stand up. When a door bangs, I jolt and spin around.

I breathe easy when Nick enters the hall. He has a bundle of carrier bags; a French roll sticks out from one of them.

He eases down bags and walks through open double doors, his tone concerned. 'How are you feeling, Kate?'

I shrug with a fragile snort and say nothing. I don't have any words.

'I left you a note on the coffee table.'

I turn and see it. 'Oh, right, I must have missed it.' Like I missed a lot of things.

His hand touches my arm, reassuring me. 'Come on, you have had a nasty shock.' He guides me back to the sofa. 'I had food in, not much, so I went and raided one of my restaurants.'

'You shouldn't have bothered on my account, I'm not hungry.' How can I eat?

He mocks me warmly. 'That's because you've never tasted my cuisine.'

I gaze up in surprise. 'How can you be so jovial when you say Greg murdered your sister?' I don't bother pointing out that I'm next.

'Being maudlin is not going to bring her back.'

'Yes, I understand that, but how can you be so flippant?'

He sits down next to me, careful not to disturb Timmy. He reaches out for my hand. It's warm, soft in my cool palm. 'Greg made my sister's life hell with all his lies, but she could not see, always making excuses for him. To have to stand back and watch was torture for all of us. Now she is at peace without that bastard. Why should I be broken again? It is certainly not what she would have wanted.' He squeezes my hand lightly and presses on. 'When we were children we made a promise to each other. That whoever died first, the other one would carry on with their life. And not wallow in mourning.' He removes his hand. 'I am a man of my word, Kate.'

I whisper, 'Okay.' I guess there's nothing else to say to that.

He stands and rubs his hands together. 'So, does Timmy like steak?'

With that, his ears prick up and his body shoots to Nick's feet in an instant. I can't help but produce a small chuckle.

Nick grins. 'I take that as a yes.'

I watch Timmy trotting behind his new best friend towards the kitchen. He's loved up with Nick. Funny how he never took to Greg, almost like he knew. I take a mouthful of wine. No wonder Susie and Martin had acted strange. Nick must have told them everything. *Could Greg have committed murder?* I stare blindly and think about the man I married. A conman, yes, but a murderer? That's a different league altogether. I go over what Nick said. *Why would he lie?* The insurance policy plays on my mind. And I recall Amy's words…*the plan.* My heart thuds and I stand up. *Fed up of waiting…* is what she had spat out.

THIRTY-THREE

The smell of steak wafts from the kitchen. Briefly, I take a peep in. Timmy is engrossed, watching Nick's every move. Nick takes a sharp knife and slices mushrooms on a wooden chopping block. His movements are professional, probably trained like Keith Floyd. Next, he finely chops garlic. It looks like he's enjoying it even under such harsh circumstances. He rests the knife for a brief second and stares out the floor-to-ceiling window.

I step away as he returns to cooking Timmy's steak. I venture back over to the glass bi-fold doors and stare out at the city lights. Nick's sister must have enjoyed this view. Did she ever feel small, lost and alone like I do now? Did she ever suspect Greg? Could she have ever imagined his intentions? The doors are easy to slide across. For some reason, I have the urge to create the same pose as in her photograph. I stretch my arms out. Head tilted back without the smile. That's the bit I can't do. Did Greg want me to find out about him? Was that part of his plan? One to lure me to another balcony and push me off? Make it look like an accident, like Nick's sister?

I flinch when Nick speaks. 'It is okay, it is only me.'

I stare blankly and say, as more of a statement, 'They planned to kill me too.'

'They?'

I step forward. 'Amy and Greg.'

'Sorry, I only knew about Amy and what took place when Susie enlightened me this morning.'

I touch the bruise on my face and sigh. 'I'm surprised you didn't know about his mistress.'

'I knew Greg was a womaniser. But I knew nothing of Amy. And If I am honest, I would say you were his next victim. I would be a liar if I did not acknowledge that, no matter how painful it is to you.'

I dig my nails into my palms. 'Why didn't you tell me? Why didn't you go to the police if you suspected Greg was out to murder me?'

He tries to guide me to sit down inside. I brush his off his hand to challenge him, snapping, 'At the party, you could have told me then.'

He tilts his head to the side. 'Imagine if I had. What would you have said?'

I'm silent.

'I have no doubt you would have thought me mad.'

I storm past him to slump on the sofa.

'Or would you have rushed home and packed your bags and booked the next flight out of town?'

I bite my lip and shrug. 'I guess not.'

Silently I agree and breathe out. 'Why me...I can't believe it. I'm shocked...'

He butts in quickly. 'Of course you are. And you have every right to be.' He stares at me and asks, 'Why you? Why my sister? I cannot answer that.'

Timmy pads in with a forlorn expression. Nick grins

modestly. 'I would say he wants his steak, the one I left to cool down.'

I pick up the wine bottle, not realising it's empty. 'I guess he does.'

'I will get another bottle, but may I suggest that you might want to unpack your clothes. I placed them in the master bedroom just in case.' He pauses before suggesting, 'That is, unless you would like me to take you home?'

I sort of half-laugh. 'I don't think that's wise, especially after what you've told me.'

'Good, then I can prepare something to eat. Food is the answer to everything in my book, and life must go on even under such dire conditions.'

I follow and watch him slice up Timmy's steak. He sets it down on a plate in the corner of the kitchen next to a bowl of water. My dog gobbles it up like he's not eaten for days.

'I'll show you the master bedroom,' says Nick. I walk behind him as he adds, 'Call me if you need anything.'

Inside I lean against the closed door. Tears fall, and I slip down and bury my head in my arms. After a while, there's a gentle tap on the door. 'Sorry to disturb you, Kate, but Timmy is restless. I think he's worried.'

I wipe my face with the back of my hand and scramble up. 'It's okay.'

'I brought you a glass of wine – thought you might need it.'

I bet my eyes are bloodshot, not that I care. 'Thanks.' I notice he's changed into a dark Boss tracksuit.

He sort of hovers and glances at the case still on the bed. 'Okay, I'll leave you to it.'

I expect Timmy to stay but I'm surprised when he stares up at Nick and follows him out. 'I thought you said he was troubled?'

'He was. But I know why he has his sights on me now.'

I raise an eyebrow.

'It might be best if you see for yourself.'

The Moroccan coffee table is laid with various dishes. French bread is spread which what looks like garlic butter. It certainly smells like it.

Nick gestures. 'This is my special mushroom and herb dip. That one is juicy large tomatoes sliced in feta cheese vinaigrette. And I'm just about to bring out fresh olives.' He grins. 'But it's the steak coming out next – perhaps what Timmy is after.'

My tummy rumbles. Surprisingly I feel hungry. 'It looks very nice.'

Nick signals playfully. 'Please take a seat, madam, while I fetch the wine.'

He returns, seeking approval. 'This is a fine Merlot from the Mpougiouris Estate, a favourite of mine. I'm sure you will agree.'

Given any other time, the setting could stand for romance. I brush the thought off. 'I'm sure I will.'

Nick brings out more dishes, then bends slightly to click his glass with mine. 'Happy Christmas, Kate.'

I huff. 'Some Christmas, I'd almost forgotten.'

He jokes, 'Not quite the turkey dinner, but I guarantee you, just as delicious.'

Timmy watches every bite we take, especially the fillet steaks, and Nick remarks, 'Cute boy. My mother's dogs have the same habit.'

I think that's his attempt to keep the conversation light, but we more or less eat in silence. After, I wipe my mouth with a napkin and fold it neatly on my plate. 'That was very nice, thank you.' After sipping wine, I admit, 'I have to confess, I didn't think I'd be able to eat.'

For some reason, Nick appears uncomfortable, like he wants to tell me something. 'Glad you enjoyed it.'

I suppose he wants to talk more about Greg. In a way, I guess there's more to come. I might as well start. 'So, how did your sister meet Greg and what else do you know about him?'

'Greg was born in a council flat, the heart of the slums in Birmingham. He acted the life of a playboy, insinuating he had come from old money. Most of his life was spent in and out of care homes. His mother was a drug addict and died early. She was just a kid herself.'

I gasp.

'Judging by your expression, I guess the version you heard was completely different.'

I scoff, not sure what to believe anymore.

'My sister met him via the internet. I do not know what possessed her to take a chance with online dating. Unfortunately, she did. She broke up with her boyfriend of five years and she insisted it was the only way to meet someone else. I reckon Greg caught her on the rebound because shortly after he moved in here. It was way too fast; the family and I were not happy. He seemed to have a hold on her, which, as I know now, was the start of his control over her.'

I explain how I met Greg after being stood up by Jason. 'Wrong place, wrong time,' I express miserably. 'Who could have predicted that?'

His tone is grim. 'So it would seem.'

'Anyway, the reason Matt – that's Voleta's boyfriend – and her relationship dissolved was because she was unable to conceive. That suited Greg, because he did not want children. That is what he played on – her vulnerability, the key part to reel her in under his control.'

Nick perches forward. 'Kate, are you okay?'

I bury my face in my hands. *What a fucking bastard.* After a minute I look up and cry, 'He said he couldn't wait to have babies.' I sniff. 'That was part of his charm, what I wanted. What I thought we both wanted.'

'Unfortunately, he is a master of lies.'

Nick gets up to fetch more wine. On his return, seated opposite me, he seems anxious when he ventures, 'You know the night we spent together.'

I'm not sure I want to hear this and I feel a blush rise up my cheeks. He too looks just as uncomfortable. So why is he mentioning it? Then again, shouldn't I be the one to confess?

He presses on. 'Nothing happened between us.' He gives me a small shrug. 'I did not want you to think I took advantage.'

Did I hear right? 'What do you mean, nothing happened?' How can he say that? How can that be true? *I'm pregnant?* I don't want Greg to be the father, not now. Not ever.

He edges forward, his tone puzzled. 'You seem shocked.'

I stare into space as the implication sinks in. There's no doubt then: Greg's the father. *What the hell am I supposed to do now?*

I pour out a good measure of wine.

'Kate, are you okay? Would you like a glass of water? I know everything is such a shock; it cannot be easy for you.'

'No...I'm fine. I'm okay with wine, thanks.' Should I even be drinking? I guess not. But telling me nothing happened – well, it's another shock piled up on the rest.

I half-listen as Nick starts to speak again. 'On the night before Voleta and Greg were due to go on holiday to Greece, they dined out.' I pay attention as he continues. 'Earlier in that day she had appeared on edge, and because I could not get her alone from Greg, I decided to come here and have a snoop around.'

I'm a little confused. 'Greg allowed you to have a key. That surprises me.'

Nick crosses his leg. 'Greg maybe the master of lies, but as a narcissist, they tend to become complacent, especially when they think everything is under their control. That is when they slip up and make mistakes.'

I lean back and rest my glass on my knee. 'What do you mean?'

I can see this is painful for him.

'Over time, as he gained control over my sister, she would not listen to any of the warnings from the family, including me. It was as if she had been taken over by an unseen force.' He takes a sip of wine before resuming. 'So I staged an argument with her, gave her an ultimatum. It was him or me. She, of course, chose him. But that is what I wanted her to do for my plan to work, which it did.'

'How? I don't understand.'

'From my bunch of keys, I ripped off her door key and tossed it at Greg's feet. I told her there was no need for it.' He edges forward. 'Greg's expression gleamed with triumph, but it wasn't as victorious as mine as I discreetly patted my spare key in my pocket when I stormed out.'

Nick stands and lets Timmy out. He looks like he needs to breathe in the cold air. He turns around to state, 'I am not proud of what I did, but it was the only way I could keep an eye on her. I could not save he, and that is what I have to live with.'

He steps outside and watches Timmy sniff around. He then wanders back inside. 'When I found the life cover on my sister, I was concerned – naturally. I phoned her over and over, but her phone was switched off and I never got to speak to her again.'

I get up and pat his arm with a wilful shrug. 'Sorry for your loss.'

'Anyway, I took the documents, and the next morning I pretended to be Greg and cancelled the policy.'

HOW DID I NOT SEE

'You did the right thing. I suppose I need to find mine and cancel that too. But what is strange is that there are no documents at the house.' I shake my head. 'No bills, no nothing.'

Nick offers, 'They could be at the apartment he is staying at.'

'Maybe.' Then a thought pops up and I question, 'How come I kept bumping into you? Like at Jo's party. Next around the corner from where Greg's supposed business was.' I frown, adding, 'And all that time, you knew but said nothing. I don't get it.'

His tone comes across as diplomatic. 'Like I said before, would you have listened?'

Disappointed tears lurk behind my eyes. If only he'd told me earlier, then things might have turned out differently. Or like he said, would I have listened?

'I was determined Greg would never get away with it again. So, Kate, I had him watched, the same as you.'

My head snaps up. 'It was *you* I felt was watching me?' I glare at him. 'And all that time you knew my life was in danger. How could you have not told me?' I gape and question him sarcastically, 'So if you were so concerned about me, why didn't you go to the police?'

'And tell them what exactly? That Greg planned to murder you for the insurance money? You cannot arrest someone when they have not committed a crime. And you simply cannot charge a man who has taken out a life insurance policy either.'

THIRTY-FOUR

I turn away and slosh out wine, not caring if I spill it. I can't believe he didn't warn me. I don't care what he said. *He should have told me*. After all, he had plenty of opportunities. But what is his real motive? Use me for his revenge.

With a glass in hand, I storm out and head for my bedroom, slamming the door behind me. I stand at the window and stare out at the rain. Tears fall and I wipe them away. Everything could have been so different. As he said, would I have believed him? Even I have to admit my doubt. I suppose him not being the father is another worry off my mind. In another way, it's a curse. To think at first Nick that was a killer, only to find it's my husband. How can I have a murderer's baby? What will I tell *he* or *she* as they grow up? I slump on the bed. More to the point, will I be alive to see it? *After all, my husband has set out to kill me for insurance money?* It's surreal, like the situation is happening to someone else.

I delve into the black fog of my brain for fragments of that night in the study. What document did I sign? Could Greg really have taken out life cover? One thing is certain: first thing in the morning, I have to speak to him. I have to know the real *truth.* I also need access to the apartment; he must have papers there. Tomorrow morning I will visit him; he has to see me. But how do I search around with him there? How do I even know my life will be safe? What if Nick is lying? Who can I trust? That's easy: no one. Certainly not my husband, and definitely not Nick – not now, after what he told me. And all that time I thought it was Jason. I stand and search the twinkling street lights below. Idly I wonder whatever happened to him. My life could have turned out so different. Perhaps he had an accident; whatever it was, it's too late for me.

THIRTY-FIVE

I stand rigid under the balcony of my husband's apartment. His statement thrown at Amy crawls around my head. *'You can't be pregnant from me because I've had the snip.'*

When the blood-red mist evaporates, it's replaced with rage. His lie catches in my throat and I can hardly breathe. All those months he lied. *The deceitful lying bastard .I suppose that's kinder than killing me,* I think irrationally. All these *fucking* months, telling me he wanted a baby, our *baby.* A thought is triggered. *There's no baby. I'm not pregnant.* I don't know whether to laugh or cry. It also means Greg knew I'd slept with someone else. He didn't even question me, knowing it could never be his. That explains his actions when I told him. My whole marriage was based on his lies. He tricked me. That's why he refused the tests. My mind churns through the past, over and over.

I blamed myself for not conceiving because of what happened at such an early age. What choice did I have after my dad had brutally forced himself on me in a drunken rage? I knew I was damaged inside. The doctors said I'd be fine, but to me, there was always hidden doubt lurking. The rapist, of course, would never be found. My dad threatened to kill my mum if I ever told on him. All that time and I thought it was my fault that I was unable to conceive. I kept the secret from my *husband* to save him from the pain I'd suffered. To think this is how I've been rewarded. I feel a snap inside me; it pulls away like I've been split in two.

The clouds darken and a thunderstorm claps. Lighting strikes across the sky. The hairs on the nape of my neck rise. My father's face flashed over mine, whisky strong on his breath; beads of sweat ran down his dark skin. His eyes snapped shut, grunting his way in. Screams echoed in my head. A sock was stuffed inside my mouth. I'd focused on a crack in the ceiling. I'd imagined the plaster, it getting bigger and bigger and then raining down on my dad, killing him. There's rage so powerful building inside me; it crawls and bites. It seeks revenge for the injustice served to me. It wants to hurt back. Hunt down those responsible. One is already dead, but the other one will soon follow. There's no other way; it's *him* or *me*. I imagine Voleta's approving face urging me on. The line is crossed with no way back. More like I'm being pushed over it.

I jolt back, hearing Amy scream from above, 'You're a liar, Greg, a dirty fucking liar.'

I snarl my lips with slight pleasure. So, Amy was knocking off someone too? How ironic. I stare up at Greg's balcony and focus on the railings. Their presence presents me with a strange notion. I step back, not caring if *he* sees me now. My thoughts turn wild. I imagine him fall, crashing onto the footpath, his skull cracked open. Thick blood draining away with all his fucking lies down into the gutter where he belongs. For some strange reason, I remember a famous couple. They were so loved up once. But years later they publicly loathed each other with such a vengeance. I'd never understood how their love changed to such hatred. *Now I get it*. Only I never imaged it would happen to *me*.

I'm startled when Amy flings open the security door. She storms out, her long black coat flying behind her. *Well, he's not getting away with it*. Not now, not ever. I will not have him treat me this way, and from nowhere a plan begins to formulate. For all I know, Amy is his next victim after me. Greg doesn't care who he hurts.

Fuelled with a new sense of purpose, I race after her. 'Amy, Amy…'

She stops to spin around. 'What the fuck are you doing here?'

I almost lose my nerve when I remember how hard a punch she packed. But I need her help. Anyway, there's a small chance she might have forgotten. Plus the bruises are covered with make-up. I have to try and win her over. So I put aside for the moment the fact that she was in on the plan to have me killed. That old proverbs flashes in my head: keep your friends close but your enemies closer.

'I heard what Greg said.'

She puts her hand on her hip. 'So, what's it to you?'

Without the aid of alcohol, I notice she is much younger close up. At a guess, I'd say twenty. There's no softness about her. It's like she's been dragged up and forced to fend for herself. And I know how that feels.

'I guess he lied to both of us – me in particular.' I soften my tone for more impact. Then stupidly, I blurt out, 'I'm sorry I slapped you.' What did I mention that for? Quickly I add, to get her on my side, 'I should have punched Greg instead, and hard.'

Her stance lightens slightly. 'Yeah me too, the lying bastard.'

I think hard of what else to say and then it clicks – our connection. 'So when's the baby due?' Well, it was. I can't even process that thought yet.

Her hand darts to her belly. 'I only did the test this morning.' She wipes a tear away quickly and sniffs. 'I thought Greg wanted a family, a baby of his own.'

In a perverse way, I feel sorry for her. 'I guess he took advantage of both of us.'

Her face then hardens. 'You can talk, you were fucking someone else. I bet you don't know who the fuck the baby's dad is.' She jabs her thumb upwards to Greg's balcony. 'That prick up there, or whoever – but we know it isn't him, now, don't we?'

I hold in my anger and shrug out my lie. 'You're right, I don't.' I sense she's livid with the other guy as well as Greg. 'That's men for you – bastards, the lot of them.'

'You can say that again,' she spits out. 'That fucker said he'd look after me. You know what, girl, you're well rid of him. And he fucking owes me money. The *money* I earned for the tosser.'

I have a prickly sensation and my heart begins to thud. So I venture slowly, daring to ask, 'What do you mean? He owes you money?'

Her laugh is sarcastic as she scoffs. 'For an old bird, you're sure a thick one.' She puts her hands in her pocket, feeling around for something. 'Do you think I'd fuck *him*…for nothing? Shit, I must have left my fags upstairs.'

I try to hide my shock. I calm the bile attempting to rise. I shallow hard as a set of implications tumble around my head. Jesus, how much more can I take? She could have passed on gonorrhoea…I could have AIDS. I fumble for the car keys in my pocket.

'Fuck me, there's no need to look like that. I'm not a fucking leper,' she sneers. 'I wasn't brought up with a silver spoon in my gob like you.'

I can't help but gape. Me? Silver spoon? *If only she knew.*

'You know what, fuck you.' She turns on her heels and stomps off.

I watch her storm off, too stunned to move, and my head screams, *Do something. Don't let her go. You might not get another chance.* I force my legs to chase after her again. 'Sorry, it's the shock of everything. Look, slow down, I can help you with money, pay you what he didn't.'

That catches her attention. She stops and demands, 'How?'

I fumble out my mad, wild idea. 'Why not reverse the plan?'

Her blue eyes narrow. 'What do you mean?'

I scan around the empty road of office blocks. 'I know a place where we can talk in private. It's just around the corner. I'll buy you some cigarettes.'

She shrugs and tags along. 'Whatever.'

It seems an age since I last made this walk with Greg, when I thought he was my loving husband on the run from the mafia. *How did I not see?* I was blind with my eyes wide open, that's what. I dread what else I'm going to find out about him. What more can there be? My pace is slowed seeing the trusted old tired pub as we turn the corner. If ever I need a drink, it's now.

The old man and his dog are in the same place. He must have been here at 9am on the dot. The limp Christmas tree is up, without its flashing lights. The nice bottle of Shiraz has gone. I turn to ask, 'What would you like to drink, Amy?'

'Double rum and Coke.'

I order, then rummage in my purse for change, which I hand her. 'I'm not sure where the cigarette machine is.'

'We walked past it in the hall.'

I watch her go and wonder whether she should be drinking alcohol – not that's it's any of my business. Why am I even thinking that? I also question my sanity. What am I doing here? I guess shock can muddle up your brain. It's certainly tangled up mine. I carry our drinks to a corner. I chose the same table that I sat with Greg, only because it's next to the open fire.

Amy returns, reeking of smoke. She plonks down and swigs her drink. 'So, what's the plan then?'

I shiver inwardly at the word. Not so long ago I was the *plan*. Red wine is sipped, more for Dutch courage, before I whisper carefully, 'Do you know what happened to Greg's last wife?'

She seems surprised. 'His last wife?'

So, she doesn't seem to know him as well as she claimed. I bet a lot of her stance is an act. For the first time, I take in her white trainers and black mini dress. 'How old are you, Amy, just out of interest?' Not that it matters.

'How old do you think I am?' Her question sounds cocky.

Surely she can't be younger than twenty? I'm uncertain and offer, 'Twenty-one.'

'Everyone thinks I look older than fifteen.'

I reach for my drink and drain it before she has a chance to see my reaction. *Fifteen.* What the hell is Greg playing at? I attempt to calm my racing heart and ask, 'Did… Greg… know your age?'

She knocks back her drink, then adds, 'Of course he knew. I was in my school uniform when he picked me up in his flash car.'

'Er…you'll have to excuse me. I need the loo…' I make it just in time to retch violently into the toilet. I can't take much more of this. My heart is going to explode. My fingers shake when I drag out the paper from the dispenser to wipe my mouth. Limply I flush the loo handle. I then search my reflection in the chipped mirror. Sunken eyes stare back. Lines have appeared that were not there before. I almost expect to see wisps of grey hair.

When I return, I blink. My handbag has vanished and so has Amy. Lucky for me, I have my phone and car keys in my pocket. I stumble out into the inner hall. As the main door opens, I see a flash of her puffing on a cigarette. My bag dangles from her arm. She's laughing and chatting with an older man. Swiftly I return to our seats and compose myself. I fiddle with my wedding ring and quash down the thought of Amy, fifteen, with Greg. How could he? She's just a kid, for Christ's sake. Dear *God*. To think I fell in love and married a monster. A predator…*A paedophile*… I feel my blood drain from my veins. I jump up and order a very large brandy.

'And I'll have another too,' says Amy, handing over my bag. 'I didn't want it stolen while I had a fag outside – you can't trust anybody around here.'

There's no answer to that. 'Thanks.' I knock back my drink and order another. *What the fuck else am I going to find out?*

I feel the air closing in; I need to leave. As I hand her her drink, I casually ask, 'Do you have a key to Greg's apartment?'

She looks over her glass. 'Why?'

'Well, I want to have a look around, and if it makes you feel any better, he also owes me money too.'

'Typical. So what's this reversed plan then?'

I guide her back over to the table. I consider whether to call the police and drop Greg in it. He is, after all, breaking the law. I whisper, 'What Greg did to you was wrong. We can report him; I'll come with you to the station.'

'If I bring the coppers to my mum's house she'll kill me. She's the one that got me started on the game – payback, according to her, for bringing me up.' She shakes her head. 'No fucker's going to help me.'

'I don't know what to say, but sorry.' *Bloody hell. I wasn't expecting that.*

Amy shrugs. 'Whatever.' She stands. 'I'm going for a fag.'
Desperate for air, I say, 'I'll come with you.'

Outside she lights up and I venture, 'I'm sure you knew Greg took out an insurance policy on me.'

'Yeah, I know, and then he planned to bump you off, but he's full of shit. He'd never go through with it. He's a blagger.'

'That's where you're wrong, Amy.' A quick scan around confirms we are alone on the footpath, and I feel safe to continue. 'I've since found out that he did kill his first wife.' I can't believe I'm having this conversation with a fifteen-year-old girl. And I try to persuade her again that we can go to the police, but she's having none of it. Instead, I offer cash in exchange for her key to Greg's apartment.

'What do you plan to do then?'

Knowing her age and vulnerability, I decide to leave her alone. I can't use a child in my plan. 'Look, just forget I mentioned that, and I'll sort out some cash for you.' Bloody hell, is that not like I'm just Greg's pimp now? What a mess. And yes, the thoughts of killing Greg are stronger than ever.

Under drizzly rain, we head to where she knows there's a cash point in the next street. It's strange to be walking alongside her and I sense this nightmare is only going to get worse. This time I don't dodge puddles and have more thoughts of drowning in one. I jolt when my phone rings. It's Nick. Earlier I unblocked his number. I silence the call; I'm in no position to speak right now. The phone is shoved back in my pocket and I pull my purse from my handbag. Pushing the card in the machine, I begin to wonder. How do I know she's going to give me the right key? I know she's only fifteen but she appears a lot older for her years – plus is she telling the truth? The numbers are punched in and I think about how to handle this.

Carefully I place the notes into my purse and turn to her. She drags on her cigarette and then blows smoke rings like a child blowing bubbles. She looks so young and helpless. She is also cunning behind her child-like demeanour; I recall the scene on Christmas Day. 'Look, Amy, after all that's happened, how do I know you're giving me the right key?'

The finger with chipped nail polish flicks away her snub end. 'Fuck me, now you're starting to wise up.' She shrugs. 'I need some stuff from the flat, so you can come around and have a nose now, but first I want the cash.'

'No, you said I could have the key. Plus I don't fancy going there right now.' God knows what I'll do. I could end up pushing him off the balcony. 'No, I need time before I can face Greg.'

She laughs sarcastically and scoffs. 'He won't be there now; he'll be down the pub getting pissed up, probably fucking that bitch Jane who works behind the bar.'

I'm about to add, *He doesn't drink*. Then I think better of it. My husband is no longer someone I know. Again I try to persuade her to hand over the key. In the end, I reluctantly go with her. However, she does relent when I offer her more money to keep the key for a couple of days. I tell her I'll give her my number if she wants the key back. Secretly I've no intention of doing that. I want her as far away as possible from Greg.

In silence we walk side by side past office blocks; for a brief second I wallow at my husband's admission. All those wasted fucking months, yearning. I bunch my hands into fists. *He deserves to die.*

'He wasn't going to kill you,' Amy says, breaking into my thoughts.

I stop, just as we reach the pub, and turn to her.

'He's all mouth, gobbing off about the plan to bump you off. He's a fucking conman alright, but he hasn't got the balls to follow through.'

I'm tempted to go back to the pub to tell her over a brandy. Instead, I hurry her along and explain what happened to Nick's sister. At first, she's in denial. Quite why I have to explain is beyond me. After all, she's only a child, but I feel the need to warn her. With the apartments coming into view, I glance up at the balconies. The thought of pushing him over the rails returns, stronger than ever.

Before we enter the block, I insist on checking the underground car park. I'm aware of what Amy said; I just want to make sure he's left the building. I'm not taking any chances. Besides, I don't trust myself, and no way do I want Amy witness to my crime. The dust-covered car is still there. Noting the absence of his Range Rover, I breathe easy.

'Satisfied?' moans Amy, unimpressed.

'I'm just going to check around the corner.' I need to be certain.

She raises her eyes in protest and pulls a packet of Silk Cut cigarettes from the pocket of her trench coat.

After we exit the lift, I follow her. Amy inserts the key and I trail behind her into a spacious hall. The light oak floor follows through into the open-plan sitting room. The spotless kitchen is to the left. I'm sort of amused, as the only thing Greg didn't lie about was his fetish for cleanliness. A couple of brown sofas and a coffee table furnish the open-plan room – that's about it. It's almost like it's waiting for the owners to hang up pictures and place down rugs to drown out the boring white walls.

Amy makes her way to the bedroom to stuff a carrier bag with clothes. I check out the patio and step outside. There's a sense of strangeness, glancing down from the seventh floor to the concrete below. It seems a lifetime since I stood down there. Was it only a couple of hours ago when I heard another of Greg's lies? I would say that was the worst one ever. The vision of the city blurs. Grey clouds gather and mentally I say goodbye to the Kate I once was. She vanished under the balcony. I suck in the cold air like it's my first breath, the first time on the planet. It feels surreal, as though I'm starring in a horror film with no end in sight. I've crossed the point of no return; a line has been crossed. The revenge plan is set in motion. *Greg* deserves everything that is coming to him. I want him to suffer as I have. Feel the pain, eat it and breathe it. I grip the black railings tightly. I image Voleta being hoisted, tossed over into the wind, her beautiful face a mask of fear. Did my husband plan to kill me in the same way? Or did he have something else in mind? Perhaps to ply me with booze and shove me down the stairs of our home, my neck snapping on each step. What better than an authentic arrest when I was banged up in a police cell for being drunk? Was that planned too?

What would have happened to Timmy? I release my hands; no need to worry about him now. I've no intention of leaving planet Earth. If anyone is to go, it will be *Greg*, not *me*. I study the railings. They shouldn't be too hard to loosen. Next, I imagine my confrontation with him. *His smug smile, smoking.* More lies dripping from his lips. I back him into the railings. But the vision suddenly stops. How do I get it to look like an accident? I can hardly push him; someone might see. I sigh and bite my lip. Maybe I could stage an argument – sort of poke him in the chest? Make it look like soft jab, but push hard. *I don't see any other way.* It's either *him* or *me*. I can't take the chance of looking over my shoulder for the rest of my life. Can I get away with it? *What choice do I have?* Wouldn't that make me as bad as him. Idly I study the view of the city doused in rain. Christmas lights flick on and I spot a small child dancing below, holding her mother's hand. Her blonde hair is tied in pigtails with red ribbons; the scene presents me with a thought. The hair on the nape of my neck spikes up and briefly I close my eyes. I'm one hundred percent sure Greg lied about that little girl's death too. *That lying, cold-hearted bastard.* Cold air fills my lungs and another thought snaps me from my trance. Somehow I could goad Greg from below; there's every chance he'll lean on the railings and then boom... bang... *dead.*

Knowing Amy is taking her stuff and leaving Greg, I feel safe to carry out my plan. She will never need the key again as Greg will no longer exist. All will be over.

I search around and find a handful of Greg's clothes hung up in the wardrobe but nothing else. Drawers are opened and slammed shut. Amy puffs on her cigarette from the balcony, waiting for her cash. I stand in the kitchen, frustrated. There's nowhere else to look. There's no papers, no documents, nothing.

'Do you know where Greg keeps his paperwork, like bills?' I call, moving towards her.

She shrugs like she doesn't give a damn. 'Are you finished?' she says, stepping inside, locking the doors behind her.

'I guess so,' I respond flatly. My handbag is on the island. I delve inside, searching for my purse. There's no point staying any longer, so reluctantly I hand over five hundred pounds. 'This was all I could take out in one go.'

THIRTY-SIX

I've hardly slept, going over my plan of revenge against Greg. Although I'm up early, I do not need to rush downstairs, as Timmy is still with Nick. I need time alone to prepare. The Roman blinds are pulled open and I head for the shower. Drying off, I throw on jeans and a jumper.

In the kitchen I pour hot water into a mug for coffee. Settling on the barstool, I log into the laptop and browse through hardware stores. Suddenly I bang down the flap. Shit...the searches can be identified. The stool topples over in my haste to stand. I pace the room, thinking hard. Even if I erase the searches, the evidence will still be there. I can't afford to take any chances.

Grabbing the laptop, I race upstairs to the bathroom and twist on both taps. The agony of waiting is long, and I will the bathtub to hurry and fill up. Finally, with sufficient water, I drop the laptop in with a splash. How long do I leave it? Where do I dump it? How could I be so stupid? Frantically I stride in and out of the room. I pray it will drown and sort of miraculously disappear like the Titanic. But it doesn't, and I end up yanking out the plug. Water streams from its shell when I snatch it up, and I give it a hard shake before I bound down to the garage. There I smash it on the concrete floor, but it's useless, hardly making a dent. Frantically I search around for a hammer. There's only the discarded pushchair and a couple of boxes – that's it. I bite down on my lip and kick the processor. Then I remember the hammer I used for steak, and I bolt to the kitchen. With adrenalin pumping, I race back to the garage and smash up the keyboard, pretending it's Greg's head.

After five minutes the screen is shattered, the keyboard battered – but not enough. I blow out a sigh and give up. A knife would do to unscrew the back. Back to the kitchen, I get one. I have to fiddle for a bit, but it works and the delicate components are ripped out. Their life force smashed to tiny bits of plastic. There's a carrier bag in one of the boxes, and I drop the dead parts of the mechanisms inside.

I feel hot and sweaty but satisfied. For my effort, I pour out a large glass of Yellow Tail. No need to worry about drinking now. Not that that's a big concern at the moment. What's more important is where to dump the busted PC. Maybe it might be a good idea to scatter it all around Birmingham; there must be hundreds of bins to choose from. Admittedly not the greatest of plans; I've hardly committed murder, though – well, not quite. Another wine is poured and I rethink my shopping plan to buy hardware products. It might be wise to use a disguise. The flawless solution hits me like black death when I recall the drive through Birmingham on my way home. *Perfect.* I could be anyone. No will challenge me, for fear of reprisals.

THIRTY-SEVEN

Zooming along the M5, speed is required. It is the equivalent to my racing heart. A dull sun attempts to shine behind dark clouds. I take it as a sign that heaven approves. They say the devil looks after his own. After today, no one will be able to help *Greg*, not even the devil himself. I power the Bentley with reckless disregard into the outside lane, the speedometer hitting 120. All too soon the exit I require appears up ahead. I change lanes amidst a blast of horns. That was God's chance to get me before I do what I have to do. I slow down and enter the dual carriageway of Hagley Road west.

A short time later I cruise down the high street of Small Heath. Searching for a car park, I turn up a side street. There's one up ahead and I drive onto the uneven surface. It's full of battered vans and litter spills everywhere. It's more of a loading bay, and I pull into a tight space. I cut the engine and consider whether it's safe. With a quick scan around, I wonder if I should have parked in the town centre and caught a cab instead. What if the car gets stolen? It's a chance I'll just have to take.

With time ticking on and my nerves in shreds, I decide to press on. Grabbing the carrier bag off the passenger seat, I squeeze out. In the high street, I glance in shop windows at my reflection. The sunglasses and headscarf sort of blend in with other women. I bite my lip when I spot the first bin, and when someone bumps into me, I freeze. It's a small kid. His mum glares at me, grabbing his hand to drag him away. It's as if she knows my guilty secret. I don't care about it because I realise I've made another fatal error. My prints are all over the laptop, plus the newspaper the parts are wrapped up in. I take deep breaths and force my jelly-like legs forward. What can I do? Nothing. I convince myself that I'm not committing a crime – not yet, anyway. Then I judge that I can't linger here any longer. I have to proceed with the plan. The packages must be dumped in bins dotted along the high street; I've no other choice.

With the last one gone, I hear a fist bang against a glass window. I freeze and steel myself to gaze around. A grey-haired Asian man waves furiously at his young assistant. He seems to have knocked the table outside, spilling a tray of onions. I sigh and scuttle on for the next part of my plan. Further up, I spot just the right shop. I peer at the display of mannequins layered in traditional burkas. I hesitate and want to bite my lip, but it feels sore. Before I enter I silently go over my prepared statement just in case any awkward questions are asked. I'm conspicuous and nervous under the unfriendly glare radiating off two female assistants. Their dress sense is identical to the models in the window and I give a faint smile as a sort of peace offering. It does nothing to thaw out their coldness, so I turn to a rack of garments. My fingers shake slightly as I linger over a black georgette four-piece burka set with a nose piece and chador. There's no need for all of it; however, I'm not keen to hang around any longer.

At the till I mumble that it's a present for a friend. The rest of the transaction is completed in silence. It's a relief to vacate the store. That's something I'm not keen to do again. I just want to get this over with, so I hurry along for my next stop.

There's an internet cafe further up on the opposite side. It takes a while before I can race across the busy road. At a close glance, my speed dwindles as I take in the yellow chipped paint around the dirty windows. Now I wish I'd brought gloves. I hesitate by the door, willing myself to venture in. I promise myself to buy disinfectant wet wipes and to clean off the germs I know are breeding inside. *Come on, Kate, it shouldn't take long.* The aroma of sweaty socks hangs in the air. Further into the shop, I wonder if the computers would be better suited in the Black Country Museum. Taking a seat, I remove my sunglasses. It's not long before I gather up my research. I write in my pad the list of items required to loosen and dismantle screws on balcony railings. There's a surprise when I google about falls from balconies. There's quite a lot that has been caused by faultiness. It presents me with a positive angle.

Outside, the dark clouds cover the sky. Heavy rain threatens. I shiver and worry about the plan; can I go ahead with it? I remember Greg's intentions. What choice do I have? It's *him* or *me*. Until our divorce, I'm not safe. How can I wait that long, constantly looking over my shoulder? How else can I be free to stay *alive?* Mine is not the best of plans. *What choice do I have?* I scurry along in search of a hardware shop, where again, cash will be paid. No one could suspect what the tools will be used for. *Why would they?*

THIRTY-EIGHT

Pulling into a side street near Greg's apartment, I park up. The burka set is torn from its bag off the passenger seat. I shake a part of it with dread. *I'd hate to have to wear this for real*, I think as I wrinkle up my nose with distaste. Later I'll drown in a hot bath of scented bubbles to wash off the smell and, just as a precaution, I'll shower and wash my hair too. With a sigh, the black clothes drop into my lap.

Heavy rain beats against the windscreen; it matches my mood. I wonder again how I fell for Greg. *How did I not see all of his lies?* Did I have stupid tattooed across my forehead? How could he do this to me? How could I fall for not only a conman, but a killer too? I bet my dad's arms are folded, a smug expression plastered over his face. *'Like I said, the brat was born stupid.'* His mantra is engraved in my head and I question whether he's right. What about Nick's sister? She didn't look stupid. She fell for Greg, same as me. I suppose I have her to thank for saving my life – one she sadly missed out on living to the full. I wipe away tears of pity for me and for the terrible last moments of her time on Earth. I watch the rain; it rolls down the windscreen like Voleta's crying out for revenge.

Cars zoom past, sending up sprays of water. I concentrate and unravel the headscarf. There's a sense that I should get a move on and not waste time self-pitying.

I discard my jacket and wiggle the burka over my head and body. Adjustments are made to the face cloth. It's uncomfortable, that's for sure, and not great for breathing either. How do these women cope?

It's surreal being covered head to toe with only a slit for my eyes as I exit the car. At first, I stumble, getting used to the cumbersome outfit. The only advantage is that I'm able to conceal the bag of tools underneath it; other than that I find it a total nightmare.

Steps are carefully trodden as I aim towards the main security entrance. Thankfully I had the good sense to park up somewhere that I didn't have to cross the road. There's no way I would have coped draped in this get-up. My main focus is on the footpath so I don't trip up and pray I don't bump into anyone. Would they even recognise me? I shouldn't think so. The access code has been memorised from watching Amy and I punch in the numbers. My heart is on high alert and I fear it will explode any minute. I scuttle in with my head bent down, especially for the security cameras. But there's no way I could be identified in this, surely? I'm tempted to take the stairs so as not to see anybody. However, I don't think my nerves will hold out – plus there's my awkwardness with the burka.

The lift button pings when I jab it with sweaty fingers. Seconds later the doors whoosh open and I slip inside. I grip the carrier bag tightly. When the doors slide across, I peer out. The hall is empty and I force my jelly legs to apartment 707. I feel suffocated, fiddling in my pocket for the door key. My fingers shake inserting it into the lock. Then I freeze and yank it out, darting to the stairwell exit. What if *Greg* is inside? I curse my stupidity for not checking the underground car park first. And there's no point trying Dean again; besides, the tracker is bound to be flat by now anyway. I can't search the car park with my nerves ready to break any minute.

Instead, I decide to bang on his door. Hopefully, I can scuttle off quickly and hide in the stairwell. Not the best of plans, I admit. Hopefully if Greg answers he'll think it a poor prank by a fellow neighbour. With the carrier bag a hindrance, I shove it in the corner at the top of the stairs – I'm sure it will be safe for a minute. I take in a deep breath and rush as best I can to bang Greg's door twice. I almost trip in my attempt to reach the safety of the stairwell. With the outer door open a fraction, my heartbeat pounds in my ears, waiting for Greg. All is silent and I bite my lip. I hang on until I can no longer stand it. He must be out. He has to be.

I steel myself to venture back into the hall, my hearing on high alert. Once inside the apartment, I peer into the bedroom. Empty. I still linger, though for sounds from the en-suite. *Nothing.* Next, I poke my head in the open-plan room. The sliding doors are closed and I take in the railings beyond. Remembering the bag, I gasp and turn in a panic. A sigh of relief escapes me, seeing the carrier I stupidly left behind.

Back inside, I start to rip off the burka, then think better of it. If I'm spotted on the balcony, no one can identify me with this on. Plus, as a precaution, I leave the key in the lock, and for extra security, I bolt the door. If he does return, I'll threaten to call the police and expose his relationship with Amy. What else can I do?

The YouTube video instructions looked easy – maybe for a man, yes. I try again using the screwdriver, easing the bolts in the right-hand side of the balcony. One hour later, dripping in sweat and with an aching hand, I've managed to loosen them, but it's not enough. I'll just have to come back tomorrow and try again. I'm too nervous to say longer; Greg could return at any time. I think it might be a good idea to hide the tools here, as it seems pointless lugging them around. The wardrobe is not an option; with only a few of his clothes hung up and a couple of pairs of shoes, the carrier bag will stand out. I go back to the open lounge and scan around. One of the brown sofas is pushed up against the wall. I fumble to kneel and look underneath. If I shove the bag right at the back it should be okay. Standing up, I move and see the island blocks the view of under the sofa. *Perfect.*

In the hall, before I can press the button for the lift, the doors whoosh open. I stumble backwards when Greg storms out, his ear glued to his phone. I catch his fleeting distasteful glare aimed at me. Automatically I cast my glance downwards. My legs shake, stumbling into the lift, and I repeatedly bang the ground-floor button. Just as the lift doors begin to close, a hand appears. I stagger backwards and hold my breath. When a young woman enters, I bow my head, saying a silent prayer. It's the footballer's girlfriend, the one who I spoke to last time I was here. I stand rigid, listening to her tap on her phone. And it seems I have blended into the walls of the lift.

THIRTY-NINE

The following day I arrive back at the apartments. I've spoken to Nick and told him I need time on my own and asked him to keep Timmy. I'll pick him up later. It just so happens that the parking space I used yesterday is free, as if it was waiting for me, along with the miserable, dreary clouds for rain. I shiver and zip up my fake-fur jacket. This time I'm checking out the car park beforehand. I gaze up to the balcony and visualise Greg backed into a corner. *Then whoosh, down he sails and lands on the concrete.* Of course I, the grieving widow, will claw back what's rightfully mine. The insurance company will claim faulty railings and all will be well. I do wonder about Amy's dreadful situation. But what can I do? I can't intervene in her welfare. Plus she's hardly someone I can stay friends with. What if she lets on that I gave her money for the key? I stop and bite my lip. But we never exchanged numbers. Then I close my eyes for a second; I've only bloody forgotten to dress in the camouflage. But I'm thrown from my thoughts when I hear Amy's angry voice from above.

'I want my money, Greg, and your wife said she'd tell the police if you didn't cough up.'

I gasp. I never said that.

Greg yells, 'What the fuck are you gobbing off to her for?'

She argues back, 'I'll do whatever the fuck I want.'

There is a noise like a slap and Amy screams. It focuses my senses and instinct alerts me to step back under the balcony. I'm just in time, as Amy's body lands on the footpath with a loud crack. I gape. Her skull is split open. Her brains surge forward, forming a carpet of bloody grey mass.

My internal feelings stop. I'm unable to drag my stare away. A trail of red liquid gathers speed headlong to my boots. I detach myself from distant screams. I think it's me. I can't tell. And why is my face wet and blood running up my jeans… or is it running down?

FORTY

There's a man outside the ambulance, hovering. I think he called out my name. His face is memorable, then it's gone as the doors close. My boots are stained in blobs of crimson. It sets off tingles, like an army of ants crawling over my body. There's a lightness in my head and my hearts speeds up. I feel as though I'm floating, and my breath is hard to catch. The memory of Amy flashes up, her head smashed. A policewoman steps inside. She lingers for a statement. How can I talk? All I see is Amy's broken body on the footpath, blood everywhere. I know she's dead. Someone said.

The young constable is persistent. She asks my name. I mumble out my details and the realisation of Greg's link with underage Amy sinks in. There's a fear she'll hear the guilty sound of the beat of my heart. There's an urge to push her out. I want to clamber into the driver's seat, speed off into the darkness, never to be seen again. *Greg* should have fallen to his death, not poor *Amy*. The blame is mine. It was me who loosened the screws on the railings. *Me.* I'll be done for *murder.* My mind detaches from my body as though torn apart. There's a chance I'll be banged up forever. I cover face with my hands.

What will happen to Timmy? What was I thinking? How did I not *see* the consequences of my stupidity? Because of me, that poor girl is *dead*. I've killed a child. There's no turning back. There's blood on my hands. I stare at them.

The police officer informs me she'll be in touch. I gaze at her blankly. I blink over and over, begging myself to wake up. This has to be a nightmare. From a distance I hear my name again; the voice is familiar, but I'm unable to place it. My brain's function is like someone has switched it off or forgotten to charge it.

A female voice speaks. 'It might be best if we sedate her.'

Another person's tone agrees, and then there's nothing.

FORTY-ONE

I flinch when I feel someone stroke's my brow. A face appears when I snap open my eyes. Nick. What's he doing? Where am I? This is not the master bedroom.

He reaches for my hand. It's resting on the cotton sheets. He gives it a delicate squeeze before dragging a chair near to the bed I'm in. 'Hello, Kate, try not to speak if you do not feel up to it. You've been witness to an awful accident.'

It all flashes back. Amy's head split on the footpath. I stare at my hands. They are still stained with her blood.

He pats my hand. 'But do not worry. You are in safe hands at a priory in Birmingham.' His tone sounds reassuring. 'You are okay – no broken bones, just suffering from shock, which is to be expected. And don't worry about Timmy; he is fine at the apartment.' He clears his throat. 'I am not sure if you are aware, but you have been here overnight. It's seven in the evening.'

I feel light-headed and I struggle up. Nick assists me, rearranging the pillows for more comfort. I see Amy's face the last time she was on Greg's balcony. Why did she visit him? *Why?* She must have gone back to demand her money. I sigh and bite my lip. How could I have known she'd do that?

'Kate, are you okay? Would you like a glass of water?'

I stare up blindly, forgetting Nick is here. 'No, thanks.' I'm not sure what I want right now.

He then blurts out, 'Greg has been arrested for murder.' And I'm sure I catch a glimpse of a tiny self-satisfied smile, but it disappears when I utter, '*Arrested?*'

'The accident took place last night; you have been asleep for a long time. Do you remember what happened?'

I question again. 'Murder…? I don't understand.' Shouldn't the police be questioning me?

'He is under arrest for the murder for of Amy.' He shakes his head. 'I never put him down as a sex predator. I am sorry to tell you that, Kate. She was only fifteen. I suppose with make-up on she looked a lot older. I admit, from her photographs in the news, she did look older than her years. And there is me thinking I thought I knew all there was to know about Greg.' Next, he says, more to himself, 'The policeman was not joking when he said it was a kid under the forensic tent when I was there last night.'

I'm confused on two points. One, with Greg's arrest and two, what was Nick doing at the apartment?

He walks over to the window to put a distance between us. 'The car park is down below. I bet it has a nice view in the light surrounded by a canopy of trees, dominated by woodland.'

His strange actions are unnerving. Why is he chatting about outside?

He pulls the blinds open, almost like he can't face me. But why? Unless he knows something?

'Apparently, the police found a bag of tools in Greg's apartment. It looks like he attempted to hide them. They were used to loosen the screws of the balcony's railings. It's clear to the police he wanted it to look as if Amy fell by accident. It seems Greg made a fateful error in leaving the bag behind.

They reckon he lost his temper with Amy. They think his plan went wrong and then he had no time to hide his equipment. It is an open and shut case.'

I freeze, not sure if I heard right.

He pulls the white vertical blinds shut. 'I am privileged to this information because I have a friend in the police force.' He turns around. 'Greg will go down for a long time, Kate. They have all the evidence they need – and the motive, of course.'

I mutter, 'Motive?' I don't understand.

'Witnesses heard Amy's shouts. She threatened to expose Greg having underage sex with her. According to the source, they had been arguing for most of the day. That is when he must have snapped and pushed her.'

I can't believe what I'm hearing. I close my eyes, wanting to be alone. I need time to think.

'Sleep tight, my love,' says Nick. I only open my eyes when I hear the door open and then close.

The police think it's Greg...

Do I confess? Something else bugs me, but right now I have enough to worry about.

FORTY-TWO

MONTHS LATER

From the bedroom window, I watch a man hammer in the for-sale sign. I don't why the estate agent is bothering, really. They've found a keen buyer already and I just have to hope the solicitor can prove ownership. I move to sit down next to Timmy on the bed and stroke the top of his head. There wasn't a great deal of Greg's stuff to pack up. What there was I'd given to charity. I'm not sure that was such a good idea. I don't want anyone else to be tainted by him. Anyway, I did, so it's too late for regrets. Our wedding photos I burned in the garden. The silver frame also ended up in the charity bag. I couldn't bear to look at the reminder, even with a different picture in. The Bentley's key fob on the side is a loan from Nick. That was another shock when the bailiffs arrived and loaded the Mercedes onto the back of their tow truck. Greg had not paid the lease on it for months. That's no surprise anymore.

Greg has asked to see me from Winston Green prison. I stand up and sigh. It has to be done. No point prolonging the inevitable any longer. In the mirror I admire curls of my natural hair colour, its dark roots of my origin restored. The first time Nick saw it, he liked it. Said it suited me. The idea was to rid of the old Kate. I thought somehow it would erase the past. But nothing can do that. From the wardrobe, I choose a fawn cashmere coat and slip it over a wool jumper and jeans. I was uncertain of the dress code for a prison visit, as this time his invitation has been accepted. Stamped and approved. There's a gift I want to present him with anyway. Call it a farewell gesture, something to remind *him* of *me* – perhaps of *Amy* too, and *Voleta*.

The circle of guilt I feel is endless; nothing can stop it. Another sigh escapes me and the if-only theme spins around in my head like a lost ball in space. I bite my lip to stop it from trembling. What future would Amy have had with a mother like hers? I close my eyes for a brief second, fighting down the memory of Greg's trial. Amy's mother had hissed and spat at him. Her thick finger had jabbed the air from a tattooed arm. Her snarl had revealed broken teeth. In some ways, it fitted the image I had of her. It's certainly a recollection I want to banish. I want it to disappear into the black hole inside my head, the ones Yellow Tail has claimed. The habit is gone for good. There's no room for drunken demons to dance around in my head accusingly. I'm quite capable of that in sober mode. I'm accountable and I know it. My actions alone were the cause of Amy's death. Plus I didn't see any point of attending the counselling sessions Nick had booked. How could I confess the truth? That has to stay locked away, but it doesn't. It comes creeping up and I'm unable to stop it. In one way it's replaced the feeling of being watched. I'm the watcher, watching *me*. The revenge I so wanted feels empty and dead. The burden of mentally being chastised over my mistake whirls on and on, like a wheel that never stops turning. There are, of course, moments when I do forget, and to look at me you'd never guess my shameful secret, my dirty deed. It was against Greg and not Amy, especially after she confessed her age. Yes, I admit she looked young, but I'd never guessed she was still just a child.

The building of Winston Green looms ahead. I shiver even though the heater is on. It's an ugly, monstrous site, a gloomy existence which probably has horrors inside. It's also the final place for my husband. Just a pity hanging was banished.

'Why haven't you come to see me before?' is his first question. 'You know I've been framed, don't you?'

I compose myself. 'Who would want to do that?'

He scoffs. 'Fucking Amy's family, for a start.' He sits forward and lowers his voice. 'She told me she was twenty, the bitch.'

There's a lot I want to say. What would be the point? I read up all on the traits of a narcissistic person. It summed up Greg to perfection. I sit back, fold my arms and suggest, 'How about we set up an appeal?' I fight down the urge to say what I'd like to say and do to him.

His stare is distrusting, leaning back in the plastic chair. 'There's something different about you.' Then it clicks. 'You've dyed your hair.'

Dyed my hair? I batter down a bitter sigh. He doesn't even know me. Quite quickly the thought is dismissed, and I return to my plan. For the impact I want to create, I unfold my arms and edge closer. 'I know all about your drug addict mother, and that you were dragged up through your childhood.' I offer a heartfelt smile. 'It can't have been easy for you.' This is to suggest I'm on his side, that I understand the pain he went through. It's my part to play right now to gain access to what I want.

He sneers like I don't know what a shitty upbringing is. I ignore his expression and force myself to carry on. 'But we're still married, for better or for worse.' I stare into his eyes and add, 'I said that, and I meant it.' These lines have been practised, along with the scene, otherwise I'd have failed to say what I need to.

He stares, as if considering whether to believe me or not. I sigh and say, 'Well, I guess from your silence you don't want my help after all to set up an appeal.'

I'm about to stand when he quickly responds, echoing my words. 'What do you mean, to set up an appeal?'

I pull documents from my coat pocket. There was no choice but to roll them up there, as my handbag and briefcase were not allowed in. I fold out the papers and carefully arrange them on the round synthetic table that separates us. Letters of exchange are clear on the headed expensive sheets from a well-known solicitor.

Greg seems impressed, leafing through the pages. 'Looks like you've been busy.'

'There's a summary on how the appeal will work. Of course, there are hefty fees, which you can see. We would have to sell the house, but that could take a year or more. The solicitor recommends that we act fast if you are to have any chance of success.' I hold my breath while he flicks through the documents. I want to bite my lip; instead, I dig my nails into the palms of my hands under the table.

I then whisper, edging closer, 'When I met solicitor, I sort of hinted about bribery. He wasn't keen at first. But I assured him there could be a decent amount of cash in it for him. I'm too afraid to ask him about my cash. It might unsettle him.'

'Busy little bee, aren't you?' His eyes bore into mine. 'But what's in it for you?'

A guard wanders over; his stare is uncomfortable. When a prisoner shouts at the woman in front of him, the guard marches over and orders the bald guy to quieten down.

I lean back and gently muster, again with practised precision, 'I still love you, Greg, no matter what you've done.' Those words, spoken from my lips, don't sound like me. It as if someone else has stepped in.

His tone is dismissive. 'Why should I believe you?'

I shrug, gazing around, and I fold my arms again. Then I unfold them to deliver my final statement as I gather up the documents. 'Look, it was a silly idea.' I allow the words to dryout in the air before I roll up the papers in readiness for my pocket again. 'Guess I didn't think this through, because I don't fancy ending up where you are, and especially not for bribery.'

'No, Kate, I guess you don't, babe.' His smile is full of charm – the one I fell in love with. 'So then, how do we start this appeal?'

His narcissistic tendency is incredible, and I press down the urge to smack off his conceited, smug grin. 'The solicitor wants his cash in advance and heavy fees for the barrister.' I shake my head. 'But I don't have that kind of money.'

Greg nods like he's going over his limited choices. I place my hands under my legs and cross my fingers, daring not to breathe as I wait for his reaction.

He chews his bottom lip, casting his eyes around and then back to me. 'There's a spare key hidden in the garage. It's for the lock-up I use to keep my private papers in. You'll find the address too. That should sort you out with what you need.'

I raid my memory for a suitable answer. I didn't expect him to fall for my plan so soon. I manage to nod and mumble, 'Okay.'

My legs wobble through security doors. At one point the guard asks if I'm okay as he unlocks door after door for the way out. With the prison behind me, I take in the fresh air and stare up at the clouds of grey on the horizon.

FORTY-THREE

In the garage, the key is exactly where he said it would be. I turn it over in my hand, wondering what it will expose. Before I leave, I let Timmy in from the garden with a promise to be home soon. There's a missed call from Nick. I'll call him later. The only thing on my mind is to get to the storage unit in Small Heath.

There's a hold-up on the M5, and I tap the steering wheel impatiently. I wonder if I'll find my insurance policy. The traffic in the outside lane starts to move and quickly I manoeuvre into it. Up ahead I spot the advert for the up-and-coming detective series. I recall the first time I saw it. It seems like it happened in another lifetime. Dean finally got in touch to say he retrieved the tracker long before the fatal accident. I settled his bill in cash – with a discount, of course. And no, I did not require his service again. Somehow I don't think his company will survive. Not that that matters anymore. I was just relieved I chose his rubbish service; in fact, he never connected me with Greg. That was something to be grateful for.

Uncertain of the location, I punch the address in the sat nav. I bite my lip and wonder nervously what I will find in the lock-up. Will my money still be intact or long gone? Does Greg own the house or the apartment?

The blue and yellow storage warehouse is easily spotted with such vibrant colours. There's a relatively empty car park at the front. My tummy churns, pulling onto it. Before I left the house, I googled the premises. Good job, really, as ID is required, and I read their terms and conditions. So, with Greg the only authorised person to the private storage company, I have every suspicion of being denied access. In effect, *Mrs* Anderson doesn't have permission, unlike *Mr* Anderson. However, there's sort of a plan I've formed – not the best, but it will have to do.

Worried about being observed, I overcome my nerves and stride over with determination. I want to give the right image, and it appears luck is on my side. At the counter in reception, I place what I hope is a flirty smile on my face. I aim it at the young man, his name badge reading Morgan. He already appears flattered. And I compliment him on his neat appearance. I tell him his mum must be proud of him. It's the distraction I planned, and my hopes remain that he'll verify the name Anderson and not concentrate on the *Mrs* which is on my ID. It works, and I'm shown to where the security door is and buzzed in. It's amazing what a few flattering remarks can do.

Number five is found with relative ease. My fingers shake, inserting the key into the small padlock. I stand still for a moment in the silence under a glare of strip lights and security cameras in the long hall. Pressure builds up, ready to combust as I prise open the door. The room is similar to a small shed, only made of bricks. There's nothing else other than a briefcase on the concrete floor. I search for a light and flick it on. With nowhere to sit, I kneel down and flip open the briefcase. I stare at the locks and silently curse. My palms are sweaty, and I dig in my nails, almost too scared to open it, fearful of what I will find. But Greg did not need for it to be locked, so it shouldn't be.

I take a deep breath and slide the catches each side. Instantly they both fly open and I pop up the lid. Photographs are bypassed in search of evidence of my money. Tears well up when I find a TSB statement dated a couple of days before Amy's incident. Clipped to the top appears to be the passcodes. I slump back against the wall and read the statement again, brushing under my eyes. It's all there in black print, the full amount of my cash.

With no time to waste, I pull out my phone and log on to Greg's account, changing his mobile number to mine. I'll have twenty-four hours for it to accept before I can transfer the funds into my account. I bite my lip, but there's nothing else I can do but wait. There's no way Greg can access the cash now; even so, I can't help but feel apprehensive.

Next, I carry on snooping. There's a document. I gasp, pulling it out. Oh my God. It's an insurance policy. *Mine.* My heart thuds in my ribcage and I glare at it. It's my signature alright. *Bloody hell.* Words fail me. There's no way I willingly put my name to that. It seems I was worth the same as Nick's sister. Five must have been Greg's lucky number, until his luck eventually ran out. I waste no time ripping it up.

Resuming my search, I find various other accounts with money in. Funds he must have conned out of other women. But who are they all? He's hardly going to offer that information to me. I'll think of something, but not now. There's a will from Mary Ryan it states she left the house to Greg along with various other cash and belongings. *She sounds like an old lady with a name like that.* The neighbour never mentioned this Mary. Then again, she was so full of herself and her brood, I'm surprised she even remembers me. I have a horrible feeling that Greg swindled so many other women. Did he kill them too? Surely the police would have been alerted? There must have been families who'd have alerted the constabulary if any woman had gone missing, or did he pick on those like me?

I dig further and open a brown envelope. There's a sharp intake of breath and the bricks of the unit close in on me. I know the face in the photograph. *Jason.* What's Greg doing with pictures of him? It looks like the same one he used on the dating site, the main one. Hairs on the nape of my neck freak out. *Did Greg murder him too?* Is that why his profile disappeared? Hang on, there are more pictures of different men. Was Greg gay? Suddenly I drop them like they're contaminated, as though Greg's acts can taint me. But what do they mean? What was he up to? I don't understand. What I do know is that I knew nothing of his real life, the one he kept hidden. Why I didn't see through any of this?

I force myself to delve into the case again. My hands feel cold and shaky, pulling out a travel laptop from the flap compartment. Passwords and names are taped to the front of it. It appears they are for dating sites. One of them is where I met Jason. That's a bit of a coincidence.

Quickly I power up the machine and log onto a dating site, Heart & Kisses. Strangely, there's Jason's profile. *How odd.* Then it hits me, bright and clear. *Greg* posed as *Jason.* Of course. That's how he caught Nick's sister. He set me up. It all makes sense. I'd opened up to Jason – that's how Greg knew about my money. Found out everything about me. *Well, almost.* The brick walls stare back. He planned it all, right from the very first message. The fated meeting and being supposedly stood up. *All fucking lies, the whole lot of it.* I go hot, then cold. I burn with livid rage. The photographs of the other men were used as aliases too. *How did I not see?* I was well and truly conned. But not stupid, not that that makes a difference anymore. And all along I thought it was fate. My true love had been found. I even considered Jason as being out for some sort of revenge. *What a fool I was.*

I rest my head on the wall and a kaleidoscope of memories with Greg shimmer by. The *perfect life.* I thought I had it. Then I fast forward to the crime I committed and sad, sorry tears fall. How can I live with the fact that it was me and not Greg who was responsible for the child's death? Of course, I argued with myself that I should confess to the police. As each day trundled on, I lost my nerve and I questioned my revenge.

Then a thought escapes from my tangle of emotions of when I was on the balcony unscrewing the bolts. How did they loosen on their own? Perhaps the rain was a factor? But I doubt it. I go back to that day. I'd dripped in frustrated sweat unable to unscrew anymore. Then I'd ripped off the gloves and shoved them in the carrier bags, along with the tools. I freeze and gasp. *The gloves.* With all that happened, I'd completely forgotten about them. I stand and pace the small unit. *They are stained with my finger prints.*

When the overhead fluorescent light unexpectedly buzzes, I tremble. More so when the door is slammed and heavy footsteps echo down the hall. I shrink back against the wall and my mind runs on delirious notions that the police have come to arrest me. *They've found the gloves.* Greg will be freed and I'll take his place. My knees shake when the door swings open.

'Kate, are you okay? You look like you have seen a ghost,' Nick asks, concerned.

My shoulders slump and I manage to nod, then mutter, 'God, you scared me.'

'Sorry, I did not mean to. Anyway, it looks like you have found Greg's stash of papers.'

The thoughts of the gloves are shoved to a waiting box in my head as I suspiciously question, 'What are you doing here?' *And how did he know where to find me?*

He carries a guilty stance. 'I just wanted to make sure you were okay.'

I demand this time. 'How did you know I was here?' Something feels odd, off-kilter, and silently I wait until he speaks.

There's a trace of guilt when he confesses, 'There is a tracker on the Bentley.'

Apprehension crawls over my body as I stupidly repeat his words. 'A tracker?' Why didn't he mention that before? My skin tingles; he must have known I was at the apartment the day before the accident. He knew I lied when I told him I was somewhere else. *He's bound to suss what I did.*

'It is okay, Kate; I am not the bad guy.'

A shiver rattles through my body when he pulls out black flimsy gloves from his overcoat pocket. *The ones I used.*

'I think you left these behind.'

I stare at them and then back at him. My brain is on no-go mode. It feels as though it's left my head altogether.

He admits, 'I know I should have told you before, but it never seemed the right time. Naturally, I was concerned when you made another trip to Greg's apartment. So I sent a guy over to check you were okay.'

I steady myself with the help of the wall and my mouth dries up.

'He used to work for a construction company building apartments with balconies.' He seems apprehensive when he presses on. 'When he found the hidden tools, he knew what they were used for and so he called me, naturally concerned, knowing what had happened to my sister.'

I hold my breath and blood pounds in my ears.

'I knew Greg would never have been so daft as to leave any evidence around should he have contemplated another move like the one with Voleta.'

He lightly touches my arm. 'Do not look so worried – I am on your side. I will never let anyone harm you again.'

Although I hear what he says, I have a bad feeling of what else is to come.

'Pete was confused at first. Then we concluded the bolts would have been stiff and awkward for a woman to loosen. I guessed your idea was, because Greg smoked, you planned to engage him in an argument from below; he would then lean over the balcony, and the rest you know. So, with a flash of anger, I told Pete to finish the job off.' His head shakes. 'But I swear, I did not know Amy would be there.'

I sink onto the concrete floor. My emotions are all tangled up. But one thing stands out: it was *him* not *me* that caused of Amy's death. It doesn't make it right, and I feel my anger rise.

Nick kneels beside me. 'Kate, I was building myself up to tell you, but the right moment just never appeared. I know it sounds like a lame excuse.'

'You knew all along but kept it to yourself. You made me feel as if it was my fault.' I brush his hand off my arm. 'Don't touch me,' I say accusingly. 'You even sorted out counselling.'

He insists, 'I thought it might help.'

I fume, 'Help…how could that possibly help? Help might have come in the form of you telling the bloody truth. That's what help would have done. You know what, I've had all I can take,' I snap, gathering up documents and shoving them back in Greg's briefcase. 'I'm going home, but then, I guess you'll know that from the tracker details.'

'Kate, do not leave like this, please, I beg you.'

His hand is brushed off again as I leave and storm out. Then I turn around. 'How did you get in here?'

'My friend owns this place.'

I open my mouth then clamp it down. Typical. 'What a coincidence,' I mutter sarcastically, marching on. And I don't even bother to ask how his so-called buddy got into the apartment.

Nick doesn't give up as I throw the briefcase on the passenger seat.

'Goddamn it, Kate, talk to me.'

I slam the Bentley door and start the engine. I just want to go home and cuddle Timmy and cry into his fur. *How dare he not tell me?*

He bangs on the window. 'I love you, Kate, and I would never intentionally hurt you. You have to see that.'

That catches my attention, and I swing the door open and fly out, demanding, 'You love me? Yet you made me feel Amy's death was my fault.' Furiously, I wave my hands around. 'When all the time you knew, and you claim to love *me?*'

'Come on, Kate, be reasonable. After all, you did loosen the screws in the first place.'

I bite my lip. *That I can't deny.* But he has no right to say that. And then a backlog of tears spring from my eyes. 'I didn't know Amy would fall.'

Nick gathers me up as I sob into his chest. He strokes my hair and whispers, 'It is okay, darling, I am here, and no one will ever hurt you again.'

After a while when I look up as his warm smile beats down. His thumb gently eases under my eyes. 'I meant what I said. I love you. And look, Kate, casualties happen in war. They also take place in real life too. Of course, Amy's death was heartbreaking, but that wasn't your intent.'

He pulls a packet of tissues from his inside pocket and hands me one. I sniff into it, listening as he presses on. 'Your circumstances were created by another person, an evil one with no thought or consideration to you or anyone but himself.' He connects his eyes with my watery eyes. 'None of this is your fault, Kate. You were pushed to the edge by someone who wanted you dead. It was, after all, *you* or *him*.'

I sniff and blow my nose. 'I should have gone to the police instead.'

He implores me. 'As I told you before, on what grounds would they have arrested him?'

I stare down at the tarmac, knowing he's right. Then I look back up and dispute, 'It still doesn't make what I did right.'

'I know that, Kate, but what choice did you have?' He grabs my arms as if to shake sense into them. 'Think of what he put you through. All the lies he told you, you put your trust in him, you fell in love with him. You wanted his child.'

I turn away as bitter tears form.

'I know it's easy for me to say. But you have to move on, let go of the past. No amount of grief and blaming yourself will ever bring her back.' He steps back for his final admission and locks his eyes on mine. 'What you have to consider and be proud of is, you have stopped him from hurting others. In effect, your actions and mine have saved their lives.' He shakes his head sadly. 'It is impossible to save everyone. Put it another way, Amy's mother was supposed to have protected her child, not sold her out for money. If anyone is to blame for her death, it is her.'

I sigh and reluctantly sort of agree. 'I guess so.'

'Come on, I'll drive you home and pick up Timmy. I do not want you to stay on your own in that house. Pack a few things and at another time we will get the rest of your stuff.'

I welcome his offer, and for once I feel a slight release on my conscience, knowing we were both to blame.

Later, when we talk more, I'll tell him when I knew of Amy's real age. I hear his diplomatic answer at the ready. '*She wouldn't go to the police because her mum threatened her, what choice did you have?'*

He kisses my hand. 'I meant what I said, Kate, and we can move on from the past, put it behind us.'

FORTY-FOUR

Timmy is on the balcony with Nick, the kind, considerate man I'm falling in love with. It's a beautiful spring day and the air has a hit of warmth. There's no smile on my lips, though. I'm off to see Greg later. A journey I'm not looking forward to one bit. Aimlessly I wander into the kitchen to make a herbal tea. Greg is never going to divorce me – not now, not ever. So how can I accept Nick's proposal of marriage? I touch my belly, knowing this time for real a seed grows; this time the doctor has confirmed it. My dream has come true. I sigh and smile. Nick is over the moon. His family is over the moon. Susie is delighted and already hinting at being godmother. It's funny how things have turned out. You just never know what life has in store for you. If it's a girl, we've already decided on Voleta, and Nick if it's a boy.

Later in the day, I fidget on the plastic chair in Winston Green prison. I feel no pity as Greg wanders over. He's lost weight. His skin is pale. For the first time, I see him differently. There's no handsome charm, there's no softness in his eyes, only the face of a cheap, despicable sex offender and murdering thug.

He slumps down heavy in the chair and growls, 'Where the fuck have you been?'

A sickness grows inside me and I stand, which nudges the chair backwards. There's no need to be in his presence any longer. I realised from the last visit that I wasn't allowed to bring in my gift for Greg, so I photographed it instead. It will still have the same impact. But first, I need to clear up something. 'Oh, by the way, the solicitor's letters weren't real.' And I make as if I'm heading over to the vending machine, more so because of his reaction.

Greg attempts to get up, but a prison guard marches over, demanding that he stay put.

I address the guard, whose muscles bulge under his uniform. 'Could you give him this picture, please?'

He hesitates, confused, staring at the photograph. Then, with a shrug of his shoulder, he flicks it over to Greg.

Reluctantly he grabs it off the concrete floor and casts his eyes over it, then he turns it over like he's going to solve the mystery. 'What the fuck is this?'

'It looks like a bolt from a balcony. It reminds me of the ones used on your railings, I think.' I let the words linger before I smile lightly.

Greg snarls, 'It was you, you fucking bitch.'

The prison guard holds him down while others race over.

Greg screams as I leave the visiting room, and I can't help but turn to blow him a goodbye kiss. It was just too tempting not to.

A week later I receive a call. Greg is dead. He got into a fight of some sort.

With the help of another private detective, I'll try to return the money I found in Greg's accounts back to the rightful owners…